wild awake

wild awake

hilary t. smith

KATHERINE TEGEN BOOKS
An Imprint of HarperCollins Publishers

Katherine Tegen Books is an imprint of HarperCollins Publishers.

Wild Awake
Copyright © 2013 by Hilary T. Smith
All rights reserved. Printed in the United States of America.
No part of this book may be used or reproduced in any manner whatsoever without written permission except in the case of brief quotations embodied in critical articles and reviews. For information address HarperCollins Children's Books, a division of HarperCollins Publishers, 10 East 53rd Street, New York, NY 10022.
www.epicreads.com

Library of Congress Cataloging-in-Publication Data
Smith, Hilary T.
Wild awake / Hilary T. Smith. — First edition.
    pages cm
Summary: "The discovery of a startling family secret leads seventeen-year-old Kiri Byrd from a protected and naive life into a summer of mental illness, first love, and profound self-discovery."— Provided by publisher.
ISBN 978-0-06-218468-9
[1. Family life—Fiction. 2. Mental illness—Fiction.] I. Title.
PZ7.H64923Wil 2013   2012045524
[Fic]—dc23   CIP
                                                                                        AC

Typography by Michelle Gengaro-Kokmen
13 14 15 16 17 LP/RRDH 10 9 8 7 6 5 4 3 2 1

First Edition

For my family

chapter one

It's the first day of summer, and I know three things: One, I am happy. Two, I am stoned. Three, if Lukas Malcywyck's T-shirt was any redder I would lean over and bite it like an apple.

Lukas and I are sitting in his basement, which is my favorite place in the entire world. Last summer, we covered the walls and ceiling with carpet remnants we found behind the Flooring World on South Granville and strung up yellow Christmas lights to replace the nasty fluorescents. Now, it's our band room. Lukas's drum kit is set up in one corner, and there's a stand for my synth.

Except at the moment, I'm holding the synth in my lap

and making laser noises while Lukas sits beside me on the blue couch. His arms, sculpted from hours of drumming and daily man-yoga, are draped over the cushions, and his eyes are bright with strategy.

"We need a new band name," he says.

"What's wrong with Snake Eats Kitten?"

"Too jokey," says Lukas. "I was thinking Sonic Drift."

I twist the knobs on my synth, then stab a key. It makes a sound like a xylophone crossed with an atomic bomb. I plunk out a xylobomb version of "Twinkle, Twinkle, Little Star."

Lukas cringes. "Do you *have* to do that?"

I ignore him and keep playing.

"Sonic Drift sounds like music for dead people," I say. "It's too—" I fish around for the word, a task rendered more difficult by the fact that my brain keeps getting distracted by the soft electric twinkle of the Christmas lights on the walls. "Too conceptual," I finish with a scholarly twirl of my hand. "It's like something you'd read in a textbook."

Lukas sits up. "Exactly. It's abstract. It sounds like the name of a serious band."

"It sounds like the name of a pretentious band. Snake Eats Kitten is accessible. You were there Saturday night—people loved it."

"People thought it was *funny*. There's a difference."

I lean over to put my synth on the floor. There's a box of

old books next to the couch marked DONATE. I pull it over. "Is your mom giving these away?"

I paw through them and pull out one called *The Adolescent Depression Workbook*. Lukas's mom is a social worker, and their house is crammed with stuff like this. The book's cover shows a goth girl sitting against a brick wall, her kohl-rimmed eyes gazing out from beneath the edge of her tattered black hood. She's holding—absurdly—a graphing calculator. Like she ran a few equations, found out the world is more effed than you can possibly imagine, and is just chilling by this brick wall, waiting for the zombies to arrive. I open it up and flip through the pages. "Okay, Lukas, I'm going to test your level of adolescent depression."

"Come on, Kiri."

"I thought you wanted something deep. This'll help us dig into our psyches." I give Lukas my best psychiatrist look. "In the past fourteen days, have you felt worthless?"

"Can you be serious for one second?" says Lukas. "We need a better name before the semifinals."

He tries to snatch the book away from me, but I pull it out of his reach.

"This *is* serious. Don't you want to find out if you're depressed?"

Lukas lunges across the couch and tries to wrestle the book out of my hands. With his body that close I can smell the lavender laundry detergent on his T-shirt, the eco-friendly stuff his mom buys. I take a big sniff while he pries my fingers off the book. Lovely.

"Lukas, Kiri, dinner's ready," calls Lukas's mom from upstairs.

At the word *dinner*, I relinquish my hold on the book and Lukas tosses it to the floor. Goth Girl lands facedown on the carpet. Sorry, Goth Girl. Good luck with the zombies.

"I still say Sonic Drift," Lukas says as we tromp upstairs.

"All right, Sonny Bono. Take a chill pill."

Upstairs, Lukas's mom is taking some kind of scalloped-potato thing out of the oven. The edges of the sliced potatoes are golden brown and swimming in cream. Petra Malcywyck sees me and waves.

"Kiri, *piekna*, would you grab me that oven mitt?"

I get it for her, and she lifts the casserole dish out of the oven and sets it on top of the stove. Lukas disappears into his room to change. He claims that drumming makes him sweaty, although I've never seen nor smelled nor tasted anything resembling sweat on Lukas's perfect body.

"How is your summer, Kiri? How are you surviving in that house all by yourself?"

Mrs. Malcywyck—Petra—is Polish and a total babe despite being in her early fifties and having completely gray hair. She has a really high voice but a serious manner, like Minnie Mouse addressing the United Nations.

"It's been good so far. I'm getting a ton of practicing done."

Which reminds me I need to go home soon and practice some more. I thought about telling Lukas I didn't have time for Battle of the Bands on top of the International Young Pianists' Showcase, but when a golden sex god begs you to make the musical equivalent of hot, sweaty love with him, it's pretty hard to say no.

"It doesn't bother you at night to be alone?" says Petra.

I smile brightly. "Nope."

Petra furrows her brow and mutters something in Polish. "When your mother told me they were planning to do this trip, I said to her she must be crazy."

As we speak, my parents are on Day Four of the twenty-fifth-anniversary cruise they've been planning for years. It's their first time going anywhere, ever, and they fretted over it like they were expecting a baby: shopping for Travel Clothes, reading Travel Books, taking a whole rainbow of Travel Pills for the obscure and possibly imaginary tropical diseases they would otherwise almost certainly contract abroad. My brother, Denny, was supposed to come home from college to stay with me, but at the last minute he decided to spend his summer torturing sea urchins at the marine biology lab instead.

My parents' decision to leave me at home alone is a sensitive subject with Lukas's mom, who believes—to paraphrase—that they are one trill short of a sonatina.

Petra takes down olive oil and balsamic vinegar from a shelf and starts making vinaigrette for the salad.

"And what will you eat?" she says.

"I eat cereal."

"And what will you eat with this cereal?"

"Soymilk and a banana."

Judging by the look she gives me, I might as well have said I was eating my cereal with malt liquor and Adderall. She shakes her head and whacks the salad tongs against the side of the bowl.

"I am afraid you will starve to death with this cereal. This can go to the table."

I take the salad bowl and carry it to the kitchen table. Besides the scalloped potatoes and salad, there's fresh bread and butter, green beans, and a plate of roast chicken. How Lukas manages to be so skinny while eating Petra's cooking every day is a mystery on par with metaparticles.

"And what will happen if you hit your head on the floor?"

I'm trying to figure out how, exactly, I would manage to hit my head on the floor, when Lukas comes out of his room in a fresh pair of jeans and a white T-shirt, and I'm still high enough that I just gaze at him while Petra calls Lukas's dad in from his study for dinner.

After a dinner full of typical Malcywyck-family repartee over the fine distinction between *electrosoul* and *electrofunk* as pertaining to various obscure seventies bands, Lukas and I load the dishwasher while Petra packs enough leftovers to last me a month. By the time she's finished, the stack of Tupperware is practically scraping the ceiling. She packs them into two canvas grocery bags and hands them to me.

"Take this home. You will eat something besides this banana and cereal."

When I say thanks, Petra squints at me. "You will call if there is anything wrong?"

"Yes."

"You will lock the doors?"

"Yes."

She holds my gaze a few seconds longer. Petra has this way of looking at you that makes you want to confess things you didn't even know you were hiding. It's a social worker trick, and if you're not careful, it'll nail you every time. She burned me with it last fall when I was so stressed out over auditions for the Showcase, I started crying at their kitchen table. I had to grin like a freaking used-car salesman every time I saw her for weeks after that to convince her I wasn't some kind of Depressed Teen like Goth Girl on the book downstairs.

I give her a dopey smile. *No problems here, lady.*

"You want to stay for a while and watch TV?" says Lukas.

"Uh-uh. I need to get home and practice."

Petra crosses her arms.

"Kiri. You are sure you don't want to stay?"

I hesitate. Lukas's dad puts his hands on Lukas's shoulders and squeezes them, waiting for my answer.

Something about that gesture that makes my heart twinge, and for one disorienting moment I'm aware of myself, standing in their kitchen, loaded down with containers of their food. *This is not your family.*

I think about my parents snug in their Luxury Berth, and Denny snug in his lab.

I think about the practice schedule I taped to the lid of the piano this morning, with lesson days filled in with yellow highlighter and self-imposed deadlines (memorize Bach; bring Chopin up to speed; play entire recital with eyes closed) circled in blue.

I think about the grocery money Mom left on top of the fridge, and the taped-up reminders to water the azaleas and take out the recycling.

I smile at Petra and shake my head.

"No thanks," I say.

I spend the six-block walk planning which piece I'll tackle first when I get home. But when I put my key in the front door, I can hear the telephone ringing inside.

And that's when things get weird.

chapter two

"Hello?"

I drop the bags of leftovers on the floor and press the phone to my ear. It's probably Petra calling to make sure I made it home safely, even though you can barely put in a pair of earbuds in the time it takes to walk from Lukas's house to mine. I roll my eyes, getting ready to deliver my nightly report on the state of the deadbolts.

But instead of Petra's authoritative chirp, I hear a long, rasping garkle.

Great. It's one of Dad's clients.

"Byrd residence," I say, this time in the drippy professional tone my dad prefers us to use in situations like this.

There's another long pause. I hear someone coughing.

Finally, the old coot speaketh.

"I want to talk to Al."

"Is this concerning a home health-care equipment rental issue?" I coo.

Silence. Then, "I said, is Al Byrd there?"

He sounds just like my grandpa Bob used to sound on the phone—suspicious, almost hostile, like he doesn't quite trust that the person on the other end of the line is really who they claim to be and not an imposter.

"He's busy at the moment. May I take a message?"

I pick up a pen and doodle on the message pad.

Date: heart.

Time: star.

Caller: stick figure with a long, squiggly beard.

"May I ask who's calling?" I say.

There's another pause, as if my words are reaching him after a long delay.

"This is Doug Fieldgrass."

I draw a row of tulips in the "Message" field. Then a swarm of bees. Taking detailed and accurate phone messages is a serious matter, as Mom and Dad reminded me about a million times before they left.

Doug Fieldgrass, whoever he is, clears his throat.

"Listen, this is Al Byrd's number, right? Sukey's old man?"

At the name Sukey, my attention snaps back to the phone. Sukey's my sister. My *dead* sister. The one we never, ever talk about.

"Uh, yeah," I stammer. "Yes. This is the right number." I attempt to regain some of my well-practiced Telephone Poise. "May I ask what this is concerning?"

I'm just trying to keep myself from freaking out, but even I can hear how coldly impersonal those words sound, how carefully neutral the tone of voice. What am I doing? I stand up straight. My fingers tighten around the pen.

"Doug? You there? I'm Kiri. I'm Sukey's sister."

There's a rustling, scratching noise like Doug just dropped the phone.

"Aw, hell," I hear him mutter.

There's a loud beep.

The line goes dead.

For one whole minute I stand there frozen with the phone in my hand, and in that minute I'm twelve again, called downstairs from my bedroom to hear the terrible news. I can smell the lasagna that was baking for dinner, hear the music I'd left playing upstairs, feel the shock of pain as sure and sudden as a yanked-out tooth before Mom and Dad had even said a word.

A trapped fly buzzes in the window and the fridge hums as it cycles on. I come to my senses and punch the call-return button. After two rings, there's a muffled *click*.

"Lissen," slurs Doug. "I ain't going to call again. You want her stuff, you get yourself down here and take it. This place is shutting down soon, and I don't have a lot of time."

"What stuff?" I say, no longer trying to hide my agitation. "Who are you?"

He says a few words I can't make out, something about Sukey's things in a closet. I bite back my frustration. *Freaking ENUNCIATE, dude.* But I know if I snap, he'll hang up again.

"Where are you?" I say, wrestling my voice into a strained semblance of patience.

He mumbles an address. I grab the message pad and scribble it down.

"Columbia? What's the cross street?"

"I'll wait outside the building," he says, and hangs up the phone.

I stare at the address I've just written. Columbia Street is all the way downtown. My parents still won't let me drive a car by myself because of Sukey's accident—though they'll never admit that's the reason—and it's easily a half-hour bike ride away. The idea of going is so absurd, so completely and totally out of the question, it stuns me temporarily. My brain flops like a fish at the bottom of a boat.

I shouldn't. I know I shouldn't.

But screw it. It's for Sukey. I grab my house key off the counter and go.

chapter three

I wheel my bike out of the garage and hop on. As I pedal down the street, my stomach tingles like I just ate a whole bag of Pop Rocks. I can't explain how urgent this feels. How breathless I am, not even counting the hills. As I charge up the bridge that crosses to downtown, I can hear the clinking of sailboat masts in the marina below. Ahead of me, the glittering angles of downtown beckon dangerously, like a drawer full of knives. I barrel through the intersection as the light turns yellow and glide up the store-lined street.

In a way, I feel like I'm going to see Sukey herself, not some questionable acquaintance who drunk-dialed my house. I imagine her standing on the corner, waiting for me in her zebra-print jacket and jeans.

Hey, Kiri-bird, she'd say. *I hear you're in a band.*

It's just me and my boyfriend, I'd say modestly, although Lukas and I aren't officially dating, not yet.

That's rad, Kiri. You got a demo for me?

In my imagination, I'm finally as cool as her, not a pathologically chirpy ten-year-old who turns red every time she drops an f-bomb.

Look at you biking around at night, she'd say with a mischievous tilt of her chin. *You're turning into a little badass.*

As I pedal down the street, I can almost smell Sukey's hair spray on the breeze, catch a whiff of her strawberry bubblegum. Around me, the city blocks peel away like pages in a book I'm rifling through to find a single, highlighted sentence. But when I pass the Woodward's building with its giant red *W* lit up with yellow bulbs, I slow down and skid to a stop.

Here's where things get tricky.

This particular block of West Hastings Street marks a not-so-invisible boundary between downtown proper and the seventh circle of hell. Keep going past the big *W* and you're in the Downtown Eastside, a place to which every creepy metaphor has already been applied: It's the urine-smelling haunted house in the city's squeaky-clean carnival, the one demented fang in its professionally whitened smile. Not a place you want to be after dark unless you're scoring heroin or shooting a Gritty Documentary.

Not a place I expected to be after dark, either. Wasn't Columbia supposed to be a few blocks back?

I keep riding east, pedaling so slowly my bike starts to wobble. I can see crowds of homeless people ahead, thick knots of them. From a distance, they almost look like nightclubbers: the same unsteady motions and drunken shouts, the odd woman in a short skirt and smeared makeup lurching down the street in high heels. I don't want to keep going, but somehow my bicycle carries me forward, its tires whispering against the pavement, until I'm stopped at the intersection.

While I'm waiting for the light to change, this dude on a rusty kiddie bike pulls up next to me. He's wearing an old jacket with faded green sleeves. He has sandy yellow hair and caved-in cheeks, and he looks like a cadaverous duck.

"Nice ride," he says.

I fiddle with my gear charger. "Thanks."

"Got a smoke?"

"Sorry."

He grimaces, gives his bike a kick-start, and wobbles through the intersection against the red light. I watch him go, trying to quiet the alarm bells clanging inside my chest. *Don't freak out. He wasn't going to hurt you.* The light changes to green. I start to ride through, but instead, I make a ragged right turn and pedal up Gore Avenue into Chinatown. Somehow, the sight of the red lampposts makes me feel safer, as if the Chinese dragons carved into them can protect me from the freak show going on a block away.

By now it's past dark, and I'm mad at myself for coming down here without looking up directions first. I thought I knew where Columbia Street was, and I was sure it came before Main Street, but now for all I know I've been riding parallel to it this whole time.

Should have called Lukas. Should have tried Mom and Dad. Shouldn't have come down here at all.

I'm so busy debating whether I should just go home that I don't notice the broken glass on the road when I ride right through it. I hardly hear the soft hissing sound of my back tire deflating. Nope—I don't notice anything until the thump of my rim riding the pavement jerks me back into reality.

I get off my bike and drag it onto the sidewalk to inspect the damage.

The back tire is completely flat. When I run my fingers around it, I find a tiny green shard of glass lodged in the rubber.

Shit. Shitshitshit.

I start walking, dragging my bike beside me like an awkward, clomping, injured horse. It thumps along beside me, but I try not to slow down. As dodgeball has taught us: Slowness shows weakness. Weakness means a ball in the face.

I don't think I need to elaborate any further.

A couple more guys on bikes reel past me, carrying bulging garbage bags full of empty pop cans on their backs.

"Hey!" I shout after them. "Where's Columbia Street?"

The one on the left turns his head. He's wearing a denim jacket with a black hoodie underneath. With the trash bag on his back, he looks like a punk-rock janitor.

"Two blocks thataway."

"Thanks."

He gives me a lopsided salute, and they disappear around a corner. I hurry my bike in the direction he pointed. When I see the green sign that says COLUMBIA in white letters, my knees go loose and weak. I recognize this place. I don't know why, but I do. Something about the red brick buildings makes my memory spit and cough like an engine that can't quite start up. I stand still, straining my ears, as if someone might whisper the answer.

Nothing. Just car sounds, tree-hush, the hoots and squeals of police cars two blocks away.

My hand moves to my pocket for the piece of paper with the address, but it's not there. I check the other pocket. Empty. I rack my brains for the street number, but draw a blank.

Suddenly, this doesn't feel like an adventure anymore.

Actually, it feels a lot like I'm standing on a sketchy block in the Downtown Eastside with a flat tire and no idea where I'm supposed to be or who I'm supposed to be meeting.

Nice work, Kiri. Way to be a badass.

I've stopped in front of a Chinese grocery store with a metal screen pulled down over it for the night. There's a bakery next to it, and across the street there's a six-story brick building with an old plastic sign above the door that says IMPERIAL HOTEL. There's some classy-looking buttressing around the first-floor windows, but whatever its former glory, it now looks like a National Register of Historic Places building crossed with a meth lab.

Where are you? I plead silently, but Sukey doesn't answer, and Doug doesn't appear.

There's a pair of crouched figures in the doorway of the hotel who look at me and mutter to each other in a way I don't like. A moment later, one of them takes out a needle and starts shooting up right in front of me.

Just when I think things can't get any more messed up, the yellow-haired homie who asked me for a cigarette at East Hastings rolls up on his bicycle and hovers next to me, his body so close I can smell the stale sweat on his jacket.

"Can I ask you a personal question?" he says to me with breath so thick with liquor it makes my head spin.

I strangle my handlebars.

"I'd rather you didn't, dude."

His face twists up.

"You're an uptight pussy."

That's it. That takes the freaking cake. I grab my bike and run the hell away from Columbia Street.

chapter four

"Got a flat?"

The guy who just spoke to me is standing outside a club where a speed metal band is thrashing away. I can hear the muffled bass and shrieking vocals, like they're murdering something onstage. I nod without making eye contact, thinking, *I've dealt with enough sketchy dudes for one night.* I feel like I've been trudging along for hours, but I've only just made it back to the part of East Cordova Street where I can finally stop pretending to be holding a can of pepper spray.

His voice wafts after me. "I've got a spare tube at my place. If you need it."

I tell myself this is some kind of sleazy trick to get me to go home with him, but I can't help glancing back just in case.

He's huge. Hagrid-esque. A bulldozer crossed with a gorilla. So big you can't take him in with one glance. He's like one of those enormous Group of Seven paintings at the art gallery— you have to back away to get the whole picture. Which I do. Rapidly.

I'm guessing he's Denny's age, maybe a little younger. He's wearing a black T-shirt and black pants ripped off at the knees, and a stud belt circa 1999. He has a broad, pale face, spiky black hair, and brown eyes. His wallet is attached to his belt loop by a chain, and his industrial-strength arms are sleeved with tattoos.

So very *not* the type of guy whose spare tube I want in my tire.

"No thanks," I say.

I keep walking. Now that I know someone's watching me, I get all clumsy. When I yank my bike to the right to avoid what looks like a pile of human feces, the handlebars buckle in toward the frame, and one of the pedals scratches my shin. I feel like kicking my stupid bike. *Stop it. I'm just trying to get us home.*

The number 17 bus blows past, its weird fluorescent lighting making the passengers inside look like items in a vending machine. I can see a bus stop up ahead on the corner, so I grab my bike by the handlebars and run for it. The bus slows down,

21

and I'm so relieved I start mentally composing the grateful speech I'm going to give the bus driver. Something that will flatter his or her heroic nature while playing down the fact that I don't have my bus pass or $2.25 in exact change.

The light on the corner turns green, and the bus roars on with an insulting discharge of exhaust. I stop, panting, dizzy with disbelief.

That's when I reconsider Homefry's offer to fix my tire.

No, "reconsider" implies careful deliberation.

That's when I say *screw it* and turn my bike around. I swagger down the sidewalk, trying to look like that whole chasing-a-bus thing was just something I did to be ironic.

"Hey," I say, wheeling my bike to a halt in front of him.

He's looking down at the pavement, squashing his cigarette with a skate shoe. I decide to be brave. At least the guy's close to my age. If he turns out to be a mofo, I'll just whip out my imaginary pepper spray and blast him to smithereens.

"I changed my mind about the tire. If the offer still stands."

When he looks up, I fix him with my best don't-mess-with-me stare. I run through a quick mental checklist: *not drunk, not homeless, not obviously a crackhead*. Even with the stud belt, that puts him head and shoulders above pretty much everyone else within a twelve-block radius of where we're standing. His brown eyes flicker over my bike before looking at me. He nods his chin toward the door of the venue.

"You wanna hear the set first?"

I shake my head. "I don't have ID."

"It's all-ages."

"No thanks. I need to get home."

He glances into the venue, and I can tell he's weighing his desire to hear more screamo with his desire to deal with and possibly rape-murder me.

I decide to cut my losses. "You know what? It's cool, I'll just walk."

He turns his eyes back to me, his expression still curiously flat. I'm starting to wonder if maybe he is on drugs, one of those evil downers that steals your soul.

"Nah. Let's go."

I waver. "You sure?"

"Yeah. I'm just a block away."

I glance down the street. On the one hand: stud belt. On the other hand: trudging all the way back home with my stupid busted bike.

Well, if it comes down to it, I'm pretty sure I could outrun him.

I nod. "Okay."

"It's this way."

He starts walking, and I lope along next to him, wheeling the bike between us. He doesn't talk, so I fill the heavy silence with charming banter.

"What band was that?"

"Pax Satanica."

"You into metal?"

"Not really."

I wonder why he offered to fix my tire if he's just going to be surly and monosyllabic. Maybe he's not used to talking to people. Maybe he's on a bad trip and I look like some kind of bicycle-wielding demon.

Either way, I shut up.

We turn onto a residential street lined with old wooden houses with rotting porches and bars on the basement windows, the kind of neighborhood that used to be dignified but now feels beleaguered, like a scuffed antique nightstand at the Salvation Army.

"I'm Kiri."

"Skunk."

That shuts me up again.

We stop in front of a white stucco house with a drooping pink roof and sagging white gutters, like a wedding cake left out in the rain. There's a little lawn in front of it, bordered by a dilapidated fence that comes up to my waist. Skunk lifts the metal latch on the gate, and I follow him through. There's a flower bed next to the house with a few bedraggled clumps of those pink and purple flowers they sell outside the hardware store for ninety-nine cents—pansies or posies or something like that. It looks like an animal's been digging them up.

Perhaps, I think to myself, a skunk.

Instead of going up the stairs and through the front door, Skunk goes down a concrete walkway along the side of the house. A motion-sensitive light comes on a few seconds later, and I see old cigarette butts in the gravel on the side of the path. I'm half expecting to see three or four more Skunk lookalikes hanging out in the backyard, drinking Jack Daniels while their pet pit bulls growl and strain against their chains.

We come around to the back of the house, where there's a small concrete courtyard with a couple of rusting chairs, a toolshed, and some potted plants. There are no pit bulls—at least, none outside. His meathead friends must all be at the Pax Satanica show. The house backs out onto a gravel alleyway with chain-link fences smothered in blackberry canes. There's an old brown van parked behind the house, next to the garbage and recycle bins. Skunk takes out his keys and unlocks a sliding glass door. I'm all set to refuse to come into his creepy rape-hole, but he doesn't invite me in.

"I'll be right out."

He slides the door open and goes inside, coming out a moment later with a cardboard box. He puts the box on the ground.

"Can I see your bike?"

I hand over my bicycle. He flips it over as if it weighs

nothing and pulls up the lever to release the back tire. I watch incredulously. Skunk's hands look like they were made to demolish buildings, not disassemble delicate bicycle parts with the grace and fluidity of a heart surgeon.

"You a bike mechanic?"

"Nah."

He roots around in the cardboard box, pulls out a little plastic hook, and pries the tire off the metal rim. It's unnerving and a little gruesome, like watching someone skin a rabbit. I wince when he reaches under the tire and pulls out the rubber tube like a long black piece of intestine. He holds it out to me.

"You want to take this home and patch it?"

"Uh, sure." I take the tube.

"It's not a big tear. Should patch up just fine."

"Yeah."

Now I'm the one being monosyllabic. I stuff the damaged tube into my pocket.

He reaches into his box again and pulls out a new tube. He uncoils it and sticks the plastic stem through the stem-hole in the tire, then wraps the tube the rest of the way around the rim. He picks up the plastic hook again and starts forcing the edge of the tire back onto the rim with the new tube nesting inside it. His motions are so quick and smooth you can tell he doesn't need to think about it at all. He looks like one of those Japanese chefs you can watch making sushi rolls through the glass window at Miyako on West Fourth, who pat down the rice, lay down avocado and crabmeat, roll it into a cylinder, and chop all in one seamless motion.

In ten seconds Skunk has the tire back on the wheel and is filling it with air from a wheezing hand pump. He pops the wheel back onto the bike, locks down the lever, flips the bike upright, and hands it to me without saying a word.

"Thanks for the fix," I say.

He nods.

A breeze blows through the courtyard, and I shiver. Time to be going home. But just when I'm about to say so, Bicycle Boy talks to me.

"Where's your helmet?"

I can't help it. I am an Eyebrow Person from a tribe of Eyebrow People; I raise my eyebrows. "You smoke cigarettes and you're asking me where my helmet is?"

He shrugs. "People drive like jerks."

"I'll be fine."

I squeeze the brake levers on my bike and glance toward the walkway. Suddenly it feels very, very late.

"I should get home. Thanks for helping."

He nods again. I stand there for a second to see if he has anything else to say. He doesn't.

"All right. Peace, man."

I turn my bike around and wheel it toward the side alley.

The tires feel firm and healthy. My bike feels whole and reassuring, back to its old reliable self. Even though I'm worn out, I'm kinda looking forward to the ride home.

"Hey."

I stop and turn my head. For a second, I think he's going to ask for my number, but instead he takes something out of the cardboard box and tosses it to me. I catch it. It's a little blinker light. When I press the button, its white LEDs start to flash on and off.

"Thanks."

I snap it onto the seat post of my bike and give Skunk an awkward wave good-bye. He picks up his box and stands there watching as I walk my bike down the side of the house, as if to make sure he put the wheel on right.

I get to the street, hop on, and don't stop pedaling until I can see the lights on my front porch.

chapter five

"I can't believe you went down there. You *do* realize that guy who called you was running a scam."

Lukas unscrews the glass jar with the fuzzy green nugget of weed at the bottom. He reaches in, breaks off a tiny chunk, and places it in a silver grinder. Lukas packs a bowl like it's a Japanese tea ceremony: formal, lengthy, and full of cryptic little steps that absolutely have to be done the right way.

"Oh, come on, Lukas—"

He cuts me off. "Let's see. Calling people on the phone, telling them you have valuable heirlooms belonging to their dead relatives and all they have to do is meet you downtown alone at night to pick them up. Sure, Kiri, doesn't sound like a scam at all."

"He didn't say he had anything valuable, he just—"

"He could have knifed you. He could have stolen your bike. I mean, no offense, but wasn't your sister kind of a druggie? What if it's one of her druggie friends?"

"Sukey wasn't a druggie. What makes you think she was a druggie?"

"Didn't she die of an overdose or something?"

"No!"

"How'd she die, then?"

"She was in an accident."

"What kind of accident?"

"What kind of accident do you think? There's a *reason* I'm still not allowed to drive."

I say it a bit too vehemently. Lukas glances up.

"Sorry. I'm just saying maybe it's a good thing you didn't find him."

My cheeks flush. At the time Sukey died, I was a giggly seventh grader whose idea of a good time was playing my favorite Disney songs on the keyboard over and over with my equally giggly friends. I know there are details about the accident that Mom and Dad have never told me, and a pathetic little part of me is grateful for that. Just thinking about the *possibility* of details makes my mouth go dry and my stomach clench like I'm going to throw up—if I knew exactly what she had been doing, or where she had been going, or who she had been fighting with on her cell phone before she crashed, I'd feel sick for the rest of my life.

Lukas takes the lid off the grinder and taps the weed out onto the book on his lap. *One Flew Over the Cuckoo's Nest.* I gave it to him for his birthday. He unzips his pencil case, takes out the teak pipe he got at the Balinese import store on Commercial Drive, and packs the weed into it carefully like he's tucking it into bed. His eyes narrow in concentration.

"Why don't you ask your dad about it?" says Lukas. "Your parents can get email on their cruise ship, right?"

I reach behind my head and massage the muscles in my neck. Even though I didn't get home until late last night, I still got up early and practiced piano for five and a half hours before coming over to Lukas's house, just like my schedule said, and I can feel it in my shoulders and back.

"My dad would just tell me I shouldn't have gone down there."

"What about your mom?"

"She never knows anything about anything."

When confronted with any kind of life situation, Lukas can be trusted to direct you to one of two handy flowcharts:

1. Ask Parent A ➡ *Ask Parent B*

or

2. Ask Parent B ➡ *Ask Parent A.*

If your problem cannot be resolved by talking to Parent A or Parent B, both charts direct you to *C: Problem Not Worth Solving.*

Which he does right on cue.

"Why do you want to find this Doug guy so bad anyway?"

"He has her things."

"What things?"

I cross my arms. "Never mind. It doesn't matter."

"What things?" he insists.

Sometimes, I hate Lukas.

"Well, he didn't say *specifically.*"

Lukas lets out a self-satisfied grunt. "See? I told you. Scammer."

He flicks his silver lighter and takes one long puff. He closes his eyes when he exhales, and I watch the smoke pour out from his lips and float up past the top of his head. Lukas never takes more than one hit, as if his senses are so refined that anything more than the slightest puff would leave him more baked than a tray of cookies. He hands the pipe to me. "Here."

I flick the lighter over the bowl and suck too hard. Lukas has been trying to teach me the right way to smoke weed for months, but I always end up burning the back of my throat. My eyes water. When I open my mouth, a huge cloud of smoke billows out, like I swallowed a burning building. Lukas watches me critically.

"Try to hold it in longer before exhaling."

I shut my mouth again before the rest of the smoke escapes. It's hard to hold my breath with Lukas watching me like that. I nod, cheeks puffed out, wishing I'd chosen a slightly sexier expression to freeze my face in.

"And don't draw so much in at once."

I let out my smoke, gasping. "No kidding."

I put down the pipe to take a breather. The room seems to sharpen, like I'm looking at it through the lenses of a new and miraculous pair of glasses. I gaze at the Christmas lights. "Lukas, did you ever notice that there's a pattern in the ceiling that looks like the Big Dipper?"

Lukas smiles, which inexplicably makes me think of clean-faced Russian peasants singing folk songs, and reaches out to gently pry the pipe from my fingers. "You, my friend, are a little high."

"I'm going to go back there and find that guy. I don't care if he's Hannibal freaking Lecter."

"All right, Nancy Drew. Hand over the piece." Lukas's fingers close around mine, trying to extract the pipe, which I have suddenly decided to hang on to.

"Just a sec, it's almost cashed."

Lukas has been teaching me stoner terminology to go with my smoking lessons: *cashed* for used up, *piece* for pipe. I think he's worried I'll make us look dumb in front of the older, cooler bands we'll naturally start hanging around with after we win Battle of the Bands if I don't learn proper form.

He tugs at the pipe/piece, rolling his eyes. "You're impossible."

"Come on. One little hoot."

"Fine." Lukas leans back while I take one last puff. When I surrender the pipe, he looks at me with the pseudo-exasperated fondness of a person who has been made, against his better judgment, to laugh.

"Ready to play now?"

I nod, beaming. Victory is mine. "Yup."

Playing music with Lukas is almost as good as doing Other Things with Lukas. He's been playing drums since he was ten, and I know my way around a keyboard, and neither of us is interested in playing drippy singer-songwriter covers like some of the other so-called musicians at our school.

And yes, when I say that jamming with Lukas is almost as good as doing Other Things with Lukas, I mean *those* Other Things. We have Done Things right here in Lukas's basement. Steamy things. Things that make my lady-parts glow with heat just thinking about them.

What Other Things have we done, you ask?

We kissed. Once. And Lukas put his hand on my leg. And I touched his earlobe with my finger.

It happened on the blue couch, after we'd each had half a glass of wine on Lukas's seventeenth birthday. Which was only twenty-seven days ago.

Since then I have replayed that erotic trifecta—the kiss, the hand on the leg, the finger on the ear—over and over and over again.

Lukas's forehead was warm. That's a weird thing that stayed with me, how warm his forehead was when it brushed mine, as if there was a little fire right inside his skull. I wanted to press against it so it burned me like a branding iron. I wanted a mark, something to prove that this rapture had really happened to me, to us. But when I leaned in to kiss him again, Lukas pulled away with a dazed or possibly dazzled expression, as if his senses were so refined he could only take one hit off the gravity bong of our mutual desire without getting completely fershnickered. So instead I took a safety pin when I got home and very carefully etched a tiny flame on my right ankle, just beside the bone.

In the slow, dreamlike days that followed, I touched the flame over and over again, thinking about him. The skull-burning intensity of that one kiss, I reasoned, was only a prelude to the intensity of Other Things still to come.

But the next time I saw Lukas, we didn't go to Kits Beach and make out on a blanket like I'd more or less planned.

Instead, we went to Kits Beach and had a three-hour discussion about how we shouldn't date because we're in a band together and it would be higher and purer to Focus on Our Art than to give in to undeniable physical attraction. Actually, I think Lukas used the word *fleeting*. Fleeting physical attraction. He said he was afraid it would get in the way of our music. This all based on some crackpot theory of Lukas's that love and music are a zero-sum game, as opposed to, say, the most explosively pleasurable combination ever invented. Like if we started dating, we'd spend all our time boning and wouldn't practice anymore. *I just want to focus on the band right now,* said Lukas.

I nodded and tried to be mature about it.

That makes sense. Yeah, I totally think so too.

But let's just say I haven't completely managed to convince myself he's right.

After jamming, when I'm about to go home, Lukas remembers he has some tracks he wants me to listen to. I sit on his bed while he downloads them onto my iPod. I like sitting on Lukas's bed. It smells nice and feels faintly forbidden, like touching Lukas's earlobes now that we're Focusing on Our Art. When Lukas hands me my iPod, the brush of his fingers practically gives me a stroke. I glance at the floor, then look up at him.

"Hey, Lukas?"

"Yeah?"

"You wanna come over to my house and watch a movie?"

By which I mean: Lukas. I have an entire *house* just sitting there. That's four beds and two couches, three if you count the short one in the basement. That's kitchen counters and carpeted floors. That's twenty-five hundred square feet of red-hot lovemaking just waiting to happen. Come over and be seduced by my wanton ways.

"You mean like right now?" Lukas says.

"Uh-huh."

I nod in what I hope isn't *too* suggestive a manner, but just suggestive enough to trigger Lukas's unconscious primal urges.

He stretches and yawns, casting a glance at the digital clock on his tidy IKEA desk. "I don't know. Me and my dad are going to Zulu tomorrow morning."

By which Lukas means: Kiri. Me and my dad are going to get up at seven a.m., go to Zulu Records right when it opens, and spend the next eight hours meticulously poring over twenty thousand dusty old used records. What could possibly be more stimulating?

I groan and dig my fingers into my eye sockets in a gesture of despair. "Maybe another night this week, though," says Lukas. "Have you seen *Zardoz*?"

"No."

"Oh, man. You're going to freak out. I'll get the DVD back from my cousin and we can watch it on Friday."

I smile all the way home. Lukas is coming over to watch a movie.

As my grandpa Bob used to say: If that ain't a date, I'll eat my hat.

chapter six

That night, I can't stop thinking about my failed attempt to meet Doug Fieldgrass on Columbia Street. I wonder who he is, and how he knew Sukey. I wonder why it took him five years to call. Lukas was probably right: It's some kind of scam, and I was stupid to even go. But there's a crazy little hope-squirrel running around inside my head, chattering, *What if it's real? What if it's important?* and it won't shut up no matter what I do.

I turn on some music and curl up on my bed with my Sukey Box, sifting through the photographs and trinkets I've looked at so many times I hardly see them anymore. Even though there's nobody home, I feel self-conscious sitting there with the door open. I hop up and close it guiltily, as if Mom or Dad is about to walk down the hall and catch me in my self-indulgence. I gaze at the picture of Sukey and me at my insect-themed seventh birthday party, wearing pipe-cleaner antennas and paper wings, and sniff the cigarette I stole from her purse one time but was too chicken to smoke, the paper gone soft and limp from so much handling. Usually I find these objects comforting, but tonight they frustrate me. Whatever that Doug guy has, I want it.

As I sort through the box, I rack my brain for ideas, theories, anything that could explain the phone call without arriving at *scam*. I think back to my disastrous bike ride, the broken glass and lost address. What I really should have done is asked him to drop off Sukey's things at our house—but then he'd know where I live, and what if he really is a sketchball?

I'm just about to pile the photographs back into the box when I spot it: the glossy five-by-seven card announcing an art opening: *6:00 p.m. at razzle!dazzle!space, e. pender @ columbia, feat. new works by sukey byrd and leon klemmer.* My eyes skid over the words *e. pender @ columbia* like a scratched record.

Holy crap.

I read the card again. Of course. That's why I recognized Columbia Street. How could I have been so stupid? I was just a block away when that creep on the bicycle scared me away. Hell. Sukey's friend was probably there waiting for me that whole time.

The art show was our first time seeing Sukey in almost two months. Mom and Dad had kicked her out of the house the day she turned eighteen, which suited Sukey just fine, because she'd been threatening to go live at her boyfriend Leon's art collective—Dad called it a loser collective—anyway. We got there late. Dad spent half an hour looking for a parking garage because he didn't want to park the Nissan on the street. Then we had to walk six blocks, and Dad kept barking at Denny and me to walk faster because there were homeless people on East Pender who were presumably planning to eat us for dinner if we showed the slightest sign of slowing down.

The place was hard to find, just a dirty white industrial-looking door in the side of a brick building. There was nothing to mark it as an art gallery from the outside, no plate-glass window with paintings on display, not even a street number. Sukey had given Dad directions over the phone, but he still seemed mad as he stood in the rain, fighting with the metal doorknob for a good thirty seconds before noticing the buzzer on the wall.

Inside, the room was dim, crowded, aswirl with people who all seemed perfectly at ease in such a covert location, who looked like they went to art shows behind unmarked doors all the time. I spied a table set up against one wall with trays of cheese and crackers and dozens of upside-down plastic wine glasses with their feet in the air. I cheered.

"I'm getting crackers!"

I started toward the table, but Dad grabbed my arm.

"Why not?" I wailed. I was ten years old, but still reverted to four and a half when I was upset.

His nails pinched my skin.

"No."

I stayed, tears of frustration hot in my eyes. Minutes crept by.

Men in shiny shirts helped themselves to cheese and crackers. Women with laughs like tropical monkeys sauntered past arm in arm. We stood there in silence, damp and grubby from the rain, like janitorial equipment someone had forgotten to put away. Sukey was nowhere in sight.

Denny pulled out his Game Boy and disappeared into the little green screen. Mom hummed tunelessly, playing with the straps on her purse. Dad stared grimly into the middle distance, his hand still clamped on my shoulder. They didn't take off their coats. I watched, limp with despair, as the party went on without us.

Then Sukey appeared in a short purple dress and silver heels that made her legs stretch almost all the way to the ceiling. Her long black hair was swept into an attractively messy high ponytail into which she'd stuck brown and orange feathers. The feathers gave her an exotic look, like the trickster raven in the

Northwest Myths and Legends book I was reading for school. Best of all, you could see her new tattoo—the silhouette of a bird on her right arm, just above her elbow.

"Jesus Christ," muttered Dad.

"Hey, guys!" she said, throwing her arms wide to embrace us all at once. When Sukey was in one of her good moods, she acted like everyone in the world was her best friend—even though her last face-to-face interaction with Mom and Dad had consisted of a screaming match after she'd gotten caught stealing champagne from the grocery store near our house for the second time in a week.

She winked at us. "Hey, Kiri. Den-Den. Have you guys looked around yet?"

"Well, we had a quick look," tittered Mom, which was so blatant a lie I twisted around, eyes wide with outrage, to glare at her.

"We can't stay for too long," said Dad. "I've got a conference call at eight."

Sukey's face flashed with something sharp and fierce, and for a terrible moment I thought they were about to have one of their fights. Leon's friends from the art collective had organized the show, and even at ten I had a vague sense that maybe that was why Mom and Dad were acting so weird. Leon was helping Sukey become a famous artist, but Mom thought he was too old for her and Dad said he was a Cradle-Robbing Junkie and that if Sukey thought he was going to help her become an art-ist, she needed to get her head checked.

Sukey and Dad stared each other down. Across the room, I could hear the monkey-women hooting and chortling with mirth. Dad's jaw was clenched, and Sukey's eyes had narrowed to smoldering points of black. But just when it seemed like things were about to get really nasty, she broke eye contact with Dad and smiled at me and Denny instead.

"Kiri, Den-Den, did you see there's pink lemonade?"

The mention of pink lemonade was almost more than I could stand. My face crumpled. "Dad said we couldn't have any."

I fought back the tears that were stabbing at the corners of my eyes. Beside me, Denny stared into his Game Boy screen and Mom kept up her wheedling hum.

"Oh, honey," said Sukey. "Come with me."

Without so much as a second glance at Dad, she took my grubby hand in her soft, vanilla-scented one and led me on a personal tour of the gallery. Our first stop was the snack table, where she poured me a cup of lemonade, rose-pink and thick with sugar, the kind that leaves sour flecks of lemon pulp on the back of your throat after you swallow. I remember the clear plastic cup and the square paper napkin I used to hold my Ritz crackers, salty and oily to the lemonade's sweet. We took our snacks and made a slow circle around the crowded room, stop-ping in front of each of Sukey's paintings. Every five seconds, another one of her friends would tap her on the shoulder and she'd spin around, beaming, to greet them.

"Hey, Neale," she'd say—or Wanda, or Feather, or Björn. "This is my little sister, Kiri." Their kindness, when they smiled at me, was mixed with bafflement, as if they could hardly believe that such a rare and dangerous creature as Sukey was related to such a plain and pudgy one as me.

When we said hi to Leon, he plucked the yellow flower he was wearing out of his buttonhole and slid it behind my ear. Leon was half Japanese, half German, and for a Cradle-Robbing Junkie he looked awfully dashing in his suit.

"Her name was Ki-ri, she was a showgirl," he sang, twirling me around like a ballerina while Sukey clapped her hands and laughed and laughed. When he was finished twirling me, he twirled Sukey, then dipped her like a tango dancer and kissed her on the lips. I looked on in awe and jealousy. The rules that applied to everyone else didn't apply to Sukey: She laughed and cried and yelled and danced without checking Dad's face first to see which one she was allowed to do. It was like she didn't even know you were supposed to.

Sukey's friends reminded me of the acrobats in Cirque du Soleil, which Dad's business partner, Sydney, had given us tickets to see—like at any moment they were about to swing from the ceiling, leap from the table, walk on their hands. They smelled like fizzy drinks and twitched a little, like mice.

I'd never met adults like that before and hardly believed they existed.

"Kiri's a fabulous musician," Sukey told them. "You should hear the songs she plays on her keyboard."

Whenever Sukey spoke, it was like I was eating one of the magical cakes in *Alice in Wonderland*. I grew taller and taller until my head bumped the ceiling, and the unhappiness of an hour ago shrank to the size of a pebble on the ground.

We paraded around the room, eating cheese cubes and chatting with Sukey's glamorous friends, while Mom and Dad hovered awkwardly near the exit, checking their phones and talking to no one. Every time I glimpsed their drab and miserable figures from the corner of my eye, I'd pretend I hadn't seen them. I wished they would disappear so I could join Sukey's glittering tribe and be one of them, happy and wild, with highheeled shoes and feathers in my hair. But when we finished our circle of the gallery, they were still there, bored and impatient, waiting to claim me like a lost piece of luggage plucked off a baggage carousel.

"Bye, Sukey," I said, but Leon the Junkie had already twirled her away.

I paw through the box, eager for more. At the bottom is a painting Sukey and I did together when she came to visit on my twelfth birthday. She was twenty then, almost twenty-one—a semi-adult, and as wondrous to me in her adultness as a movie star. I lived for Sukey's visits, basked in them, and clung to each murmured confidence as proof that I was the person Sukey trusted most in the world.

"Artists need their own space," she said, flicking her paintbrush across the paper we'd spread out on the kitchen table. "As soon as you can, Kiri-bird, get yourself a room just for making music. You'd like that, right? You can't make good art in Mom and Dad's living room. It's scientifically impossible."

There'd been some kind of drama with the art collective a few months back and Sukey had moved into her own place, a little studio where she could paint in peace. I'd never been there, but she'd told me all about it. She'd been working on a big painting ever since she moved in, and was already talking to some underground gallery about showing it when it was done. We hadn't been to any more of her openings since the one at razzle!dazzle!space, but maybe Mom and Dad would let me come to this one. Denny could drive me; he was sixteen. Sukey promised she'd let me know as soon as she found out when it was going to be.

"I've been working on a very avant-garde composition," I informed her, pronouncing it *avant-grad*.

Sukey laughed, a slow-motion twinkling of the vocal cords. I had a garage-sale Casio keyboard then, not even a real piano, and I was always making up songs with dramatic titles like

"Heartstorm" or "Prelude for a Broken Wing."

"You gonna play it for me before I leave?" she said.

I shook my head.

"Come on, Kiri-bird. I don't know when Dad's going to let me see you again."

Technically, Sukey was banned from even visiting our house after Dad found out she'd stolen some money last time she was here—for paint, Sukey told me. For jars of gold and arsenic and ochre. This birthday visit had taken some high-octane pleading on my part, and even then Sukey was only allowed in the kitchen and living room and not upstairs.

"It's not finished yet," I said.

Just then, Dad appeared to let Sukey know it was time for her to go home, which was no longer the same thing as our home.

"Can't she stay for dinner?" I said, playing the birthday card for all it was worth.

"That's okay, babe, I have to get going anyway," said Sukey, which probably meant she was fiending for a cigarette. "But let me give you your present."

I fidgeted with anticipation, wishing Dad would leave the room. He was standing there with his hairy arms crossed, watching her warily, like he thought she was going to give me something inappropriate he was going to make her take right back—birth control pills or a stolen piece of jewelry.

"I didn't have time to wrap it," Sukey said, pulling something out of her bag, but when I saw what it was, I was too happy to care. It was one of her bird paintings—she'd done this matching pair while she still lived here, and I'd been begging her to let me have one forever. The one she gave me had the words *we gamboled, star-clad* spiraling out over the birds in silver paint. The other one said, simply, *daffodiliad*.

"You're the BEST!" I kept saying over and over as I danced around the kitchen with the painting in my hands. I was still squealing my thanks when Mom came downstairs to talk to Sukey—or try to—before she left.

I didn't open the card taped to the back of the painting until after Sukey was gone. It said:

Hey, k-bird. Hang this in your room, and I'll keep the other one hanging in my studio. Be cool and don't be a faker. Love, S.

For the next few weeks, I worked furiously on my new composition. Hunched over my keyboard, I made up strange chords, bold rhythms, soaring melodies. Maybe I could play it at Sukey's art opening—we could even put my name on the card, *feat. kiri byrd on keyboard*.

I called and called Sukey's cell phone to tell her about this idea, but she must have lost it on the beach again, because she didn't pick up. Mom said not to worry; Sukey would call me back soon. I lay on my bed planning the details of our show: the crackers and lemonade, the clothes we'd wear.

When she died, it was like my house burned down.

chapter seven

The next morning I dress carefully, putting on ripped jeans, a vintage blouse, and the dangly beaded earrings that used to belong to Sukey and that have lived on my dresser ever since. If Doug Fieldgrass was calling from razzle!dazzle!space, he's probably the curator. I want to look hip and mature and artistic when I meet him; I want to look like Sukey.

Why's the gallery closing? I'll ask sympathetically. *It's such an interesting space.*

I try Doug's number three times, but he doesn't answer. I sit at the piano, telling myself to be patient, but after practicing for ten minutes, I decide to ride my bike downtown anyway.

Maybe he'll be at the gallery, and if he isn't, at least I'll know where it is for next time.

In daylight, Columbia Street seems way less sketchy. The Chinese grocery store is open, and there are wooden trucks of produce out on the sidewalk in front of it, long, hairy daikon radishes and bundles of bok choy and mountains of tangerines for fifty-nine cents a pound. The white lettering on the awning says MONEY FOOD ENTERPRISES, which I find impressive in its bluntness. In my neighborhood, even stores that sell nothing but lotto tickets and flavored cigars have names like Willowtree Natural and Organic Market. As I ride past on my bicycle, I can see old people with canvas shopping bags moving around the bins of dried fish and mushrooms, chatting in Mandarin.

Past MONEY FOOD ENTERPRISES, Columbia Street extends into Chinatown proper, with the pagoda-style roofs and dragon flags and a zillion little stores selling paper lanterns and mysterious plastic cooking utensils of indeterminate function. There's a restaurant piping out the twangs and trills of Chinese opera, and old ladies in floppy hats pushing fold-up trolleys down the sidewalk.

I ride up and down the block a few times, looking for the gallery. When I can't find it, I cruise down East Pender. No dice. There's a vacant lot that worries me, surrounded by a newly erected chain-link fence. I wonder if they've relocated, if the old building's been torn down. I pause next to the curb and call Doug's number, which I carefully programmed into my phone before leaving the house. It rings interminably, just like the three other times I tried to call him this morning.

Where Columbia meets East Pender, there's a small grassy park with cherry trees, an overflowing garbage can, and a few benches. I put away my phone and ride past the park very slowly, trying to figure out what to do. There are some people lounging on the grass under the cherry trees, two men and a woman, listening to music on a yellow plastic waterproof radio and passing around a tall brown bottle in a paper bag. Their shopping carts are parked next to the bench, piled high with clothing and recyclables. I'm biking so slowly it's obvious I'm either lost or looking for something, and one of the men calls out, "Whatcha looking for, honey?"

I stop and put one foot on the curb to stay upright. The sun's so bright I have to shield my eyes to look at them.

The man looks me up and down and chuckles. His skin is tanned to the color of old pennies, and he has ropy muscles like when he's not busy boozing he spends all his free time pumping iron.

"Your boyfriend run off on ya, sweetie?"

The woman sitting beside him punches him on the arm.

"Don't give her a hard time, Don. She's a baby."

She's wearing a pink corduroy jacket with fake fur around the collar, and she has the same round face and big boobs as my mom.

"I'm trying to find this art space," I say.

"The what? Speak up, baby."

"There's supposed to be an art space here. Somewhere on this block."

I feel awkward standing on the curb like this, squinting into the sun, shouting at her over the traffic noise like a dumb tourist asking for directions to Stanley Park. But I don't feel comfortable going onto the grass, either. It somehow feels private, like a front porch or a living room, and I'm reluctant to get any closer without an invitation.

Fake Fur Woman nudges her companion in the ribs.

"She's looking for the art museum, Don. You're in the wrong place, baby. You gotta take the number nineteen bus all the way downtown and get off at Granville. The bus stops right over there. You can stick your bike on the front, they got racks."

She's giving me directions to the big modern art gallery downtown. I squirm. It would be useless to explain. Instead, I nod and look where she's pointing.

"Okay, thanks. You guys have a good one."

"Take care of yourself, baby."

The guy named Don says something I can't make out, and I hear Fake Fur Woman telling him to shut up and be nice to that little girl. "She's looking for the *art museum*, Don!"

I wave good-bye to them and go a little farther down East Pender, scanning the storefronts for anything resembling the brick warehouse where Sukey had her show. There's a smoke shop and a convenience store, but nothing with the scuffed white door I remember. Then I come to some apartment buildings and a parking garage.

A parking garage like the one we circled the neighborhood for half an hour looking for on the night of Sukey's show.

I hurry back to the convenience store and ask the old Punjabi guy at the counter if he knows of an art space in the area. He glares at me like I've just asked if I can use the employees-only bathroom and shakes his head, muttering, "No."

I wander down a few alleys and even get excited at one point and knock on the door of what turns out to be a shelter for runaway teens. The spiky-haired woman who answers the door says the Freedom from Drugs Group doesn't start until one p.m., and I back away awkwardly, mumbling something about coming back later.

I look up razzle!dazzle!space on my phone's crappy internet browser, but either it doesn't exist anymore or it's too hip to have a website. I'm just about to ride home in defeat when I hear someone shouting at me.

"Hey! HEY!"

For a second I think I dropped something. I brake hard,

feeling my pockets for phone, wallet, keys. All present and accounted for. I scan the busy street until my eyes locate the person shouting.

He's lurching down the sidewalk on crutches, one denim pant leg pinned shut below the knee. His face is partly shadowed by the brim of his baseball cap. He has the body of a retired gym teacher or a summer-league soccer coach: square build, with strong-looking arms gripping his crutch handles and a sagging belly.

I'm still sitting on my bicycle. I warily dismount and lift it onto the sidewalk, already preparing my defense: *No, I don't have any spare change, I don't want to answer a personal question, no, no thank you, no.*

He catches up with me and I manage to sneak a quick glance at his face before looking back at the road, which I am pretending to scan for a friend's car. He has grizzled cheeks, lips so stained from smoking they're almost gray, and eyes too big for his head, like golf balls stuffed into sockets intended for marbles. When he speaks, his breath is sour with beer.

"You the kid came down here on the bike Tuesday night?"

I blink at him uncomprehendingly. He wobbles closer, his eyes flitting over my face, my clothing, and lingering on my earrings.

"I'll be damned," he mutters. "You are Sukey's sister, aren't you?"

When he says her name, my nerves light up. Those two syllables coming from a stranger's mouth, coming from *this* stranger's mouth, disorient me completely.

"Doug Fieldgrass," he says, extending a petrified claw. My ears ringing, I reach out and shake it.

"Kiri Byrd."

chapter eight

I don't like the way Doug smells, or the tattoo on his left arm identifying him as a member in good standing of the Hells Angels. I don't like the tallboy of Coors Light sticking out of his pocket, or the fact that he's as tipsy as a turtle at eleven a.m. I don't like the way he stands too close to me, breathing into my face like a boy at an eighth-grade dance. I don't like the reproachful tone of his voice, as if I've done something shameful and I don't even know what it is.

This is not the Doug I came here to find.

The Doug I came here to find is an artist who's been running razzle!dazzle!space for years, who knew Sukey back in the day, who will lead me through the white door to the echoey gallery and hand me a stack of canvases wrapped in brown paper that he just happened to find in the storeroom the week before.

This Doug lets a loud fart rip and says, "It's about goddamn time."

We shuffle down the street together, Doug with his crutches and me with my bike. I feel agonizingly conspicuous, like the sole, towering twelve-year-old at a day camp overrun by seven-year-olds. I can feel people looking at me, wondering what I'm doing here, what I'm doing with him. He has some kind of rash on his neck, the mottled purple-blue of uncooked sausage. As we walk, he talks nonstop.

"They're closing down the building, and I can't hold on to her stuff no more. We've all gotta move out by the middle of July. I say it's horseshit."

He cracks his Coors Light and takes a swig. I smell the warm, watery beer and struggle to keep my voice conversational.

"Are you from razzle!dazzle!space?"

"Razzle *what*?"

I try again: "How did you know Sukey?"

Doug swallows his beer and wipes his mouth with the back of his hand. "We were neighbors, eh. She was down the hall from me."

The knot in my chest unclenches. Sukey's art studio. It all

makes sense. But why would he wait five years to call? And why does he have stuff that belonged to her, anyway? Didn't Mom and Dad clear out her studio themselves?

Questions flit around the corners of my mind, but I bat them away. *Stop being such a Lukas,* I tell myself.

"Are you an artist too?" I babble, eager to make the pieces fit together.

"Whassat?"

"Sukey said there were lots of other artists in the building."

"She did, eh?" Doug chuckles, a rusty sound like a pair of scissors left out in the rain. "Good old Sukey. What a kid."

Doug jerks his chin at the brick building to our right. "This is the one. I saw you down there with your bike the other night, eh, but you ran off before I could come down and meet ya."

We're back at the intersection of Columbia and East Pender, across from MONEY FOOD ENTERPRISES, standing in front of that creepy hotel. Doug lifts a veiny hand and points at one of the windows on the fourth floor.

"Sukey-girl lived in that one. Four-oh-nine."

He takes another swig of beer and eyes my bicycle.

"Don't you got a boyfriend with a truck or something, honey? You won't get much home on the back of that thing."

I hardly hear him. The window Doug pointed at is a jagged spiderweb of splintered glass. There's something pushed up against it, a mattress or a piece of furniture, blocking the room from view. As I gaze at it, my elation at finding Sukey's studio turns into a cold lump at the pit of my stomach.

This can't be right.

Sukey wouldn't have lived here. Not in this building. Not down the hall from someone like Doug. And especially not behind that evil-looking window, four stories up from a piss-smelling sidewalk where even the pigeons look strung out.

I look back at Doug.

"Where'd you get my number?"

Doug turns his oversized eyes on me and lowers his beer.

"Looked it up in the phone book. Guess I shouldn't have bothered, eh?"

We stare each other down. I have the same swimmy feeling in my guts as I get before a piano recital. That trapped feeling, when there's still technically time to run away, slip out the back door, but at the same time I know I've come too far and invested too much to back out.

"She really lived here?" I say.

"Right here."

It occurs to me that Sukey might have moved here because it was the only place she could afford. Struggling artists always live in cheap places: drafty garrets, crumbling country estates, pay-by-the-week hotels in the Downtown Eastside. . . . But by the looks of the decaying humanoids slumped in the doorway of the Imperial Hotel, there hasn't been any art happening here in a long, long time.

I cast another glance at Sukey's window. "Can I come back in a few weeks?"

In a few weeks, Mom and Dad can deal with this. In a few weeks, I won't even have to get involved. The thought soothes me. Yes. I'll bike home and practice piano, then go to Lukas's for dinner.

Doug spits.

"I don't know, honey. Building wasn't supposed to come down until September, but now they're saying it might be sooner. And anyways, I'll be long gone before then."

"Can't somebody else hold it till I get the chance to—"

Doug crumples his beer can.

"You don't want to deal with it, guess it's going down with the rest of this dump. I told myself I was only going to try calling her family one more time. *We're not interested,*" he says, mimicking my dad's clipped syllables. *"I don't think so,"* he continues in the voice my mom uses with telemarketers.

A blaze of shame burns my cheeks. *They must have thought he was crazy.* I glance at his beer can.

Maybe they were right.

"Wait," I say. "I'm just thinking."

I could see if Lukas's mom would come pick me up. But she doesn't get home from work until six, and she'd ask too many social-worker questions anyway. I guess I could drag everything on the bus. . . .

Suddenly, I have an idea. It's a terrible idea and it will probably backfire. But it's the only thing I can think of that might actually work, and once I've thought of it, I can't let it go.

"I'll be back in ten minutes. Will you still be here?"

"Reckon so."

"I do want her stuff. I just need to go get—"

"Go on. I ain't going nowhere."

Doug crutches his way over to the doorway and sits down on the steps. He slides a half-smoked cigarette out of his pocket and lights it.

I get on my bicycle and pedal as fast as I can.

chapter nine

"Oh, hey. You brought back my light."

Skunk slides the door open a little wider and turns the bike light over in his fingers before slipping it into his pocket. He's blinking funny, and his hair's tousled as if he just woke up from a nap. He's wearing an old band T-shirt that makes him look like the kind of huge, soft, stuffed gorilla you win at a carnival for throwing a dart at a balloon. I know I should probably feel embarrassed about showing up at his house like this when he probably never expected to see me again, but all I can think about is getting back to the Imperial before Doug decides I flaked.

I wonder if Skunk can tell how edgy I am. I'm picking at

the rubber grips on my handlebars and dancing in place like a monkey. He rubs his eyes.

"How's the tire working out?"

"Great."

He glances at my bike appraisingly, as if he thinks I came here to get him to fix something else. Like my squeaky brakes. Or my questionable sanity.

Before I have the chance to lose my nerve, I jerk my thumb at the van parked in the alley.

"Is that yours?"

He nods slowly, his sleepy eyes still half-closed. "Yeah."

"Do you think you could give me a ride?"

I know it's a long shot. I'm pretty sure I just got him out of bed, and by the looks of it, the van probably doesn't even run. I know if some random stranger came and knocked on my door looking for a ride, I'd say hell no.

But Skunk just yawns and says, "Let me get my keys."

He steps back into the house, sliding the door and curtains all the way shut behind him. I wonder what he's hiding in there. Posters of naked death-metal chicks? Indoor grow-op? I try to steal a glimpse inside when he comes out, but he's too fast for me, and all I see before the door snaps shut is a slice of hardwood floor.

"Want to put your bike in the shed?" he says.

"Hm? Oh. Sure."

I follow him across the courtyard and wait while he unlocks the shed. When I hand him my bike, I get a shiver of anxiety, like I'm leaving an arm or a leg behind, or a baby, or a pet. As we walk to the van I resist the urge to run back and knock on the corrugated metal and say, *I'll come back for you soon, I promise.*

Skunk's van smells like cigarettes and sandalwood. The rust-colored upholstery is worn so thin it's shiny. The stereo is too old to have a CD player, and the cup holders are full of dusty cassettes that must have been there since he bought the thing. Even though Skunk hasn't asked for an explanation, I find myself babbling at him. Sukey. Columbia Street. Imperial Hotel.

He seems to get it.

There's a faded sticker in the corner of the windshield with a picture of a duck that says FRIEND OF MARSHLANDS. I point to it and say something, but we're driving down the alley and the gravel's making a racket under the tires. Skunk says, "What?"

"Are you a friend of marshlands?" I shout.

This time, Skunk says, "Yeah," and I flash him the devil horns because even if he's just saying that, that's badass.

We roll out of the alley and take a right, then left and a right again to get onto Columbia Street. I'm starting to relax a little now that we're on our way. I hate cigarettes, but I find it oddly comforting when cars smell like them. When Sukey lived at home, she smoked Marlboro Lights out her bedroom window, and sometimes if I was good, she'd let me flick the lighter.

"This it?" says Skunk.

I look out the window. It's taken us all of ten seconds to drive to the Imperial.

"Yeah."

"Want me to wait here while you grab your stuff?"

I nod, fumbling with the door handle. I can see Doug through the dusty van window. He's sitting against the wall with a couple other guys, talking. My heart bangs. I start to get out, and Skunk says, "You okay?"

The question takes me by surprise. I hang there awkwardly, my legs already out of the van and the rest of my body still inside it. I hate that question, "Are you okay?" It's like asking someone if they think you look fat. You're almost guaranteed to get a lie.

"Huh? Oh. Yeah. Of course I'm okay. Sorry. I'll try to be quick."

"No, I mean—take your time."

He glances out the window, taking in the snaggletoothed windows of the Imperial Hotel.

I give him my best and bravest smile. "Don't worry. I'll be done in five minutes, tops."

Doug and his homies are still drinking on the steps. When I walk over there, they're caught up in an argument over whether Larry stole Fink's cigarettes. Nobody looks at me. The guy who is apparently Fink is wearing a red ball cap that looks like it survived several cycles through a trash compactor. He has pale white skin and red hair that looks surprisingly delicate compared to the rest of his thickset body. The guy sitting next to Fink has a square chin and brown eyes and is wearing a denim jacket with fraying cuffs. The accused cigarette thief is not present. I make sure I speak loudly.

"Hey, Doug."

He ignores me. "I'm just saying if I see that son of a bitch come around here again, I'm gonna punch his goddamn lights out," he says to Fink.

"Hey, Doug, can you—"

"And if he says it's a free country, I'll say look, buddy—"

"Um, Doug?"

The guy in the jean jacket glances my way. "Doug, I think the little lady wants to talk to you." He elbows him in the side and jerks his chin at me.

"Oh, hello!" says Doug, as if I've just dropped in from outer space. "You're back."

"I'm back."

"And you want to ask old Dougie out on a date."

Fink and the denim-jacket guy start laughing, wheezing through their teeth. Even though I'm grateful for Skunk's van, suddenly I wish I had called Lukas's mom after all—she would have come up to the door with me, and she wouldn't have taken any shit. I square my shoulders and do my best to channel Petra Malcywyck: "Actually, I'm just here to pick up my sister's things."

Doug slaps the pavement beside him. "Siddown, have a drink with us."

He holds out his Coors Light. The thought of sharing beer that's been backwashed through Doug's gray lips revolts me. I wonder if Skunk's following this interaction from the van, but I'm too embarrassed to look.

"No thanks."

"Come on. Have some fun."

Doug floats the beer can back and forth in front of me in what is meant to be a tantalizing fashion. When I don't take the beer, Doug loses interest and becomes reabsorbed into another conversation with his friends, this time concerning a stray dog someone in the building has adopted. They've named the dog Jojo, and it trembles all over unless you speak to it very, very softly.

I realize that if I don't make a stand, I could be waiting here all day while they drink. I crouch down so my face is level with Doug's and clamp my hand on his shoulder.

"Hey! Doug! Let's do this and then I'll be out of your hair."

Fink and the other guy start giggling again. Doug gives them an exaggerated raise of the eyebrows and says, "The little lady wants me to show her upstairs."

At the word *upstairs* my temples throb. I hadn't thought about what it would be like to actually go inside. But if Sukey lived here, it couldn't have been that bad.

"Why don't you give old Dougie a hand up, honey."

He belches with so much vibrato I wonder if he's been classically trained.

My eyes flick to the crutches leaning against the wall. Of course.

I hold out my arms. He puts down his now-empty beer can and grabs my wrists in a fireman's hold. The warmth and dryness of his hands surprises me, like baseball mitts left out in the sun. I lean back and pull while he wriggles up on his leg, and when he's more or less standing he clamps a hand on my shoulder to brace himself while I hand him the crutches. I adjust my footing and we almost lose our precarious balance, but we find it again and Doug gets his crutches in place under his arms and then he's standing on his own.

For a second, we eye each other, catching our breath. Doug hop-steps over to the greasy glass door of the Imperial and pulls it open. I wait behind him, casting one last glance at the bright, sunny street before I step inside, hoping it's what Sukey would have wanted me to do.

chapter ten

"We and Sukey-girl were neighbors, eh. We shared a wall."

The elevator is broken, so Doug and I are climbing the stairs to the fourth floor. The stairwell is dark, narrow, and carpeted with what appears to be pureed roadkill. So far, we are on step number twelve and making such slow progress I'm pretty sure I'll have gray hair by the time we reach the fourth floor. He places the rubber tips of his crutches on a step, braces himself, and hoists his good leg up. This process is complicated by the fact that he is totally hammered and keeps putting his crutches at crazy angles and having to start again.

"We were real good neighbors. Sukey-girl was a sweetie pie.

She gave me Snoogie. That's my kitty cat, eh."

As Doug rambles, I remember Sukey dabbing yellow paint on my nose: *I have my own studio, Kiri. Right downtown.*

Why would she lie? I would have given her my entire allowance every week. I would have given her my birthday money. I would have begged Mom and Dad to let her move back in. Anything so she didn't have to live in a place like this.

Step fourteen. Doug plants his crutch in the middle of a half-eaten egg salad sandwich that's lying on the step. He doesn't notice and swings himself up anyway, then pauses to take a rest. The stale, eggy stench of the sandwich fills up the entire stairwell. Doug burps.

"Almost there, honey."

I roll my eyes. Almost there, unless you count a million more steps full of belching, dirty jokes, and rogue egg salad sandwiches.

Doug interprets my expression correctly for once and scowls.

"What's a matter? You got a TV show to watch?"

He squints at me reproachfully. When he looks at me like that, I do feel kind of ashamed for being impatient with an old disabled man trying to climb a million stairs on crutches, even if he is an obnoxious drunk. I bite my lip.

"Sorry. It's just, my friend's waiting with the van."

"I know, curly. You got somewhere to be."

He lifts the crutch that was on top of the egg salad sandwich and we start climbing again. The sandwich, horrifyingly, sticks to the bottom of the crutch and rides along until four steps after the second-floor landing, when it finally peels off. To make things worse, Doug clams up and proceeds in wounded silence while I drag along behind him. I never thought I'd wish for Doug to start talking, but now that he's not, there's nothing to distract me and I start to notice things I'd rather not notice, like the sound of a violent argument taking place a few floors above us.

Once we leave the stale sandwich behind, the stairwell smells sweet and rank, like a recycling bin full of soda cans gone syrupy in the heat. There's trash everywhere: food wrappers; nasty, scrunched-up paper towels; shoes and clothing that look like they were dredged up from a murder scene at the bottom of a swamp. I'm pretty sure there's been a used condom stuck to the bottom of my flip-flop for the last few steps, but I'm too afraid to look. Whatever it is, I can feel its rubbery squishiness every time I put my foot down. A door slams, and a few seconds later a woman comes storming down the stairs, swearing, an orange-green bruise on her jaw.

"Watch it, bitch," she says as she pushes past me, although I get the unsettling impression she hasn't seen me at all.

I wonder if Skunk's still waiting for me. I asked him to give me a ride, not sit in his van all day while I participate in some kind of absurdist play. I should have gotten his number and called him when I was ready to go. I shouldn't have come in here at all. The only thing keeping me going is my anticipation of what's waiting for me at the top of the stairs: a box of Sukey's paintings, maybe, and some of her cool clothes.

Doug grunts and pants. I try not to breathe. We make it to the third floor and start on the last set of steps. The light-bulb has burned out, and we struggle up the trash-infested staircase in watery dimness. It's too dark to make out what's on the steps, but I'm pretty sure the mystery condom on the sole of my left flip-flop has been joined by a mystery cigarette butt on my right.

I get a queasy feeling when we pass from the third flight of stairs to the fourth. From this point on, I've gone too far to turn back. It's like that time in ninth grade leadership camp when they made us swim to an island a mile from shore. After the first twenty-five minutes, the beach was too far away to swim back to, but the island was still a green blob in the distance, and I was out there, in the open ocean, way behind the other kids, with nothing to grab on to and the bottom too deep to stand.

Tap-tap-THUMP.

Doug hoists himself up the last step and starts down the hall. The light in the hall is busted too, and the fire door is clogged with trash. The glass box that used to hold a fire extinguisher has been smashed, and there's a greasy pay phone bolted to the wall with its receiver hanging down by a mangled cord.

Doug reaches out and brushes his fingers against a battered door.

"Sukey-girl lived right here."

I glance at the door as we go past it. Some of the other doors on this floor are missing their knobs or have a hole in the wood where the deadbolt used to be. Sukey's door is the only one that has all its parts. Maybe there's a perfectly good apartment in there, where Sukey hung her bead curtain and set up her paints and easel in the corner. Maybe she lived here because it gave her a morbid kind of inspiration for her paintings. Or because no matter how dingy it was, it beat living in the same house as Dad.

Doug opens his door and goes into his room. I hover in the hallway, fingering the cell phone in my pocket, getting ready to call for help at any moment. I can hear Doug clomping around in there, knocking things over in the dark, trying to call his cat out of the shadows.

"Kit-kit-kit-kit-kit! Kit-kit-kit-kit-kit!"

I glance into Doug's room. There's a towel nailed over the window and no bulb in the ceiling fixture. All I can make out is a mattress piled with clothes, a few odds and ends of furniture, and a photo in the kind of cheap plastic frame you can buy at the dollar store. There doesn't seem to be a kitchen or a bathroom. I wonder how many floors down he needs to go to use a toilet.

A moment later Doug comes back to the door carrying something in the crook of his arm. At first I think it's some bundled-up laundry, but he hands it to me, and it's a scruffy white cat with pale red eyes and a stump where its back right leg used to be. It meows and tries to scramble out of my arms. Doug goggles at it fondly.

"This is Snoogie. Sukey-girl found her in the alley."

I am trying to unhook Snoogie's claws from my shirt. She meows again and tries to climb me like a tree. She manages to get up to my shoulder, then digs in her claws parrot-style and won't let go, surveying the world with a look of such extreme cat-paranoia I start to wonder if she knows something I don't. Doug reaches up and strokes her affectionately.

"Snoogie's a good cat."

Actually, Snoogie seems like a very bad cat. But I don't say this to Doug, whose perception has clearly been warped by love and/or cheap beer. As I watch him pet her, I start to get anxious. What if I've come all this way for nothing? What if all he has to give me is a busted old lamp or some moldy bath towel he's been hanging on to for five years? Maybe there's a good reason my parents hung up on him the other times he called. My thoughts flit guiltily to my piano, sitting neglected in a dust-spangled shaft of light. *Later,* I promise myself.

"Hey, Doug?"

"Whassat?"

Doug isn't listening. He's too busy gazing at Snoogie, who is currently attempting to climb from one of my shoulders to the other by way of my head.

"Are her paintings here?"

"Say 'gain?"

Snoogie hops down to the floor and darts into Doug's room. He finally looks at me.

"Do you have Sukey's paintings?"

"There weren't no paintings left at the end, nah. She got into one of her moods and started giving 'em away until there weren't none left. She gave one to me, big yellow painting, but those crackheads came in here and stole it. You can't have nothing nice here without someone coming around and stealing it. Hang on, I'll grab you what I got."

Doug closes the door halfway and disappears into the murk. I hear him banging into something, swearing, and pulling open a stuck door. I glance into the room and see him rummaging through a closet packed with garbage—*actual* garbage, soda cups and napkins and cigarette boxes. It's all tumbling out around his skinny ankles in a mini avalanche of crap.

Great, I think, stepping back from the door. *He's one of those crazy hoarder people.*

"Hey, Doug?" I call. "I kinda need to go."

"Hold on, honey," he hollers back. "I had to bury the bag real good so those crackheads couldn't find it."

I hear cans rattling to the floor, and a grunt of effort from Doug. "Sukey and me were like family," he wheezes. "People got to take care of each other down here. I woulda called you's sooner, but I've been sick."

I roll my eyes. *Sure. If by sick, you mean hammered.*

I poke my head through the door and see Doug hauling a big black trash bag out of the closet.

"D'you want some help?"

Doug doesn't seem to hear me. He rests on his crutches to catch his breath. I step into his room and pick my way across the cluttered floor. "What's in there?"

The cat runs out from under a wooden coffee table and jumps onto the mattress. Doug gazes after it.

"Sukey-girl's things. The manager sent someone in there to dump all her stuff in the trash after the cops left and I said, that ain't right."

Doug aims his foot at the middle of the bag and gives it a push.

"Think you can lift that?"

I eye the bag doubtfully.

"Yeah."

I grab the garbage bag around the neck and hoist it onto my back. Doug watches me struggle upright.

"You got it, honey."

"What did you say about cops?" I say, trying to balance the bag so it doesn't knock over any of Doug's stuff.

I know Sukey got in trouble with the police a couple times after she moved out, because Dad used to get phone calls late at night and have to drive down to the station. Doug ignores the question.

"Big yellow painting. Size of that window. She did it just for me. Reminded me of wheat fields. I bet your daddy's got a dozen of 'em, eh?"

"No. She didn't give him any. I only have one, in my bedroom. I was hoping you'd—"

"We always joked I was gonna be rich someday when she got famous and the paintings were worth money, eh. I said, Sukey-girl, you're gonna make me and Snoogie into millionaires."

The heavy bag is pressing into my back. I can feel myself starting to sweat. I know I should head for the stairs, but my feet refuse to move.

"Doug? Why did you say there were cops?"

He's produced another beer from some hiding spot, and now he cracks it open. His bloodshot blue eyes are wandering.

"Goddamn management didn't hardly wait twenty-four hours before they stuck the next person in there. They got this rat-faced little tweaker moved in before the blood was even dry on the floor. There's no respect around here. None at all."

I wheel around to see Doug better and knock over a half-full can of beer that was perched on top of an unplugged mini-fridge. I really wish there was a light in here, because I'm starting to feel claustrophobic in the dimness with a giant trash bag pressing on my back and my ears buzzing louder and louder with every word Doug says.

"Doug," I say in my steadiest, untrembliest voice, "what are you talking about?"

Doug reaches out to stabilize the bag before it slips out of my hands. He holds on while I get a better grip. While I'm trying to find the right place to rest the weight of the bag on my shoulder, he leans his face in close to mine and fixes me with his big drunk eyes.

"Oh, honey," he says. "Don't tell me you don't know."

chapter eleven

When I step outside again, the world feels like it's been Photoshopped: The colors are supersaturated, and the brightness levels are way too high. The garbage bag containing Sukey's earthly possessions is a huge sticky lump on my back. I feel like an insect, an ant carrying a crumb a hundred times bigger than I am. Except unlike an ant, I can't handle this load. It's too big. I can smell the panic in my sweat. I literally cannot breathe.

I see Skunk's van parked by the curb. Sunlight is glaring off the windshield. I lurch toward it, the garbage bag riding on my back like a monster, a mountain, a grotesque ball-and-chain.

Don't-think-about-it-Don't-think-about-it-Don't-think-about-it.

There's a thin, tight thread running between my heart and the crown of my head that's threatening to snap. I try to focus on getting to Skunk's van, but the world is loud and awful and heavy, and the truth is even worse. I don't know if I can make it to the van. I don't know if I can make it another step. I can feel the plastic garbage bag stretching and straining, and it's just a matter of which one of us breaks first.

Don't think about it.

I hear a car door slam.

"Kiri?"

Don't cry.

Skunk lumbers toward me. Something about the sight of his scruffy T-shirt anchors me, and I shuffle toward him like a duckling imprinting on a backhoe.

"Hang on."

I stop. Skunk lifts the bag off my back. I wait next to the van while he opens the back door and hoists the bag inside. My back and shoulders are aching from the trip down the stairs, and my heart is beating so hard it feels like it's trying to dig a tunnel out of my chest.

"You okay?"

Don't cry.

My best and most reliable Normal Voice comes out as a

high and strangled squeak.

"Yup."

"You sure?"

Rapid nodding.

"You want a ride home? You look kind of freaked out."

I decide that Skunk must be very perceptive for a person whose wallet is attached to his belt by a chain. When I get into the van and close the door, I am finally able to breathe.

Just as we're buckling our seat belts, Doug comes staggering up the sidewalk and knocks on the window. I can't imagine how he got down the stairs so fast—he must have rolled down, or used someone's greasy pizza box as a toboggan. I don't want to talk to him, but the morning has already taken such a gruesome turn it can hardly get any worse. I grab the old-school plastic handle and crank the window down. He sticks his grizzled old face through the window. His beer breath fills up the whole van. I notice Skunk sizing him up, probably wondering whether to step on the gas and rip his head off.

"Hey. Hey!"

Doug's shouting like we're across the street from him, not sitting within spitting distance. His yellow fingers grip the edge of the window like he thinks that's going to stop us from driving away.

"Honey, listen. I didn't mean to upset you back there, eh? We all loved Sukey-girl."

I don't want to hear it, and I don't want Doug's nasty beer spit spraying onto my skin. His face is huge and mottled and much, much too close.

"It's fine."

He leans his head in even closer. "I didn't mean to scare you, eh, honey? You know if you ever—"

"IT'S FINE."

His eyes widen, and he moves his head back like I'm the one shouting in *his* face while he's trying to drive away. He glances back toward the doorway of the Imperial but doesn't lift his fingers off the edge of the window. When he speaks again, his voice has gone down to a normal volume.

"Hey, do you think you could help me out with five bucks?"

I stick my hand in my pocket, fish out a bill, and push it at him. He grunts and peels his fingers off the window. I look at Skunk. "Let's go."

Skunk signals and pulls out into traffic, leaving Doug standing there on the sidewalk with his crutches. I watch his crooked shape recede in the rearview mirror.

We drive down Columbia Street, and soon we've put one block, two blocks, three blocks between ourselves and the Imperial Hotel. The farther away we get, the less real the Imperial seems, until what happened in Doug's room starts to feel fake, implausible, like something that couldn't have happened after all.

Except that it did.

Skunk reaches into the cup holder. "Coffee?"

I realize that's what I've been smelling for the past two minutes. He lifts a hot paper cup and hands it to me.

"Thanks."

"It's black."

"That's fine."

I smile at him, doing my best to keep a lid on things, secure the emotional perimeter, choke off the flood inside me like a thumb clamped over a garden hose. It's my own fault for going in there. I should have gone home and practiced piano like I wanted to.

I feel a stray sob straining at the back of my throat and take a sip of coffee to suppress it. But somehow, when I swallow my coffee I forget to not think about what Doug told me, and before I know it there's coffee all over my lap and tears washing over my cheeks and my chest hurts so bad I actually look down to see if I've been shot. I wipe my nose on my sleeve and try to jam the mostly empty coffee cup back into the cup holder before I spill it all.

Skunk is steering with one hand and feeling around under the seat for a napkin with the other. Neither of us knows where we're going. I try to stop crying and apologize, but all I can manage is a series of soft shrieks.

"I'm sorry," I gasp.

"Shh, no, it's okay."

He finds a stack of napkins in an old Taco Bell bag and hands them to me. I put them on my lap, and within a matter of seconds they're all soaked. Between sobs, I somehow blurt it out: "I just found out my sister was murdered in that hotel."

When I say it out loud, I immediately regret it. It's just like the time I told Petra I was stressed out over auditions for the Showcase: He's going to think I can't handle it. Now each time he sees me—assuming we ever see each other again—he's going to think of this tearstained freakazoid who got him to haul her murder-bag home in his van.

"I thought it was an accident," I babble through my tears. "My parents said—they never told me she was—"

Murdered.

When I get to that word, my throat constricts. I don't know who killed her or why he did it or if they caught him or what Sukey did or didn't do to bring it on. Doug didn't get that far before I bolted for the stairs.

All I heard was the word *stabbed.*

Followed shortly by the word *death.*

Skunk glances over at me and gently touches his hand to my elbow.

"Hey."

I turn my face away so Skunk won't have to witness how

pitiful I am with my messy tears and blotchy face. Outside the van, the world is surreal, going about its business with incomprehensible calm. A FedEx truck idles next to a mailbox. A man with two little kids comes out of a noodle shop holding a stack of Styrofoam take-out boxes.

"Where are your parents?" Skunk says softly, as if I'm a lost kitten he's trying not to scare away. "How do we get you home?"

He fishes in his pocket for his cell phone.

"Here."

I wave it away, sniffing back my tears.

"It's okay, I'm fine."

"Are you sure you don't want to call your mom or dad?"

"I can't, it's long distance, they're away on this cruise."

"Is there someone else?"

"No, I'm really fine."

Skunk keeps a firm grip on the wheel. "You wanna just drive for a while? Want me to take you back to your house?"

A new wave of grief breaks over me, and I can't answer him. All I can think about is Sukey, my Sukey, with her zebra-print jacket covered in blood.

We drive on in silence. Skunk flips the turn signal and does a U-turn at the green light. I wonder if he's taking me back to the Imperial to be with the other freaks and crazy people where I belong. But we drive past the Imperial and farther into Chinatown. I watch the red lampposts going by.

"Where are we going?" I croak, my voice hoarse from crying.

He signals and pulls into a parking spot. His face, flat and groggy when I knocked on his door this morning, has sharpened with resolve.

"Lucky Foo's for dim sum. And then maybe the China Cat Bakery for buns with red bean paste."

chapter twelve

Whoever says that food can't fix your emotions has never eaten a plate of salty, oily dim sum at Lucky Foo's. By the time the waitress comes by with our third pot of Lapsang souchong, I've turned from a ragged, sobbing wreck into an exhausted puddle. The dim sum we ordered is long gone. But I feel like as long as I stay here, snug and cozy in the dim wooden booth with the stone fountain burbling in the corner, I'll never have to face whatever's waiting for me in the back of Skunk's van.

I've told Skunk everything.

I told him about Sukey's art show.

And about the time she snuck me out to McDonald's past

my bedtime and we shared a chocolate milkshake.

And about the purple paint splatter on the carpet of Sukey's old bedroom that Mom never managed to scrub out.

And about the matching paintings she promised we'd hang in our bedrooms forever, *daffodiliad* and *we gamboled, star-clad.*

"And you had no idea she was murdered?" says Skunk.

"No!" I burst out, louder than I need to. "They said it was an accident. They made it sound like a car crash. Drunk driving, something like that. Mom said it wasn't nice to talk about."

"Nobody mentioned it at the funeral?"

Skunk's voice is gentle, but his eyes betray a hint of incredulity. He's right. How could you not know how your own sister died? My parents must be pretty great liars.

A little voice inside me adds, *Or you must be pretty great at playing along with them.*

I mumble into my teacup, "I didn't go to Sukey's funeral."

The silence that stretches between us swarms with unsayables. I know what Skunk's thinking.

"My parents didn't want me to," I squeak. "They said I'd be too upset."

Instead, I stayed home with Auntie Moana, in my pajamas all day like a little kid. We watched TV and made cookies, and when they came home from the funeral, Mom and Dad and even Denny made a big deal out of how delicious they were.

Later, Mom sat on my bed and gave me "the talk"—*this is what we say when people ask about Sukey's accident, this is how we act*—then asked me if I wanted to go to Central Music next week and pick out my very own grand piano.

"Didn't they tell you later?" says Skunk.

"No," I say, but I'm remembering the music store, the guitars hanging from the walls, the pianos herded together like elephants, shiny uprights and voluptuous baby grands. I felt a strange mix of guilt and anticipation as I wandered through them, testing the keys. Denny turned mean when Sukey died, lashing out at the slightest provocation, going straight to his bedroom the minute he got home from school. I had to be the good one. The talkative one at dinner. Mom and Dad needed me, it was obvious from the way they'd started lavishing me with praise for the stupidest things. The smiles on their faces when I picked out my piano said it all: Someone in our family was going to be okay, and we'd all somehow agreed that person was going to be me.

Skunk reaches for the teapot. When he does, the sleeve of his T-shirt rides up, and I see the tattoo on his upper arm.

"Sukey had a tattoo of a bird in the same place," I blurt. "What's the story with yours?"

He finishes pouring the tea and sets the teapot down, his sleeve sliding back over the delicate shape of the bird. His hand moves to his shoulder protectively.

"Nothing. It's from a band I used to be in. We all got the same one. It's stupid."

"No, it's not. Can I see it? What was your band called?"

He looks uncomfortable, like he's sorry he ever poured the tea. So far, Skunk hasn't answered any questions, not that I've asked very many. When he talks, it's always something short, a door he slides shut quickly so whatever's inside won't escape. He looks down at the table.

"It doesn't matter. It was a long time ago."

"It can't have been that long ago. How old are you?"

"Eighteen."

Three years younger than Denny. I'd been trying to guess. "Are you in school or something?"

"Not right now. I'm starting a bike repair apprenticeship in September."

I trace the rim of my teacup with my finger. "I'm in a band too."

He looks up, glad to have the attention deflected from him. "Oh yeah? What do you play?"

"Synth. I've got an old Juno." I sniff. I have that post-cry headachy thing, like my head is being crushed inside a vise. "We haven't actually played any shows yet, but we're doing Battle of the Bands this summer at the Train Room. Do you ever go to shows there? It's, like, the only all-ages venue that doesn't suck. It's pretty near your house."

The smile that was starting to form when I said I played synth vanishes from Skunk's face. It's like somebody drew a curtain: His expression goes neutral, mouth straight, eyes blank. I pick up the clay pot and pour him some tea.

"What's wrong? What are you thinking about?"

"Nothing."

"Come on."

"My band played a show there once." He shakes his head as if to dislodge the memory. "But I haven't been back."

I imagine Skunk onstage, pawing an electric guitar. I try to guess the band name that goes with the tattoo—Bird Slayer? Big Skunk and the Birds of Death? Whatever it is, it can't be as bad as Sonic Drift. I pick up my warm teacup and cradle it in my hands. "Why'd your band break up?"

"It didn't." The words seem to pop out of Skunk's mouth before he has a chance to stop them. A look of regret flashes across his face, and he hurries on before I can question him.

"They went back to the East Coast," says Skunk. "And I stayed here."

I'm about to ask him why, but the bells on the restaurant door tinkle softly, and a party of five crowds into the tiny reception area. It's almost six—dinnertime. Time to give up our table. I decide to let him off the hook.

"I guess we should go."

"Sure you don't want more dim sum?"

"I'm good."

Skunk nods. "I'll give you a ride home."

When Skunk drops me off, we trade numbers so I can pick up my bike later.

"I don't really keep my phone turned on all the time," he says, handing me back my phone after keying his number into my contacts. Which I take to mean: *I hope to God this messed-up girl doesn't start calling me.*

He lifts the garbage bag out of the van for me and dismisses my renewed volley of thanks and apologies with an embarrassed shake of his head. He looks relieved as he pulls out of the driveway, giving me a quiet half wave over the top of the steering wheel. By the time I carry the bag to the front door, he's already gone.

Even though my first instinct is to rip the garbage bag open as soon as I get in the door, that's not what I do. There's something about the house that stops me: the neatness of the shoes on my mom's prized Pottery Barn shoe rack, the muted coolness of the front hall. I pause, my fingers already tearing through the thin plastic, and force myself to lift them off.

This is neither the time nor the place, the house seems to say. *Have some self-restraint.*

I stand up reluctantly and gaze down at the garbage bag. As if on cue, the antique clock in the living room chimes six o'clock. With each sanctimonious *tong* of its bells, I feel more and more ashamed of myself.

I have duties, I remind myself. Responsibilities. While I was out making a fool of myself in the Downtown Eastside, I missed six hours of piano practice. While I was out there blubbering over private family business with a total stranger, the azaleas went unwatered and the mail went unretrieved.

I glance at myself in the mirror hanging opposite the front door. Puffy, tearstained face. Messy hair. Pitiful eyes.

I remember the day when my seventh-grade teacher called my parents to tell them I'd been crying in the bathrooms at lunchtime after Sukey died—how disappointed Dad was that I was using Sukey's death as an excuse to get attention from my teachers; how delicately Mom suggested that Sukey would have wanted me to be happy; my humiliation at letting them down.

Get it together, Kiri.

I take a deep breath, pick up the garbage bag, and carry it up the stairs. I pause in front of my bedroom, then change my mind and go one door down to Sukey's old room. Ever since Mom turned it into a guest bedroom, it doesn't feel like Sukey's at all. The walls are solid white where they used to be covered in Sukey's paintings. There's a Monet print where Sukey used to have a Nirvana poster. The purple stain on the carpet is the only real trace of her left in the whole house.

Now, my mom keeps the bed in here done up like a bed in a

hotel room, with a fancy duvet and a dozen completely unnecessary decorative pillows that you have to throw on the floor just to have enough room to lie down. There's a fuzzy white hotel bathrobe that nobody has ever used hanging from a hook over the closet door, and a bath towel, hand towel, and washcloth folded up neatly on a low Japanese table at the foot of the bed, just waiting for a guest with extremely high-maintenance Toweling Needs to show up and use them.

I pad across the carpet and place the garbage bag in the middle of the tightly made bed, then walk out and close the door.

When I sit down at the piano and turn the metronome on, I feel a wave of relief. The metronome's metal arm ticks back and forth and I play smoothly and evenly, never missing a note.

Three hours pass quickly, by the end of which I am as calm and steady and reasonable as the metronome itself.

See? I tell myself as I slip into bed. *Everything's under control.*

chapter thirteen

For the next three days, I am a model of self-discipline. Up at six. Practice until eleven thirty. Eat some leftovers straight out of the Tupperware without even warming them up. Water my mom's azaleas. Bring in the mail. Drill my pieces some more. When I go over to Lukas's house for band practice, I tell him what happened and make him promise not to tell his mom.

"I *knew* you should have called your parents before agreeing to meet that guy," he keeps saying, which is not the reaction I was expecting, but he gives me this sweet, awkward hug and even walks me home at the end of the night, telling me to call if I need anything.

Each time I pass Sukey's old bedroom on my way to the bathroom, I can hear the garbage bag in there, whining like a ghost. I don't open it. I can't open it. I tell myself I'll open it once I've practiced for a few more hours.

I practice for a few more hours.

I still don't open it.

The piano is a sleek black submarine that carries me deep, deep down, until the surface world is nothing but a muffled shimmer. I practice carefully, paying attention to each note. I polish my pieces the way our neighbor, Mr. Hardy, polishes his vintage Thunderbird. Slowly. Obsessively. As long as I'm sitting at the piano, the entire universe is under my control. Eighty-eight keys, ten fingers. Sheet music is dependable. The notes don't change when you're not looking. You don't open your book one day to discover that your pieces have switched from major to minor, or that the fast ones have gone slow, or that the melody has changed beyond recognition, leaving your fingers to stumble over unfamiliar notes. You don't have to be brave, just careful.

When my parents call to give me an update on their snorkeling adventures in the Caribbean Sea, I keep my voice bright and interested. While Mom tells me all about the tropical fish she saw in the coral reef this afternoon, I plan out exactly what I'm going to say, how I'm going to bring it up.

I found out about Sukey—too accusatory.

One of Sukey's old friends called—too complicated to explain.

"Your dad saw a giant sea tortoise. How big was it, Al? Three feet? We just bought an underwater camera."

For some reason, hearing my mom chatter on about their cruise makes my throat go thick and soggy. It's like they're on this sunny planet where everyone's happy and nobody has bad news, and I'm this evil astronaut coming down from outer space to ruin it all. When I finally speak up, I don't even tell them about going to the Imperial.

What I say is, "What happened to the person who killed Sukey?"—as if I had known how she died all along.

I thought they'd freak out when I said that. I thought they'd say, *Oh, Kiri, how did you find out? Did Denny tell you?* and they'd fuss about how sorry they were for lying to me and ask if I was okay.

But instead they act like I asked if they know where the blade for the blender is because I want to make a banana smoothie. Mom demurs and Dad says something dismissive, and somehow we're back on sea tortoises and piano. The conversation feels like one of those shopping carts whose wheels lock if you try to push it past the edge of the parking lot. There are things I want to say, but I just can't.

"Did your program for the Showcase come in the mail yet?" Mom says cheerily.

"No, but—"

"Do you know if you'll be competing with that Japanese boy?"

"He's Korean, Mom. I don't know. Did Sukey—"

"What?"

The connection is bad. Our voices are echoing on top of one another, piling up like cars in a highway wreck.

"I found a bag of Sukey's things," I enunciate loudly. "In the basement."

A little white lie, but whatever. At this rate, it would take about a million dollars' worth of long distance to explain the truth.

"Don't make a mess," says Dad. "I don't know who was rooting around down there last, but they left a snowboard right in the middle of the floor where somebody could trip over it and break their neck."

I don't think he heard me right. I clench the phone in frustration.

"There's a pianist on the ship who plays during dinner," says Mom. "You could do that for a summer job when you're in college."

I imagine myself in a cruise ship dining room, wearing a sequined dinner jacket and tootling out jazz standards while people like my parents eat lobster.

"Sounds good, Mom," I lie. "Sounds really, really good."

I go back to the piano and try to practice some more, but my hands start shaking, and no amount of scolding myself will steady them. I can't stop thinking about Sukey. I can hear her screaming with every note I play. I can see her face reflected next to mine in the piano's shiny surface, the same dark hair on our shoulders, the same blood running through our veins, leaking out, spilling on the floor.

I force myself to play the Beethoven.

Then play it again.

Then play it again.

But halfway through the third time, tears pool in my eyes until I can't even see the keys. I stop playing, peel myself off the piano bench, and stagger to the phone to call Lukas. He'll come pick me up. Petra will feed me borscht and lemon cake and let me sleep on the fold-out couch in the Malcywycks' tiny living room. She'll hug me to her solid, round body and tell me everything's okay, and later, once she's gone to bed, Lukas will take me in his arms and tell me the same thing.

I start to dial the Malcywycks' number, but a little voice in my head sneers at me.

Is that how you want to be? You want them to think you can't handle things? Go crying to Petra. I'm sure Lukas will find that very attractive.

I push the voice away and keep dialing. But it comes back.

Okay, fine, you can call—but don't do it tonight. If you still feel bad tomorrow, you can call. Tonight, take it easy. You don't even have to practice anymore if you don't want to. Just don't call right now.

My finger hovers over the last digit.

I press the red button and hang up the phone.

I'm just high-strung and need a break. No reason to turn it into a crisis. I stand in the kitchen, trying to decide what I want to do to relax. I could watch TV, or take a bath, or—

It occurs to me that the best way to deal with this situation is to get completely effing blazed.

Five seconds later I'm kneeling on my bedroom floor, pulling the old wooden jewelry box out from under my bed. I pop open the lid. The small plastic bag of weed and papers Lukas gave me a while ago is sitting there, untouched. I've never smoked by myself before, but tonight seems like as good a time as any to start.

I sit on the floor for a long time trying to roll a joint, then go downstairs and root through the junk drawer for the stem lighter we use to light the barbecue. I don't even own a lighter, that's how big a stoner I am.

The barbecue lighter isn't in its drawer. I open and shut a few other drawers, but it's not there either. I bang around the kitchen looking for it until I realize there's a perfectly good gas stove right in front of me. I switch on a burner and hold the tip of my messed-up excuse for a joint in the blue flame until it lights. I switch off the burner and blow out the little birthday-candle flame that has sprung up on the end of the twisted paper, put it to my lips, and inhale. The smoke tastes sour and pavementy, like a lemon candy dropped on the street. I turn on the kitchen fan for ventilation, mosey into the living room, and turn on the stereo.

This is fun, I tell myself, turning up the volume dial. The music sounds lush and comical, like something played by elves. I wander back into the kitchen and open a brand-new box of cereal. The flakes make a high ringing sound when they tumble into the bowl that somehow fascinates me. I stand at the counter smoking and shaking cereal into the bowl until I completely lose track of time. When I finally get out the milk, it's half past midnight.

I take one bite, dump the rest out in the sink, and drag myself to bed.

chapter fourteen

When I wake up, it's very bright and very warm and very twelve thirty p.m. The nightmare I was having about Sukey's murderer slinks out the back door of my mind. My mouth feels dry and sour like I just ate a gym sock, and I've got that throbbing headache that spells dehydration. I haven't practiced piano and I haven't opened the garbage bag, and now I have only twenty minutes before I have to leave for my piano lesson. From the second I open my eyes, I feel sick and shriveled and hollow in a way I know drinking a liter of water won't help.

I go to the bathroom, get undressed, turn on the shower, and step inside. As the water warms up, I remember flashes of my nightmare about Sukey. The part where I'm climbing the stairs of the Imperial Hotel with the massive garbage bag on my back, and I keep getting stuck between the railings. The part where she's waiting for me to come save her, the part where I can hear her calling me through the walls. The part where I finally get to the fourth floor and she's already dead. The part where I wake up and a spider is looking down on me from my bedroom ceiling, threatening to drop on my head.

I squeeze shampoo into my hand.

It's okay, I tell myself. *You're okay. Just breathe.*

I press my lips together and work the shampoo into my hair. It fills the shower with a happy floral scent, and for some reason that pushes me over the edge. I buckle over, sobbing, my head resting against the hard shower tiles. I remember crying like this when Sukey died, the tears harsh, devouring, total. I hadn't known I was capable of being so sad, and the discovery shocked and terrified me. It was like finding an extra door in the house I'd always lived in, and opening it to discover that the grief had carved out new rooms, new hallways, an entire bleak annex of its own. There were dark places in my mind I'd never known existed, and now that I'd seen them I knew they'd always be there, lying in wait, even when the original door had been sealed up.

I let myself cry for a minute or two, then stop as sharply as twisting off a tap. There's no time for this, no time. I have a piano lesson to get to, after all. *You can put the garbage bag in the basement until Mom and Dad get home,* I tell myself. *And you never, ever, ever have to go back to the Imperial Hotel.*

By the time I'm dressed and putting my piano books into my backpack, I feel a little better, woozy from those endorphins your body pumps out when you cry.

You're fine, I tell myself again as I lock the house and walk down the driveway. *You're just rattled from the nightmare.*

Mr. Hardy waves to me from his front yard, where he stands watering his lilac bushes with a hose. He's wearing khaki shorts and a T-shirt from Run for the Cure—standard retired-person gear. I give him a cheerful smile and wave back.

"Hey, Mr. Hardy."

See? You're fine.

My piano teacher, Dr. Scaliteri, lives way over in Kerrisdale, a forty-five-minute bus ride from my house. The Kerrisdale bus is always full of quiet foreign exchange students listening to iPods and the occasional mom in two-hundred-dollar exercise pants sitting next to a baby in a high-tech stroller. That's because Kerrisdale is the yuppiest neighborhood in the city. The streets are lined with fussy nail salons, chain clothing stores dressed up to look classy, and shops with names like Giggles and Birdy: An Upscale Baby Boutique that make you want to punch someone in the face.

Dr. Scaliteri's house is Historic and manicured to within

an inch of its venerable old life. She lives on a wide, tree-lined street with brand-new sidewalks and lots of that tall, wavy beach grass in people's front yards that's actually an invasive species. The house is all gleaming hardwood and stained glass, and the piano's an eleven-foot concert grand that looks more like a Hummer than a musical instrument. It even has that new-car smell.

While I'm playing the Bach, Dr. Scaliteri perches on a silver exercise ball, bouncing up and down and writing notes on a spiral-bound pad. She's wearing a low-cut black leotard, a dark red skirt, and silver ballet shoes. A golden pendant in the shape of a treble clef hangs between her crinkled old-lady cleavage. Dr. Scaliteri is in her sixties, but she still looks like the "piano teacher" in a low-budget porno: heavy mascara and piles of hair. All that bouncing on the exercise ball while she's giving piano lessons has done wonders for her thighs. Now and then while I'm playing, she hums or whispers something under her breath, which drives me crazy, but on the few occasions I've stopped playing and said, "What?" she literally made me wish I'd never been born.

I switched to Dr. Scaliteri from my old piano teacher, Mrs. Benjamin, right around the time my parents bought me the grand piano. She has a reputation as the toughest piano teacher in the city, and she takes only a few high schoolers. Most of her students are performance majors at the university, a tribe of pale, serious, vaguely subterranean-looking twenty-year-olds who look like they've been locked inside their practice rooms for weeks. There's tall Anna Weissberg, who plays for the symphony; Nelson Chow, who has just been accepted to Juilliard; the Fukiyama twins, Jeff and Mark, whose commitment to technical virtuosity is matched only by their commitment to wearing perfectly laundered Ralph Lauren polo shirts in cautious shades of tan and blue. Dr. Scaliteri's college students generally don't acknowledge my existence, but who knows? That could change after the Showcase.

I play the first and second movements of the Italian Concerto, a thirty-page baroque extravaganza that Bach apparently wrote to amuse himself while waiting in line to buy a Wiener schnitzel. It's a hard piece, but I know I've got it nailed. My fingers dance over the keys, breezing through one mathematically perfect trill after another. As I play, the despair I was feeling on the bus melts away. This is something I'm good at. This is something I can do.

But when I start to play the third movement, Dr. Scaliteri waves her hand to stop me. I halt, baffled, and wait for her instructions.

Dr. Scaliteri just stares at me and bounces.

An entire minutes passes, then another one. I watch the last digit on Dr. Scaliteri's desk clock switch from a three to a four. At seventy-five dollars an hour, these are expensive minutes.

We're talking over two dollars' worth of staring. Staring plus bouncing. I gaze around the room to distract myself, looking at the stained-glass window of a fruit bowl, stained-glass grapes and oranges made jewel-like by the sun. Who has a stained-glass window of a fruit bowl in their house? That window is the reason this room's always so hot. It doesn't open, so you just sit there sweating and breathing in hot, stale, exercise-ball-smelling air while you're trying to play.

Dr. Scaliteri reaches over to her desk, picks up her calendar, and flips through the weeks. Frowning, she traces a French-manicured fingernail along the pale blue boxes representing the days until she finds what she's looking for.

"The Showcase is July thirtieth."

I nod. I could have told her that and saved her eighty-five cents' worth of time, but I know that making me sit here adding up pennies while she paws through her calendar is kind of the point.

"That gives us less than six weeks."

I nod again. She peers at me over the rims of her cat's-eye glasses.

"You're distracted. Why?"

I think about the Imperial Hotel, my nightmare last night, the unopened garbage bag on Sukey's old bed. My face must betray a glimmer of guilt, because Dr. Scaliteri pounces.

"Aha. A boyfriend."

I shake my head.

"Dog died."

Shake.

"Grandma sick."

Shake again.

Dr. Scaliteri scowls.

"Then whatever it is, it can't possibly be as important as the Italian Concerto. Now let's get to work."

We work for three and a half hell-bent hours, until the keys are literally smeared with blood and my mind has been bleached to a glorious blankness, a lunar eclipse of the soul. The music is a castle I conjure around myself, a fortress of notes no feeling can storm. Inside it, I am powerful. I wield my own skill like a sword.

When I'm getting ready to leave, Dr. Scaliteri looks at me sternly.

"You cannot have distractions, Kiri. Piano must come first. Whoever this boy is"—she narrows her eyes—"you tell him not to call until August."

The powerful feeling lasts all the way home. But the badness from this morning comes back when I walk in my front door, like a hornet that was waiting all day to sting me. The can of soup I heat up for dinner burns. I bang my shin on the coffee table. When I unload the dishwasher, I drop a plate, and although it doesn't shatter, a crack spreads across it like a vindictive grin, and I don't know whether to put it in the cupboard or throw it out. Everything feels an inch out of place, just enough to make me clumsy. The garbage bag in Sukey's room is a boulder someone heaved into the pond of our house, disturbing the pebbly bottom and making the water rise to lick the banked canoes.

I can't open it.

I won't open it.

I go to bed early in an attempt to escape.

But when I've been lying there for forty-five minutes wide awake, I finally get up and pad down the hall to Sukey's room.

Hi, Sukey, I think, walking to the bed and laying my hand on the garbage bag. *It's good to see you.*

I slowly tear the trash bag open.

Sukey had an accident.

What I want to ask my mom is, who calls getting stabbed to death an accident?

The hole in the bag widens until its contents start spilling out. I watch while a portrait of Sukey takes shape before my eyes.

There are some things I recognize:

   -paintbrushes with red and black paint dried onto
      their tips;

-a little glass jar of turpentine;

-pencils and pens;

-the pair of high-heeled silver shoes she wore at her
	art opening;

-a half-finished tube of vanilla-scented hand cream;

-empty CD cases: *Nevermind, Mellon Collie and the
	Infinite Sadness*;

-a mug that says BLACK CAT ART SUPPLY;

-one of the ceramic frogs that used to sit on her windowsill
	at home, now chipped;

-a little kid's painting of daisies that I recognize as mine;

-a bag of glass paint jars with their lids stuck shut.

And some things I don't recognize:

-a rumpled denim jacket with silver hearts Bedazzled
	around the cuffs;

-a plastic purple brush;

-a cheap digital alarm clock;

-a short leather skirt with beaded fringe;

-a sparkly pink tube top;

-Zig-Zag rolling papers;

-a picture frame with no picture;

-an empty lighter;

-a small wooden carving of a bear.

And there are things that scare me:

    -empty orange pill bottles of all different sizes;

    -a weirdly stiff and bunched-up quilt I slowly realize is
        covered in dried blood;

    -an unbent paper clip with a curiously blackened tip.

chapter fifteen

That night, I don't go back to bed at all. I lay out Sukey's things like holy artifacts. I can't stop looking at them. I can't stop touching them. I can't leave them alone. I move from object to object like a paleontologist inspecting fossils, the same way I moved around her old bedroom touching everything I could find on the night Mom and Dad told us she died.

I try on the denim jacket with the silver hearts. It smells a little rancid, like french fry grease, probably from being buried under the trash in Doug's closet for so long. I want so much for it to smell like Sukey that I bury my nose in the sleeve again and again, but there's no trace of her cigarette smoke or her perfume.

I run the purple brush through my hair.

I plug in the alarm clock.

I buckle on the silver shoes and take an exploratory stroll around the room. They fit, which surprises me, and I stand there, teetering, feeling my legs lengthen like a stretched piece of gum.

I lay out the leather skirt and sparkly pink tube top on the bed and imagine Sukey wearing them. The skirt has a small yellow splatter of paint on the front. Somehow, that splatter reassures me, like at least some things didn't change after she moved into the Imperial.

I roll a joint with one of the Zig-Zag papers and smoke it, sitting on the bed. After I smoke the joint, I question the ceramic frog. He, surely, must have some comment to make about what happened, some amphibian complaint.

Mister Frog, you have been with Sukey for so long. Did you see what happened? Did you try to stop it?

I talk to the frog for a good long time. All he does is gaze at me with dumb froggy eyes. I shake him and speak severely.

Mister Frog, we have ways of making of you talk.

When I get tired of the frog, I pick up the wooden bear. It's small and light, carved out of a pale blond wood, a scrap of pine or maple. It has pointy little bear ears and a doglike snout, and one of its paws has just snatched an oblong shard of a salmon. It fits in my hand like a toy. *Hey, little bear,* I think, stroking its sleek wooden back. *It's okay.*

When I turn it over in my hand to look at it more closely, I realize there's an inscription scratched on the underside with a knife or the sharp tip of a nail: FOR SUKY. FROM DOUG.

I can't help it. I'm a sucker for sad things, I guess. I hug the bear in my hands and cry and cry.

By the time I get to the scary things, it's well past four. The light on the ceiling buzzes faintly, as if to complain about being left on for so long. I'm still wearing Sukey's silver shoes. I imagine they'll bring Sukey back if I click their heels together three times, but when I try it, nothing happens. I pick up an empty pill bottle and gaze at the ruined label. The paper is rippled as if it got wet, and some of the letters have been completely rubbed off. The part I can read says 300 MG BY MOUTH, but 300 milligrams of what? I pore over the other bottles: Percocet, Demerol, Oxycodone. They're not Sukey's, they can't be Sukey's, but why are they in the bag?

I put them down and pick up the bloody quilt. It's stiff and bunched. I pull it apart, smoothing it out with my hands. The bloody parts look like invasions of bacteria in a petri dish, billowing clouds of black. Underneath, I can make out the scraps of flowered cotton and blue corduroy. The quilt is a horror, a nightmare in my arms, but all I can think about is how much the blood looks like paint—something knocked over and spilled by a clumsy elbow. An accident. I bundle it up carefully and slip it back into the bag, leaving everything else on the frilly bedspread.

I mean to go back to bed then. I really do. But not before touching each object one last time.

When the sun comes up at five, I am twisting the paper clip in my fingers. I am using its burnt tip to spell her name on the back of my hand.

chapter sixteen

"You seem happy today," says Lukas.

Lukas and I are walking down West Broadway on our way to a party at Kelsey Bartlett's house. Or rather, Lukas is walking. I am hopping along beside him, tugging leaves and petals off every tree we pass. I felt a crazy burst of energy when I saw him waiting for me on the corner in front of the supermarket, and everything from last night seemed to slip off my shouldres like a heavy backpack. My body's a little achy from not sleeping, but instead of feeling exhausted, I'm wired. The evening air smells like a pair of old jeans baking on a clothesline, and the sky is the color of a squeezed peach. I tuck a blossom behind Lukas's ear.

"I was up all night."

"Why?"

"I opened the bag."

"Oh."

He gives me a half-worried, half-encouraging glance, as if he's afraid to ask what was inside. We're walking down the Greek block, past the little grocery store with its shelves of canned olives and tahini. A woman in a green dress pushes the door open, and the sudden whiff of baking pita bread reminds me I haven't eaten yet today. Lukas notices the blossom and bats it off.

"Want to know what was in the bag?"

I start to list the objects in no particular order. Lukas stops me when I get to the bloody quilt.

"I don't think I can listen to this."

I blink at him.

"Why not?"

"It's horrible! He gave you a bloody quilt? That's sick."

I have to admit I hadn't thought of it that way.

"He didn't seem like a sicko."

"Are you kidding me? He gave you a bloody murder-quilt he kept in his closet for five years."

I shrug and do a pirouette on the sidewalk. I know I'm acting strangely for someone who spent all night sifting through a bag of pill bottles and rancid clothes, but that's precisely the reason Lukas's presence is making me so batty with joy. I poke him.

"He has a three-legged cat. I trust a man with a three-legged cat."

"I thought you said he was smelly, obnoxious, and too drunk to walk."

"Goes with the territory."

"You *do* need some sleep."

I pluck a daisy from someone's front yard and stick it, boutonniere-like, in the pocket of Lukas's shirt. It rides there for half a block like a puppy with its head out a car window before tumbling out and doing a face-plant on Kelsey's front step.

Kelsey Bartlett lives in one of those houses that doesn't look like much from the outside, but once you go in it's all black leather couches and hardwood floors and a curiously invisible sound system that even plays music in the bathroom when you're going pee. There aren't many people there when we show up, just a few girls sitting on the couch eating celery sticks and ranch dip. When we walk in, Kelsey swoops over to greet us, wearing a purple halter dress and those stupid forty-dollar flip-flops all the girls at our school are wearing this year. Lukas's face perks up when she appears, like he's relieved to see someone who won't talk his ear off about her murder scene evidence collection.

"Welcome, welcome," gushes Kelsey. "I'm so glad you guys showed up. I haven't seen you in forever, Kiri. How's it going?"

Even though I secretly think Kelsey's kind of a ditz, I give her a big smile.

"Fine. My practice schedule is positively *murderous*."

Lukas shoots me a look, but Kelsey doesn't notice. She makes a little face and pulls me into a hug.

"Crazy piano girl. I don't know how you do it."

Kelsey and Lukas start chatting about which bands they're going to see at IndieFest this year. I try to join in, but I've been too busy to look at the lineup, and I probably won't have time to go anyway. After a few minutes I wander away to see who else is here. I say hi to my friend Angela, who's in the middle of telling a story to this girl Rhett whose dad owns the Cactus Club.

"Hey, Kiri," says Angela, sipping her Sprite. "So anyway, he came back again yesterday, and this time he brought his friend. . . ."

I listen as Angela shares the breaking news about the latest additions to her pervert collection. Highlights at six:

-her forty-year-old manager at the snack bar has a crush
    on her;
-her old boyfriend from middle school wants to get back
    together;
-Pete Vozt texted her a picture of his schlong.

I peel away from Rhett and Angela and go say hi to the orchestra kids, who are entertaining themselves by playing Chubby Bunny with the cherry tomatoes. There's no room on the couch, so I plunk myself down on Bryan Kravchenko's lap. He groans and tries to push me off.

"Get off me, yo!"

Instead I lean back and try to crush him against the couch.

"Help! Get her off me! She's crazy!"

I finally get off when he elbows me in the ribs. They start talking about a TV show and I get restless again, so I mill around the house, stealing chips off people's plates. Somebody sets up Guitar Hero and everyone clusters around the TV to watch.

All of a sudden, I feel incredibly bored.

This party is stupid.

There's nothing *happening*.

Everyone's just flirting and posing and trying to look cool. There's no greater meaning here. No beauty. Sukey was stabbed to death, and I'm supposed to stand here watching fools play Guitar Hero?

A hum of anxiety is building in my chest like a swarm of wasps. I should do something. I should make some signal to let Sukey know I'm with her. I can't just stand here.

I make another useless circle of the living room and go outside to the deck, where there's a hot tub, tiki torches, and a barbecue the size of a tank. The lid of the hot tub is off, and the water is steaming quietly into the night. It looks so warm and peaceful, I walk right over and dunk my arm in.

Kelsey's dad is manning the grill.

"Go ahead," he says when he sees me. "You can be the first one in."

The suggestion is too tantalizing to resist.

I can see my reflection wobbling on the surface of the water like the film of edible ink on a Your-Photo-on-a-Cake. I slip my feet out of my sandals, swing my first leg over the edge, and the water swallows up my leg all the way to the hem of my shorts. I swing my other leg in and stand there like a stork in the middle of the warm, bubbling water. Inside the house, a group of guys has just shown up: I can see a flock of wide-brimmed caps moving toward the chip bowls on the kitchen counter. A pair of celery girls squeak open the sliding glass door and come onto the deck to gawk at me.

"Omigod, Kiri, are you really getting in?"

"I *am* in."

And oh how brightly doth the first stars shine in the waning nectarine of the sky. This is real. This is like one of Sukey's paintings. Now if only Lukas would come out here and dance with me and the celery girls would go back inside with their tanned legs and big teeth. I scrape the surface of the water with my fingers. The celery girls squeal.

"But your clothes are going to get wet. Where's your bathing suit?"

I ignore them and turn around in a slow circle, feeling the hot jets of water whooshing against my legs. Little white petals are falling from a Japanese cherry tree and landing on the water. Little bubbles are crowning the hairs on my legs. I am the Lady of the Lake. Suck it, bitches.

"Are you just going to spin around in circles and not say anything?"

I reach up, plug my nostrils, and submerge, submarine-style, until their voices are nothing but warbling squeaks above the surface of the water.

When I come up again, the celery girls are still standing there, now joined on the deck by a half-dozen more gawking girls and a handful of lumbering Ball-Cap Orangutans that start hooting and taking pictures on their cell phones when I emerge soaking wet.

I take a quick bow, step out of the hot tub, push through my crowd of admirers, and go inside, trailing wet footprints across the kitchen floor. My random act of beauty accomplished, I make a unilateral decision to grab Lukas and bust out of here.

Lukas is still talking to Kelsey, whom I suddenly can't stand with a level of not-standingness so powerful I can hardly restrain it from leaping out of my throat like one of those snakes-in-a-can. She's telling Lukas about how much she loves waterskiing, her voice high and whiny-sounding. I wedge myself between them. "Lukas? D'you want to go?"

"Oh, hey, Kiri."

Lukas is holding a can of soda with beads of condensation on the outside. I can smell the chemical tang of the fake lemon when he takes a sip. I not so much ignore Kelsey as fail to see any point in acknowledging her existence for the second time in a single evening. Kelsey looks down at my dripping clothes.

"Ooh, looks like someone found the hot tub. I can lend you a swimsuit, babe."

I sort of nod at Kelsey, but my eyes are locked on Lukas. "Hey, Lukas? Lukas. Are you ready to go?"

The wired feeling that started when I left my house has grown into a thrumming, crackling, electrical field. I want to kiss Lukas. I want to dance down the street. There's a reason people get drunk after funerals, and I suddenly know what it is: the flip side of sadness is a dark, devouring joy, a life that demands to be fed.

"Lukas—"

Do Lukas and Kelsey exchange a look? Was that a look? Bitch, don't exchange a look with my future boyfriend!

Lukas rocks on his heels. "Actually, I was just about to get a burger."

Kelsey licks her lips in what I cannot help but interpret as a lecherous fashion. "Mmm," she says, looking me square in the eye. "Think I will too."

I cast Lukas an urgent look, but it bounces right off him. He gives me a strained smile and turns around to go outside to the barbecue. Kelsey follows him, waving over her shoulder at me.

"Bye, Kiri. Sorry you had to leave so early!"

On the walk home from Kelsey's, a car full of college boys slows down and follows me for an entire block, whistling at me and shouting, "Where's the wet T-shirt contest?" I give them the finger, but they just laugh, and when I duck into the corner store to escape them, the cashier shoos me back out again for dripping water on the floor. As I hurry down the street, my wet clothes cling to my skin, clammy and uncomfortable. When I get home, I flick on all the lights, but the artificial brightness only emphasizes how big and empty the house is.

I make a beeline for my bedroom and paw through the heap of clothing on my floor, looking for something clean to wear. I haven't done laundry in the two weeks since Mom and Dad left, and all my shirts are sour and wrinkled. I pull on an old tank top and go downstairs to make something to eat, but the carrots and broccoli have gone limp and rubbery and the bread is blooming with mold. I stand over the compost bin tossing everything out, my heart fluttering with something like panic.

I wish I'd stayed at the party. This time, I'd cooperate. I'd watch people play Guitar Hero. I'd pretend Kelsey Bartlett had even slightly tolerable taste in music. I wouldn't make a scene in the hot tub.

Bad thoughts snake through my brain. Stupid thoughts. I wonder if those boys in the car figured out where I live, if they know I'm home alone, if they're planning to come by later and break into my house. I wonder if Sukey's murderer is still on the loose. I wonder if he knows where I live. I wonder if Sukey did something bad or got in trouble with some gang or stole something her murderer is still looking for.

Once I start thinking about the murder, I can't stop, and horrifying scenes reel through my mind, all these scenarios, all these reasons. I go to the computer and type the words *Sukey Byrd murder* into the search box. The back of my neck heats up, and I minimize the window, as if I'm afraid someone will walk in and catch me snooping. It feels like I'm doing something forbidden—pawing through my parents' dresser or reading Denny's email. *It's public information*, I remind myself. *I'm allowed to know.*

But part of me knows that I'm not allowed. That I'm breaking a rule. When I reach for the mouse again, my hand is shaking. I can feel the computer screen's glare on my face. *Be brave*, I tell myself. I click the window open again.

The first few hits are for some other Sukey Byrd, a criminal lawyer in Cambridge, England, with a specialty in murder trials, but the last one's an article from the *Sun*.

I click.

The page takes a moment to load. When it does, a pop-up ad blocks most of the screen. I close it and scan the page for her name.

It's not even a real article, just a news brief: name, age, address. *Ms. Byrd, 21, was estranged from her family. There have been two other murders reported since the hotel changed ownership in 2001.*

Estranged from her family. It sounds cruel and primitive, like a tribe booting one of its members out into the desert to die.

"She wasn't estranged from *me*," I whisper at the screen.

I comb through the search results to see if there's anything else, but there's nothing. I don't get it. Where's the murder trial, the conviction, the lifetime in prison? Does this mean they never found out who did it?

Just chill, I tell myself. *Newspapers don't turn every single murder into a big story. It doesn't mean anything.*

I click the window shut and clear the search history, like I've been looking at porn or instructions for how to build a bomb. My skin is hot and I'm sitting up too straight. I feel conspicuous in the same way as when I came home from Lukas's house after we kissed on his birthday—like the truth of what

I've just done is written all over me, obvious as a clown wig, and everyone can see.

You're allowed to know, I tell myself again, but already a fine mist of guilt is settling over me. I think of my parents and shake it off. *You don't owe them anything.*

I try smoking weed again, but instead of mellowing things out it gives my worries tiny fangs and bright yellow eyes and hairy feet and sets them marching like trolls. I sit on my bed with the lights on and my cell phone at the ready, my thoughts sliding back and forth between paranoia and self-recrimination. *If you weren't so self-absorbed, you would have noticed that things weren't okay with Sukey. You would have helped her. But no, all you cared about was whether she would take you for milkshakes when she came to visit. You selfish little brat. You* knew *she didn't die in a car crash, didn't you?*

I didn't, I swear I didn't.

But you cared more about keeping Mom and Dad happy with your stupid piano playing than about knowing the truth.

I curl up into a toxic ball of grief and self-loathing, the ceiling light hot and accusatory on my back. In the morning, I promise myself, I'll get Doug to tell me the details, even the horrible ones, even the ones that will break me in ways I will never be able to fix. It's what I deserve for being such a coward. And it's the only way I can start to forgive myself for hiding from the truth for so long.

chapter seventeen

"He was a kid, eh. Young guy. Stupid. Hooked on junk."

Doug and I are sitting in a sticky, distinctly sneezed-on booth at the Sunshine Diner, one of those all-day-breakfast places in Chinatown. He agreed to put down his early-morning beer, pull a shirt on over his speckled torso, and talk to me when I showed him the wooden bear. We're the only ones here except for a table of twentysomething hipsters wearing plastic sunglasses and those really tight cardigans that make skinny people look anorexic and everyone else look morbidly obese. They're reading the menus and laughing about the spelling mistakes, debating loudly whether to order the chocorat milk or the rapefruit juice. They project this aura of gleeful self-awareness that makes me feel awkward sitting with Doug while he pores over the menu like a sacred text, hungrily and with complete lack of irony.

I clamp my hand around my glass of syrupy orange juice. "What was his name?" I say.

"Billy."

Billy. I handle the word warily, like an animal that might bite. My head has been swarming with questions all morning, but now that Doug is here in front of me, I'm too nervous to speak. I wish he would just talk, just tell me things. I tear at the edge of my napkin and twist the little white shreds into spirals, my mind shouting, *Ask! Ask! Ask!* but my lips refusing to move.

The waitress comes to take our order, staying just long enough to leave a disinfectant breeze that lingers over our table. I take a sip of my orange juice, as thick in my throat as cough syrup.

"So this Billy," I force out, my fingers working the napkin. "Um. How—um."

Doug lets out a long, hoarse sigh.

"She helped him out a couple times. Sukey-girl could never say no to anyone who needed help, even a junkie. She said he was just a kid. Said he just needed to get on his feet."

My stomach turns.

"She *knew* him?"

I'd been imagining a stranger or distant acquaintance—some random brute, senseless as a dump truck. I hadn't even considered the possibility that it was a friend. Someone who knew her. Someone she'd helped. Someone who had seen how small she looked in her denim jacket and realized how easy it would be to break her body with a fist, a knife, a pair of scissors. I feel the orange juice burning in the back of my throat and force myself to swallow.

The waitress comes again with our food but I don't see her, I just hear the clink of plates on the table in front of me and smell the suddenly unwelcome aroma of scrambled eggs. Doug reaches for the grubby ketchup bottle next to the napkin dispenser. He turns it upside down and whacks it. Dark red blobs of ketchup plop out, and I have to look away before it calls up images I'd rather not have in my head.

"I told her to stay away from that kid," he says. "He was dangerous. Shifty-eyed. Rob his own mother for a fix. Sukey used to let him stay at her place when he had nowhere to go. She'd tell me, 'Doug, he's just a baby. He's just a baby, Doug. He'll be all right once he gets clean.'"

I pick up my knife and fork as if to eat, but I'm remembering the way Sukey always gave change to the crusty punks sitting outside the McDonald's with their enormous dogs, all spikes and grunge and attitude. Some of them were nice, but there were scary ones, too, and Sukey never seemed to notice the difference. I remember one guy in particular, with long, dirty dreadlocks and a barbed-wire tattoo around his neck. When Sukey gave him our change, he asked her for a cigarette, and while she was digging one out of her purse, he walked his eyes all over her body as I half-hid behind her, unnerved.

It was him. I know it was him. I remember the faded black spikes around his neck and the way his dog growled.

"What did he look like?" I whisper.

"Crooked nose," says Doug. "Blond hair. One of those hockey players, eh."

Something like relief sweeps over me. *It wasn't the guy outside the McDonald's. It wasn't anybody I've seen.*

Doug's still talking. I struggle to catch up.

"—said he took a puck in the face during a game. His nose pointed straight to the left, like he wiped it on his sleeve and it stuck there, just like that. Made him look tricky. Sukey told him he should go play hockey for some college, after he got clean. She was always trying to tell him to go play hockey. Said he looked just like Bobby Orr."

I thought I wanted to know these things. I really did. I wanted someone to hate—a name, a face. But instead of feeling angry, I feel sicker and sicker, imagining the boyish face and bent nose, the short haircut, the pale skin. This is the person who killed Sukey? This Billy? This kid? Out of all the people in the world, what gave him the right to play with her life like a beer bottle he smashed on the pavement?

I take a bite of my toast. It scrapes my throat going down. The pain is a strangely welcome distraction. I push another dry, jagged bite down past my teeth.

"Did they have a fight?" I squeak before it's all the way down. Doug shakes his head.

"What happened?" I say.

"Kid came in one night looking for money to pay some people back. She was in her room, painting."

"She was painting?"

"Oh yeah. When Sukey-girl got her hands on some paint, she'd close her door and stay in there for days. Artistic privacy, eh. But that kid busted in there anyway. He didn't care about nobody's privacy."

My heart stops beating.

She was working on a painting. The one she told me about on my birthday. The big one, her best one yet, the one that was going to be finished soon and shown in a gallery.

"What happened next?" I say.

"Oh, honey."

"Tell me."

"You're a good kid."

"I'm her sister."

Doug takes a sip of his coffee. He puts his mug down and closes his eyes.

"I heard the kid shouting. He said he knew she was hiding money somewhere. He knew she had a hundred bucks somewhere. She had some boyfriend who used to give her money now and then. I went to get my bat from behind the mattress. I was going to go in there and knock his lights out."

Doug pauses.

"I could hear her talking to the kid, trying to make him calm down. Then she started screaming. I was down on the floor getting my bat, and when I tried to stand back up, my crutch slipped. I fell down hard, eh. She was screaming and screaming, and I could hear him knocking around in there, knocking things over, looking for her money. I yelled, 'Get out of there, you lousy son of a bitch!'"

Doug says it loud. The hipsters at the other table glance at us and snicker, and the waitress casts us a dirty look from across the room.

"Doug," I say, but there's no stopping him now.

"I got back on my crutches and started for the door. Sukey was screaming her head off, and I heard a thud like someone falling down. I got out to the hall just in time to see the kid run down the stairs. I shouted, 'I'm gonna kill you!' Then I hurried into Sukey-girl's room to make sure she was okay."

Doug stops talking and shakes his head.

I'm frozen in place, literally frozen. I can't swallow or blink or breathe. The food on the table looks lurid, surreal. Beside us, the hipsters' chatter rises above the noise of plates clanking in the industrial dishwasher. Doug's face has become impenetrable, as if we've come to a gate beyond which only he can proceed, a room only he can enter. Our waitress whisks by with the bill on a plastic tray and clears away our barely touched plates. Neither of us moves.

"What happened to him?" I say.

I imagine police sirens, blue lights flashing on Columbia Street. The kid being led away in handcuffs, his body twitching from adrenaline and withdrawal. An ambulance idling outside while the paramedics carry Sukey's body down four flights of stairs on a stretcher. Someone at the police station calling, Dad reaching out to answer his cell phone as he's driving home from work.

But this isn't the picture Doug leaves me with, this tidy TV ending of ringing phones and flashing lights. He dips his head to put on his baseball cap and lays one hand on his crutches like he's planning to get up. With his cap on, all I can make out of his eyes is a dark glitter, like water at the bottom of a sewer.

"After he did what he did to Sukey-girl, he went down to the second floor. The dealer was waiting for him with a few of his buddies. Kid went in there trying to give 'em a painting he grabbed out of Sukey-girl's room—the only one she still had, the purple one she always kept up there on her wall."

Pain lances through me. *Hey, k-bird. Hang this in your*

room, and I'll keep the other one hanging in my studio. I try to fill my brain with the pattern on the Formica table.

"What did they do?"

Doug looks around the diner as if he has only now become concerned about being overheard. He lowers his voice. "They bashed his head in with a pipe. Threw his body in the Dumpster." He drains his coffee. "No more kid."

chapter eighteen

"Kiri," says Dr. Scaliteri, leaning forward on her exercise ball and gripping my wrist. "You *must* get serious about this piano. We worked on these problems on Monday and there's no change. No change at all."

I am sitting on the piano bench, wearing a short green wrap skirt, a black tank top, and a cowrie-shell necklace. This morning I showered and brushed my teeth and even put on makeup. Securing the perimeter goes for appearances, too.

On the bus ride here I almost cried, imagining Billy barging into Sukey's room at the Imperial while we were safe in our house, a ten-minute drive away. Even though I've taken the same bus a hundred times, I looked out the window and didn't recognize a thing—as if I'd been seeing the whole world wrong, as if I'd never really seen it at all. I panicked and thought I'd missed my stop, but ended up getting off a stop too soon and walking the last ten blocks, arriving at Dr. Scaliteri's house sweaty and five minutes late.

I force myself to meet her eyes.

"I'm sorry. I've been—something came up."

Dr. Scaliteri glowers. She turns to her desk, and it looks like we're about to go through the old calendar routine again, but instead she picks up a piece of mail. She waves the envelope at me.

"Your name has come up for the master class with Tzlatina Tzoriskaya," she says.

The sweat freezes on my skin.

The master class is this elite inner Showcase-within-the-Showcase, whereby qualified Young Pianists are given the opportunity to learn an extra piece selected by the judge for its extreme difficulty and announced just weeks before the big event. It's supposed to test your ability to learn music quickly—that, and your ability to not have a nervous breakdown under circumstances almost clinically designed to produce one.

Dr. Scaliteri enunciates slowly.

"For this class, Tzlatina has selected the Prokofiev."

"Which Prokofiev?"

"The Concerto Number Two."

Only one of the hardest piano pieces ever written. My jaw drops.

"I can't have that ready that in time for the Showcase. It's a hundred pages long."

"For the master class, it must not be ready. It must only be memorized. Tzlatina will give you instruction on how to polish. It is a very big opportunity for you."

"I know, but—"

"Tzlatina is on the faculty of music at the Royal Conservatory. You will be auditioning there in the fall, yes? So you see that it is very important for you to make an impression."

My palms inexplicably start to sweat, and my eyes dart to the floor. *Get it together, Kiri,* warns a voice in my head, but that only makes me sweat harder. The piano's pedals shine back at me, dainty brass paws, and its smell of felt and lacquer presses at my nostrils. I wish I was outside, on the sidewalk, somewhere with air. I wish I was riding a bus with its windows open.

"You will not audition for the Conservatory?" says Dr. Scaliteri.

I look up. "What? Of course I'm going to audition."

Dr. Scaliteri crosses her arms. "What's happening with you, Kiri? You used to be so full of focus, and now it's distraction, distraction."

Dr. Scaliteri says the word *distraction* like she's talking about hard drugs. I recognize that tone. It's the one Dad used to use with Sukey. I blush. "I'm not losing my focus."

"Okay," Dr. Scaliteri says with an exasperated flutter of her well-groomed hands. "Okay. But you know, the other students in the competition, they come from all over the country, all over the world, from all the best teachers. They are serious piano students."

"I *am* serious."

"Then you will stop mooning around with this boyfriend of yours and you will memorize the Prokofiev."

When she's finished this little pep talk, Dr. Scaliteri calls in Nelson Chow, who has just walked in the door looking dapper in his khaki pants and a yellow T-shirt, and has me play my entire repertoire over again.

"Now, Nelson," says Dr. Scaliteri when I've just deployed the last deafening atonal slam of the Khachaturian, "do you have any suggestions for Kiri?"

Nelson puffs out his lips while he thinks. Dr. Scaliteri waits, tapping her pen on her knee. He scratches his arm.

"It sounds like she's afraid of the music."

Dr. Scaliteri turns to me brightly.

"That's interesting, isn't it, Kiri? Tell us why, Nelson."

"She's rushing through a lot of places."

"Aha," says Dr. Scaliteri, widening her eyes as if Nelson Chow has just pulled a live rabbit out of the piano and set it, hopping, on the floor. "What do you think of that, Kiri?"

I don't know what I think. My mind is in space. My sister was killed by a kid with a sideways nose.

Snap out of it.

I try to look Serious.

"What?"

Dr. Scaliteri claps her hands.

"Switch places. Up, up, up."

This is one of Dr. Scaliteri's favorite tricks, the old switcheroo. I peel my thighs off the leather seat and stand to the side while Nelson takes my place at the piano.

"Nelson, give us the Khachaturian."

Not *play* us the Khachaturian. *Give* us the Khachaturian. As if Nelson in his insufferable yellow T-shirt is some kind of saint from whom all music floweth. He starts playing my piece—*my piece*—his hands blitzing over the keys. My heart sinks. It sounds completely different from when I play it. There's something powerful in it I can't put my finger on, something commanding and deep. Nelson must have stronger fingers than I do, or better technique. By the time he finishes his piece and reverts to Standby mode, I'm so embarrassed I want to melt into the floor.

Dr. Scaliteri turns to me and displays her fangs.

"What did you notice about Nelson's playing?"

I try to think, but she doesn't wait for me to answer.

"Nelson *listens*," says Dr. Scaliteri triumphantly.

Bitch, please.

Dr. Scaliteri gives me one last long look, as if to gauge my level of Seriousness. She picks up a stack of sheet music that was sitting on her desk and hands it to me. My eyes skate over the cover page: Concerto No. 2.

Dr. Scaliteri nods at the door.

"Next Thursday or nothing," she says.

chapter nineteen

The next week is simple.

I don't think.

I don't sleep.

I don't have endless looping nightmares about a kid with a sideways nose.

I just practice and practice until the world dissolves and anything that's not piano fades away. Pretty soon, reality takes on the clean, sharp simplicity of a training montage. Cut to Kiri playing the Prokofiev, turning up the metronome one more notch, playing it again. Cut to Kiri fumbling with the sixteenth note section, frowning, and starting over, her eyebrows knit in an attitude of grim determination. Kiri tapping out notes on the kitchen counter while she waits for her instant oatmeal to microwave, Kiri doing sit-ups on the living room floor while Prokofiev plays on the speakers. Kiri working. Kiri getting Serious. Kiri practicing as if her whole life depends on it.

The kitchen sink fills up with milk-slimed cereal bowls and spoons studded with dried Grape-Nuts. My life consists of the safe little triangle between the fridge, the bathroom, and the piano. When my shoulders start to droop, I drink some coffee and keep going. There simply isn't time to stop. I have more than one hundred pages of music to memorize by next Thursday. One hundred pages in six days.

Each time I make a mistake, I pounce on it with my claws extended and wrestle it to death.

Each time I feel like resting, I think about the master class with Tzlatina Tzoriskaya and force myself to go on.

Each time I feel like crying, I tell myself to knock it off.

I think about all the money that's gone into my piano lessons, and the days and weeks and hours. I have to get this right, I just have to, or else—

I don't want to think about the "or else." Or else is a blank. A big gaping canyon. And on the other side of it is a person I don't know how to be.

By the third day, I don't have eyes anymore—I have orbital cavities. My hair hangs limp and greasy like I'm an actress at a haunted house. My back aches like I've been dragging the piano across the floor, not playing it, and my mouth tastes like caffeine. When my friend Teagan calls from physics camp to tell me a convoluted but hilarious story about the second law of thermodynamics, she stops halfway through to ask if she should, like, call me an ambulance. When Lukas's mom calls to check on me, I carry the phone to the piano and play her part of the concerto.

"It is incredible what you do with this piano," says Petra. "I am wishing we had started Lukas when he was young."

Her approval is a gold star I use to hold up all the ones whose edges have started to curl.

The metronome ticks. I lose track of days. My clothes start to smell like I just ran a marathon. Several nights pass where I don't see my bed, don't even go upstairs at all. Sergei Prokofiev starts talking to me, a constant internal chatter, critiquing my technique and making grim Russian noises whenever I miss a note. I can feel the music growing on me like a graft on a plum tree, the new leaves shooting out, becoming a part of my brain.

At one point, my parents call long-distance from Brazil to give me a detailed update on the state of the lemur population at the Sao Rodrigo Wildlife Preserve, which they visited on a recent excursion from their cruise ship. My mom gives me a full report on the distinct habits, personalities, and dietary preferences of all six members of the lemur family showcased in the little pen at the visitor center. My dad's contribution is a scathing condemnation of the boldness of the Brazilian homeless person. I pace around the kitchen while they talk, and eventually set the phone on top of the fridge and wander away.

When Wednesday night rolls around, I'm ready. I've spent an entire week Focusing on My Art, and now not only am I a honed and dangerous pianist, I have also become Serious. I'm a finely focused laser beam. Forget burning the candle at both ends—I've dipped the candle in kerosene and torched that sucker. One hundred pages of music, all safely stored in my brain. You tell me if that isn't Serious. You just try telling me that isn't some Serious shit.

chapter twenty

Not even ten minutes after I declare victory on the Prokofiev, the phone rings and it's Lukas calling to see if I want to watch *Zardoz*. The timing is so uncanny it's got to be a sign. I tell him to come over in an hour, by which I mean, *Give me an hour to prepare my sex-dome.*

I hang up the phone and launch into preparation mode.

First, I clean up the living room, fluffing pillows and draping the chenille blanket invitingly over the back of the couch. I load a good playlist onto my iPod, flick off lights and switch on lamps, gather up all the old newspapers and dump them into the recycling bin in the garage. Next, I tackle my bedroom, tossing dirty socks and underwear into the laundry bin and hanging up clothes. I spend five minutes debating whether to leave a black bra hanging casually over the closet door, then decide it looks too staged and move it to a dresser drawer. I crank open the window next to my bed so that the evening air slinks in luxuriously over the pillow.

It's not that I think all these preparations are necessary for romancing Lukas. He's a simple person with simple likes and dislikes. It's more to indulge my own sense of occasion that I whisk from room to room attending to these details. I feel like a theater director fussing over a set on opening night. I want the entrances and exits to be perfect. I want the trapdoors to swing open when they're supposed to and the bed to swivel into place on cue. I run a sound check and test the lights. I stride around the house making sure that every prop is in place. I go down to the basement and select a bottle of red wine from the wooden rack, go to the kitchen and stick a frozen loaf of French bread in the oven.

My heart fluttering, I go back to my bedroom and dig out the condom I've been saving ever since ninth-grade health class, the condom that has been hidden inside a Christmas sock stuffed inside an old running shoe wedged behind a box on the high shelf of my closet for three years and nevertheless seems to bleat its condomy presence to the world like a poorly muffled alarm clock whenever anyone comes into my room.

I put it in an easy-to-reach spot in my drawer, then on

second thought I put it back in the sock, because I don't want it to seem like I just generally keep condoms casually accessible, then on third thought I take it back out of the sock, because what kind of creepy, desperate human owns a single, expired condom they've been keeping in a Christmas sock since ninth grade?

Next, it's time for Ultimate Physical Purification. I shower, shave every body part that isn't directly attached to my skull, wash my hair, blow-dry it, clean under my toenails with one of those metal things you're not supposed to use, apply scentless deodorant, pluck a few eyebrow hairs, and moisturize everything. Twice. I imagine Sukey here with me, helping me get ready for the date.

Lookin' good, babe, she'd say approvingly. Then she'd mess up my hair, because you don't want to look like you spent time on your hair, and quickly fill me in on the sort of arcane sexual knowledge I imagine all older sisters, but especially Sukey, must possess.

I root through my closet and find the filmy blue dress Auntie Moana sent me for Christmas last year. I slip it on, my skin still warm from the shower, and float downstairs.

At 8:20 Lukas shows up with the Netflix envelope bearing *Zardoz.* He's wearing a white T-shirt and jeans and looks like a model in a Habitat for Humanity ad, like he's about to pick up a hammer and build some disadvantaged refugees a duplex.

I uncork the wine, and while it's breathing we hang around the kitchen, talking music. Lukas's eyes keep darting to my dress, which rides up my thighs in a dreadfully sexy manner when I sit on the kitchen counter, one leg draped over the other.

"Have you heard of this band called Mist?" says Lukas.

We have my laptop out, and we're listening to songs on the internet. Lukas clicks on a music video, which starts to play. It's some kind of hipster twee-pop crap, all xylophones and cutesy lyrics. I cringe.

"Lukas, this music blows."

"Just listen for a second."

I listen for precisely one second, during which said music continues to blow. I raise my newly plucked eyebrows at Lukas.

"I'm serious, why are you showing me this?"

"I was thinking we might want to move our sound in that direction."

"Are you kidding me? This sounds like it was written by the Mickey Mouse Club."

Lukas ignores me. "Hear how the synth's a little dancier?"

He hums along for a few bars. I punch him lightly on the shoulder.

"Lukas, we are not dumbing down our act. You're the one who's always saying you want us to be a serious band. Where'd you even hear about these losers?"

"Kelsey played their album at her party after you left."

"Great. Now we're taking career advice from Kelsey Bartlett?"

"She actually knows a lot about—"

"Lukas. Listen to me. *We* are building cathedrals. These guys"—I wave my hand at the laptop—"are making instant pudding."

Lukas rolls his eyes.

"No, but that's the thing. You make your first album mainstream to get radio play, then later, once you have a record deal and a following, you can slowly introduce the headier stuff. When you're established."

"Yeah. Established in sucking."

"I just think we should make our music a little more accessible for Battle of the Bands. It'll be temporary, okay?"

I raise my eyebrows. "The douchy sellout you pretend to be is the douchy sellout you become."

"Since when are you so concerned with selling out?"

"I just think we should live dangerously."

"Sure. *After* Battle of the Bands."

This isn't the kind of flirtatious banter I'd been imagining. I give Lukas a smile. "Come upstairs. There's something I wanted to show you."

I hop down from the counter, pick up the wine, and pour us each a glass. It glugs in the neck of the bottle in a way I think most waiters would disapprove of, but I don't know any other way to do it. I hand Lukas his wine and pick up mine, cradling the glass in my hand. As an afterthought, I tuck the bottle under my arm. You never know. This could take a while.

"Come on. It's upstairs."

I start for the staircase, glancing over my shoulder to cast Lukas an encouraging smile. After a slight pause, he follows me. I can hear my dress swishing against my legs as we climb the stairs. When we get to the top, Lukas's face is slightly red. He hangs outside the door when I go into my room, looking down at his wineglass like he's afraid my bedchamber is filled with scandalous things to shock his Victorian sensibilities. Part of me is glad I stuck that bra in the drawer. Another part of me is enjoying his discomfort—it means I'm doing something right.

I beckon him in.

"It's okay, Lukas. You can come in. I can't show you out there."

He looks flustered but comes and joins me next to my bed. For a moment, all I can think about is the fact that Lukas is standing next to me in my bedroom. It makes the whole room feel different. I'm suddenly aware of the nubbly carpet beneath my toes, and the notes from Teagan tacked to my bulletin board, and the way the pale blue curtains are furred with dust. Lukas is standing close enough that our arms brush, and for the second time this evening I'm aware of the delicious clean-smellingness of my own body, like a fresh-cut branch.

"See that painting?"

I point at the wall. He has to lean over my bed to see it clearly in the carefully dimmed light.

"Sukey did it."

I can hear the pride in my voice, as if I'm the one who painted the silver-edged birds. Lukas squints.

"What does it say?"

"'We gamboled, star-clad.'"

"Is that from Shakespeare or something?"

"I don't know."

"What does it mean?"

"Literally, it's about frolicking under the stars. But it can mean anything you want."

Lukas finishes looking and straightens up, his arm brushing mine again. This is my moment. I put my hand on his inner elbow.

"Shall we?"

We both lift our wineglasses and take a sip at the same time. I can feel my pulse speeding up like in the moment before you get a test handed back to you and you're still not sure whether you bombed it or got an A. The smell of French bread is starting to fill the house, warm and floury.

"Um," says Lukas, his hand darting up to touch his collarbone like he does when he's nervous. "Shall we what?"

"Gambol, star-clad."

I can tell he's thinking about it. Wondering exactly what type of gamboling I mean. Debating whether this is an acceptable breach of Focusing on Our Art. Asking himself if he can spare the vital forces necessary to give in to fleeting physical attraction and still have enough left over for his drum kit. He glances at the painting again, then down at my red bedspread, then back at me. His lip quivers. As if on cue, we both take another sip of wine.

The smell of warming bread is growing stronger, mixed with the scent of lilac bushes wafting in through the open window. For one utterly still moment, we're suspended, Lukas and I, like two tightrope walkers far above the ground.

I reach out and touch his earlobe with my finger.

Lukas jerks away like I've just burned him with a match.

"Wait, Kiri. I need to tell you something."

The warm, swimmy feeling I was getting from the wine evaporates instantly. I feel the tightrope shaking, then snapping. Then I realize I was walking on it alone. My mind races over the past few minutes, scanning them for wrong turns. Did I go too far? I didn't grab Lukas or tear off his pants or even kiss him. I just wanted to touch him, to remind him that the door was still open and I was still there, and see if maybe he was still there too. But Lukas looks so upset I suddenly feel like some kind of brutal she-rapist in my clingy blue dress.

"Um. Can we sit down for a minute?" says Lukas, his cheeks

reddening. "There's something I have to tell you."

Now I'm going from wondering if Lukas thinks I'm an oversexed maniac to wondering if He's Just Not That Into Me and has been too nice to tell me until now. When we sit on my bed, my heart breaks a little. This is how I had imagined us sitting. But if everything was going according to my imaginings, Lukas's hands would be under my dress, not lying in his lap, and we'd be exploring each other, not having another sure-to-be-lengthy discussion about why we shouldn't date.

I can hear the music playing downstairs, bright and dreamy and so utterly inappropriate for the moment we're having, I want to smash my iPod. Lukas blurts out what he has to say in a single suffocating sentence:

"Don't-get-mad-I-hooked-up-with-Kelsey."

I look away before he can see the hurt and embarrassment that streak across my face like a pair of mice running out from under the stove. Kelsey Bartlett. Of course he'd choose her over me. I know I'm not that attractive, especially to someone like Lukas, who has a perfect body—I have a big mouth and too much hair and I don't pluck my eyebrows often enough even though I come from a family of Eyebrow People and have what is basically a single unbroken line of fur across my forehead. In five seconds I've gone from feeling like a sleek, warm love-otter to a cold, untouchable frog.

Ribbit.

"I'm really sorry I didn't tell you sooner, Kiri. I didn't know you still felt that way about me."

Lukas is peering at me like I'm a puzzle, some complex piece of machinery he didn't realize was broken, but there it is, the missing spring, the snapped wire. I can't stand it when people look at me that way. So I do what I know how to do. Smile and secure the perimeter.

I take a long, ragged drink of my wine and reach for the bottle to pour myself some more. A million questions push at my brain.

When did you start liking her?

Did you kiss her first or did she kiss you?

When you say you hooked up, exactly how much hooking do you mean?

But I can't ask. I can't show him I care that much. Instead, I give him a casual shrug. "That's okay, Lukas. It's not like we were dating."

I think Lukas can tell it's not okay just by watching my efforts to pour myself more wine. First it runs down the neck of the bottle instead of pouring out, then I swing the bottle down too close and break the glass. There's a high-pitched *chink*. Wine leaking all over my dress.

"Shit."

"I'll get paper towels."

"Crap."

Lukas hops up, flees my bedroom, and all but vaults down the stairs.

"Where are your paper towels?" he calls from the kitchen.

"Goddammit."

My lap is soaked in wine and spangled with a million isosceles triangles of shattered glass. I can hear Lukas bumping around the kitchen, opening and shutting drawers. Lukas wouldn't survive a single night at home by himself: Who looks for paper towels in a drawer? I get up from my bed. "They're on the counter."

"What?"

"Bloody hell, Lukas."

I tromp down the stairs and lumber into the kitchen, a glittering, wine-soaked King Kong. I rip a bunch of paper towels off the roll on the counter and pat myself down. In the glare of the kitchen light, all my hours of preparation are completely unnoticeable. The house is just a house. I am just a Kiri. Lukas and I are just friends. And that's assuming our friendship survives this freaking circus.

Lukas leans against the counter and watches skeptically while I try to pick the shards off my dress.

"Be careful with that broken glass."

"Thanks, Lukas."

"Do you want me to get a broom?"

I've been shedding glass on the floor every time I move,

but Lukas won't be able to find the broom closet until Google makes an app.

"Don't worry about it."

"I think something's burning."

The French bread. I lunge for the oven and pull open the door. The loaf of bread I stuck in an hour ago looks like a giant charred dog turd. As the smoke detector starts screaming, I grab the ruined bread with an oven mitt and throw it into the sink, where it lies hissing reproachfully. Lukas is flapping around uselessly under the smoke detector. I manhandle him out of the way and stab the red button with a barbecue tong. I take a big breath, dredge up a smile, turn around, and face Lukas.

"Well. Shall we watch the movie?"

Lukas looks at me like I've just suggested we sterilize a ballpoint pen and give each other tattoos.

"Oh. Um, isn't it kind of late to start the movie? I was thinking I would head home."

"But it's only nine thirty."

"I've been going to bed early."

"We could make coffee."

"I think I'll just go home." He walks to the front door and hops around self-consciously, putting on his shoes. I watch him from the kitchen. "I guess I'll see you on Saturday then," he says, dropping a shoe, picking it up again, and sticking it on his foot.

"What's on Saturday?"

"Battle of the Bands."

"Oh yeah."

I try to keep my voice light, as if for me this is just another perfectly normal evening of making unwanted sexual advances, being a sloppy drunk, and standing there pathetically while the object of my affection falls all over himself trying to escape from my lovearium before it's even dark outside.

Lukas finally gets his shoe on his foot. He grabs the door handle.

"Okay. Good night, Kiri."

"Bye."

He struggles with the door, discovers the lock, lets himself out, and pulls the door half-closed behind him without realizing you have to really yank it to get it shut. It floats open again behind him, as if to add the final insult to the huge festering injury that is my life. I sigh, walk over, and shut it myself.

Then I walk back to the piano. Because now that Lukas is gone, what else is left?

chapter twenty-one

The next morning, I take the bus to Kerrisdale, sit down at the piano, and play one hundred pages of dazzlingly complicated piano music from memory while Dr. Scaliteri sits on her ball, inspecting a suspicious mole on her cleavage. When I'm finished, she looks up and says one word: "Good."

I stand up, bow, collect my books, and breeze out of the room.

International Young Pianists' Showcase? I've got that shit in the bag.

The thrill of victory is a pleasant antidote to the sludge of humiliation left over from last night, and I float past the bus stop and on down the street, my fingers tingling with bliss.

I did it. I did it. I did it. I did it. My lips keep drawing upward in a loose, dopey smile, and I can barely feel the pavement beneath my feet. I did it. I did it. So what do I want to do now?

I want to ride my bicycle.

Where is my bicycle?

In Bicycle Boy's shed.

I swivel around like an ice skater and glide in the direction of downtown.

It turns out downtown is a two-and-a-half-hour walk away, plus another twenty minutes of backtracking when I mysteriously end up near the stadium.

Along the way I buy:

-three kiwis, a plum, and a pluot, all of which I eat except for the third kiwi, because the roof of my mouth starts itching in that way that sometimes happens when you eat too many kiwis;

-a cup of probiotic frozen yogurt with blackberries that inexplicably costs seven dollars, despite being very small and containing approximately twelve calories;

-a yam roll and an avocado roll from Happy Sushi that come in a plastic clamshell with fake green grass, a wasabi turd, and a little pile of pickled ginger like fairy tongues;

-a can of Diet Dr Pepper that makes me feel insane;

-a coffee drink with Chinese characters on the can that
   makes my sweat smell like coffee and makes me have
   to pee;
-a coffee at a coffee shop so they let me use the bathroom;
-a tube of SPF 60 sunscreen so I don't get mysterious moles
   on my cleavage when I'm old like Dr. Scaliteri;
-a new pair of flip-flops after the toe-thong thingy on my
   left flip-flop comes out of its socket and I can't get it
   back in;
-a wide-brimmed straw hat;
-a pair of tweezers and some questionable depilatory
   cream to deal with my eyebrow situation once and
   for all;
-a cranberry oat square at a coffee shop so they let me use
   the bathroom;
-a blue lightbulb;
-a jumbo bag of Meow Mix;
-an acorn squash;
-henna powder, incense, and temporary tattoos of various
   Hindu deities.

On my way to Skunk's house, I stop off at the Imperial to
give the Meow Mix to Doug. The same woman who gave me
directions to the modern art gallery when I was looking for
razzle!dazzle!space is sitting on the steps in pink spandex pants

and a tank top. Her brown hair is piled up in a high ponytail on her head. She looks like Workout Barbie if Workout Barbie had aged a few years and was starting to lose some hair.

"Is Doug around?" I ask.

She shakes her head and answers in her sexy, raspy voice. "He's not here, baby. He went to the clinic for his checkup. Did you bring him something?" She eyes my shopping bags. I show her the cat food.

"Aww, that's sweet, baby. Doug loves that kitty. You should go on up and leave it in his room. None of the rooms lock around here; you can go right in."

She tells me her name is Jasmine and she used to have a straw hat just like mine. I reach into one of my shopping bags. "Do you want a kiwi?"

"No thanks, babe, I'm allergic," she says, taking a drag on her cigarette.

I climb the steps to the fourth floor two at a time, hardly noticing the garbage or the rotten air. When I get to Doug's room, I march right in and set the bag of cat food on the floor. Snoogie materializes out of nowhere and rubs herself against my legs until I crouch and drag my fingers through her scruffy fur. I imagine Sukey picking her up in the alley behind the Imperial, stroking her ears and inspecting her stumpy leg, and thinking, *This cat is exactly what Doug needs.* I imagine Doug admiring her paintings, telling her how beautiful they are, and saying *Don't let that kid Billy hang around you, Sukey-girl, he's nothing but trouble.*

Guilt and jealousy splinter through me. Those missing months before Sukey died—they're something I'll never be a part of, something I'll never get to know. It fills me with a kind of howling indignation to know that Doug and Sukey shared something without me, that Doug stole something I'd desperately wanted all my life: to be Sukey's confidant, her fierce protector, and the only one who truly loved her in the world.

It suddenly feels very urgent to get out of Doug's room. I rip open the bag of cat food and make my escape while Snoogie is busily chomping away. My skin prickles when I walk past room 409 on my way back to the stairs, and I pause there.

This is where Sukey died.

This is where Sukey *died*.

I imagine her behind this very door, painting and playing CDs on her crappy CD player. I knock softly, ready to bolt at the slightest indication that there is anyone inside. When nobody answers, I turn the knob and open the door an inch. There's a reek of stale cigarette butts and a naked mattress strewn with porn magazines. I pull the door shut and hurry to the stairs.

When I get to Skunk's place, there's a light on and music playing. I rap on the glass. There's motion on the other side of the curtain, and Skunk pulls open the door. He has a cigarette and lighter in one hand, which he slips into his pocket when he sees me. I smile. "Hey! I came to pick up my bike."

His expression relaxes. "Hey, Kiri. How've you been?"

He steps outside and slides the door all the way shut behind him, like there's something in there he doesn't want to get out.

"Do you have a cat?" I say.

Skunk looks at me blankly. I worry the edge of my flip-flop against the concrete.

"You always shut the door so quickly. I thought maybe you had an indoor cat."

He shakes his head. "No cat."

"Or an extremely vicious cat who attacks strangers. That old man who had my sister's things has a cat like that. It's called Snoogie, and it's mean as a snake."

I think Skunk's starting to warm up to my surprise visit. His brown eyes mellow and his shoulders relax.

"You'd need a cat like that if you lived at the Imperial Hotel," he says.

"A guard cat."

"Maybe I should look into getting one."

I'm not 100 percent sure, but I think the unspoken end of that sentence is *to keep crazy girls from knocking on my door.* Yes, I'm being too chatty.

"Have things been okay?" he asks.

I try to remember how long it's been since he last saw me.

Two weeks? He probably thinks of me as that crying girl who's always in trouble.

I nod, embarrassed.

"Yeah, everything's cool. I'll just grab my bike and get out of here."

Skunk presses his lips together.

"Actually—"

"Let me guess. Pawn shop. I should have called you a week ago, I know. How much did you get for it?"

I can't help it—I can't stop jabbering. When someone else is being serious, I start telling jokes. It's like only one person is allowed to be serious at a time, and that person is never, ever me.

Skunk kicks at a pile of cigarette butts on the patio. "You might be mad."

I stare at him. "Wait, you really did sell it?"

"No. I started doing some work on it."

"Oh. But there was nothing wrong with it."

A guilty look ripples across Skunk's face. "I knew you'd be mad."

He walks over to the shed, undoes the combination lock, and pulls open the metal doors.

There's my bike. Well, sort of. It's upside down and resting on a wooden workbench with its wheels in the air. The seat is off, the back tire is completely flat again, and the frame is held in place by two metal clamps. I hurry to its side like I'm a panicked relative who has just arrived at its hospital room.

"What did you do to it? Why's the tire flat again?"

Skunk steps into the shed and pulls a dirty string to turn the light on.

"The wheels were so far out of true the spokes were about to snap. Your brakes are pretty shot too."

He squeezes the brake lever to demonstrate. The brake pads kiss the tires feebly.

I cross my arms.

"It rides okay."

I don't know why I'm being so defensive about the state of my obviously defective bicycle, but it irks me when people fix things that don't need fixing. Skunk gives the brakes another squeeze.

"If you think this thing rides okay, it's been a while since you rode a decent bike."

"My bike *is* decent."

"But it doesn't ride straight anymore, does it? Watch this." He gives the back wheel a spin. I watch with my arms still folded. Skunk points. "See that?"

I glance at the wheel to be polite. As it spins, the wheel veers out to the right, then back in again. Skunk spins it a little harder. It wobbles in and out, in and out, in and out. "If you keep riding on this, those spokes are going to snap," he says.

He looks at me sheepishly. "You *are* mad."

I shake my head and try to suppress my irritation. *Stop being such a bitch-nacho.* I paste on a smile. "I'm not mad. I appreciate your help."

Skunk snorts. "Translation: Hands off my bike, asshole."

"Sorry. I just wasn't expecting Project Extreme Bike Makeover."

For the first time since he opened the shed, Skunk looks apologetic. He leans against the workbench. "If you want, I can just reinflate the tire and you can take it how it is. Or if you've got a minute, I can finish truing the spokes right now."

I pause. When I look at my bike again, my self-righteousness ebbs a little. Fine. It's maybe a little bit wonky. And I'm being extremely rude. After all, he's already helped me out twice. The least I can do is let him true my stupid spokes. I put my hands on my hips.

"All right, Bicycle Boy. Extreme Bike Makeover. You're on."

Skunk reaches for a curved plastic tool that's lying on the dusty workbench. He gives the wheel a spin and watches as it wobbles through the brake pads. After it's gone around a couple times, he stops it, gives the little metal nub at the bottom of one of the spokes a quarter turn, and spins it again.

He sticks his finger in the wheel to stop its spinning and adjusts another nub. When he spins the wheel again, that part doesn't rub against the brake pads anymore. There's not really room for both of us to stand inside the shed, but I clear a space on the workbench and sit next to my bike with my legs dangling down while Skunk works. Now that I've decided to stay, I'm getting excited about the tune-up. It's been a long time since I did anything vaguely maintenance-y on my bike. I lean forward and rest my chin on my knuckles.

"So were the wheels totally messed up?"

"Pretty much."

"What happens if the spokes snap?"

Skunk shrugs. "You'd probably go over your handlebars."

"Awesome."

"Or a spoke could shoot through the rim and burst the tube."

"That's so metal."

"Here. Listen to this."

Skunk strums one of the spokes so it resonates like a guitar string. Then he does it to another one. I sit up straight. "Hey! They sound the same."

"You want to check the other ones?"

"Sure." I hop off the bench and squeeze in beside him. When I get close to him, this scent, this whiff of cigarettes and bicycle grease and orange rinds, catches me by surprise. It's fleeting and intense and almost too personal, like walking past someone's window and catching them changing. I wonder if that's why he keeps his door closed: Otherwise the whole world would smell him and come sniffing around for more.

I strum the spokes one by one.

"That one's a little off."

"Do it again?"

I strum the spoke again, then try the spoke above it. They sound slightly different.

"Good ear," says Skunk. He hands me the tool. "Go for it."

We slowly work our way around the wheel, spinning and adjusting and spinning again. It's oddly addictive once you get started, like working the knots out of your hair when it's really tangly. Every time we push the wheel it spins straighter, until eventually it passes through the brake pads without scraping them at any point during its revolution. When we're finished with the back wheel, we flip the bike around and do the front. Every time Skunk moves, I catch that scent again, peeling paint and citrus. He smells like an old ladder left out in the sun.

When both wheels are done, Skunk lifts the bike down from the workbench and checks it over. He reaches out a tattooed arm and squeezes the brake levers one more time. I feel a surge of my initial defensiveness rising up just in case, but Skunk doesn't say anything. As he runs his fingers along the titanium posts, I suddenly feel acutely conscious of the coolness of the air against my skin. For some reason, I think about Lukas, who never wrote back to the texts I sent him trying to make light of the sex-dome incident last night. I gaze around the little shed, searching for something to distract myself. I straighten up with a jolt when I notice the shiny green electric bass that's leaning in the corner with a greasy rag hanging off its neck.

"What's that doing in the shed?"

Skunk's face is tipped down and I can't see his eyes, just his hands moving carefully around my bicycle. "I think your shifters need some WD-40."

He reaches for the blue can on the bench and gives the gears a one-second spray. I peer at the bass. It's beautiful. Sleek. Curvy. Like an exotic fruit. I want to eat a slice of it.

"Skunk?"

"Hm?"

He picks up a screwdriver and twiddles with a screw. He takes it out, wipes it off, and starts screwing it back in.

"Please explain to me why am I seeing a vintage Fender Mustang bass on the floor of this shed."

He looks to where I'm looking and his brown eyes widen slightly, as if he never noticed the seven-hundred-dollar instrument that just happens to be lurking under his grease-rag collection.

"Oh. Yeah. I'm trying to sell it. I was going to put it on craigslist."

"You're putting a vintage Fender on *craigslist*?"

Skunk spins the screwdriver around in his hand.

"Is that illegal or something?"

"It should be."

"Why are you selling it?"

"I'm not in a band anymore."

"So start another one."

He shakes his head. "I'm more into bikes right now."

"They're not exactly mutually exclusive."

"There's only so much time in the day."

"Are you expecting me to believe you just woke up one morning and decided you'd rather spend all day lurking in some crusty shed than playing that fabulous instrument?"

"Pretty much."

I chew on this while Skunk raises my bike seat by another half inch and clamps the lever down.

"I find this answer highly dubious."

Skunk gives me a look.

"I find this bicycle highly dubious."

"Promise me you will not sell that gorgeous instrument."

"Do you play? I'll give it to you."

The offer is so tantalizing, my blood momentarily freezes over with greed. I grip the edge of the workbench.

"I play keys. Not bass."

"You could learn."

"Keep it. You're going to play it again."

Skunk shakes his head. I keep at him. "Yes, you will. I know you will. At least put it in the house. If you leave it out here, it'll get warped when the temperature changes."

Sigh. Now I'm the one being all fussy about someone else's stuff. But I can't help it: Nobody owns a bass like that unless they're either rich as balls or they really mean it. Even if he doesn't think so now, I'm pretty sure Skunk really means it. Or used to mean it, anyway. I eye the bass again.

"Make you a deal. You bring that bass back inside and I'll consider fixing my brake pads."

Skunk cocks his head, wrench in hand. "What kind of a deal is that?"

"What do you mean, what kind of a deal is that? You indulge my ridiculous neurosis and I'll indulge yours. It's perfectly fair."

Skunk smiles, and when he does he looks less like a meaty thug and more like a big, shaggy bison.

"I'll think about it," he says.

chapter twenty-two

I'm sitting at the piano, listening to the metronome tick. But tonight, for some reason, I just can't make myself practice. The piano sounds too bright, like a voice in a commercial. Instead of melting into its embrace, I chafe at it, like a hug from a relative you secretly hate.

I remember my first-ever piano lesson with Dr. Scaliteri, a month after Sukey died. She stared at me for a long time, perched on her silver ball, and asked me a question that drove a wedge between that moment and everything that came before it: "Great art requires great discipline, Kiri. Are you ready to be disciplined?"

She had me play nothing but scales that day, up and down

the piano in every key, making me do them again and again if I fumbled a single note. My despair at getting them right was a strange sort of rescue from the larger despair clawing at my life, like wrestling with a difficult crossword puzzle when you're alone in the wilderness with two broken legs and no hope of making it out alive.

Great art requires great discipline.

I lift my hands back onto the keys and grudgingly start on a scale. But tonight, it's not discipline I need. I remember the time I asked Sukey where she went at night when she snuck out. It was the summer before Mom and Dad kicked her out, back when you could still hear music pounding behind her door anytime you walked by. I was sitting on her bed, watching her paint, her black brush flicking over a rectangular canvas, her hair pulled back in one of my fuzzy pink hair elastics because she was always losing her own.

"I go to Kits Beach and watch the ships," said Sukey.

"Why?"

She shrugged. "Because they're beautiful."

"That's really all you do?"

I'd been expecting boyfriends, drinking, all the usual things Sukey got in trouble for. But somehow this felt more luminously dangerous, more thrilling, like swallowing fire.

She dabbed her brush in violet and touched it to a spot of green. The lizard Sukey was painting seemed to come alive and wriggle, as if her touch was all it took to make it real. She smiled. "That's really all I do."

The memory kills me. I pull my hands off the keys and stand up. I'll go for a bike ride. Just a little one. A starter adventure. I'll go out and explore and find some ships of my own.

At first, I stick to familiar streets, making a wide circle around the neighborhood. The leaves in the treetops form a starry tunnel overhead, bathed now and then in orange lamplight. I turn left when I get to Arbutus, then right and then left again. Pretty soon I'm in a neighborhood I've never been to before, with brick houses and flower beds so perfect it looks like they were unpacked, fully grown, from a cardboard box. I roll past a park where people are playing late-night tennis under spotlights and a short strip of restaurants where the smell of frying onions is sharp in the air.

Each street I turn down is a revelation. With every push of my pedals, I can feel the map getting bigger, new squares and lines and landmarks appearing like new levels in a video game. When midnight rolls around, I'm way down in East Van, cruising down Commercial Drive. I roll down the street, eyeing the record stores and hippie clothing shops and dimly lit bars. Up ahead on my left, I can see a small crowd of people gathered in a playground, all of them on bicycles—fixies and road bikes and one recumbent covered in yellow reflectors. With their blinking lights and shiny helmets, they look like a flock of fireflies. I swoop closer to get a better look. There's maybe twenty people, mostly college kids, with some people my age and a few older-looking riders thrown in for good measure. Some of them are holding beers or flasks, and there's a couple joints going around.

I'm so pumped from my bike ride I don't feel shy at all. I ride my bike up to the edge of the crowd and nose in next to a girl in a cute leather jacket and sparkly tights.

"Hey. Whatcha guys doing?"

She adjusts the strap on her black helmet.

"Midnight Mass. We go for a ride twice a month."

"Where you going?"

"I don't know yet. We kind of make it up as we go along."

I look around at the rest of the group. My eyes wander over girls in furry-eared hats and guys with pink and silver tassels hanging off their handlebars. Everyone's talking, laughing, drinking, oddly glamorous on their tricked-out bikes. They remind me of the people at Sukey's art opening. Alive. Happy. Free.

Then I spot him.

Skunk.

He's standing at the other edge of the crowd almost exactly opposite to me, his huge body balanced over the slender angles of a black Schwinn bike.

I stand up on my tiptoes and wave.

"Skunk!"

He doesn't hear me. He's peering down at his handlebars while he feels the brake wire with his fingers, no doubt planning some completely unnecessary repair.

I back up my bike and ride around the edge of the crowd. "Skunk! Hey."

His face registers a brief moment of surprise and confusion. I roll my bike right up alongside his.

"I can't believe you're here! Do you do this every month?"

There's a joint coming our way. I can smell it, but can't place it with my eyes.

Skunk fiddles with his brake wires. "Sometimes."

"I've already been out riding for three hours. My bike's riding totally straight now, thanks to you."

His face brightens. "Good."

"I've been thinking about fixing those brake pads. Pending you taking care of that Fender, of course."

Skunk doesn't answer. We stand there in silence, scuffing the grass with our feet. I wonder if Skunk wants me to leave. Maybe I'm ruining his quiet night out with my chatter. Maybe this is the kind of thing that drove Lukas away from me: Kiri Byrd, professional motormouth.

When the joint gets to us, Skunk passes. I waver, then pass too so he doesn't think I'm a druggie. When a fifth of Captain Morgan comes around, Skunk passes again. I'm starting to

worry that he's a Mormon or a straight-edge punk like this kid
Alex at my school, who wears a Mohawk and safety pins but
won't touch a beer. I lean over and catch his eye.

"Intoxicants not your thing?"

"I choose my poisons."

"Does that mean we're robo-tripping later?"

He smiles.

"Wait and see."

I'm starting to realize that talking to Skunk is like digging
for clams on the beach. You see bubbles in the sand and start
digging, but he's digging too, and nine times out of ten that
sucker's faster than you. I cock my head.

"You straight-edge or something?"

Skunk hesitates, and for a second I wonder if I'm digging
too hard. He squeezes his brake levers.

"Not exactly."

"You're very evasive, you know."

Skunk's about to say something when a tall, skinny guy on
a red BMX shouts, "Listen up!" and everyone shuffles into a
bicycle huddle to decide on a route for the night. Somehow
Skunk and I get shuffled apart. When I spot him again from
across the circle, he's lighting a cigarette. He sucks on it nervously and lets out a long, smoky exhale. *There's one of his
poisons, anyway.*

Red BMX lays out some route options. I vote for northward.

So does Skunk. Stanley Park at night sounds like fun. I've only ever been there during the day, whenever Auntie Moana and Uncle Ed come to visit. The bike path is always so clogged with little kids on training wheels and their beaming parents that there's no point in even trying to ride around them.

Red BMX pushes off and starts pedaling down Commercial Drive. For a moment all you can hear are gears cranking and tires bumping down over the curb. I can see Skunk up ahead of me, not too far behind Red BMX and his girlfriend, Purple Mongoose. For someone who loves fixing bikes, Skunk's doesn't look like much. The taping on the handles is scruffy, and orange foam peeks out from the cracks in the saddle. You'd think someone Skunk's size would look funny on a spindly road bike, but Skunk and his bicycle fit together perfectly. When he pedals, I can see the flash of muscles in his calves.

We turn down East 7th Avenue, cutting through a warehouse district I've never been to before—blocks and blocks of buildings like monoliths or ancient tombs, so quiet that speaking feels forbidden even though it isn't; even though it can't be. I bike on the left side of the street, ready to swoop back over the line if a car comes, but none do. *How silly to have a line there at all*, I think, delighted, pedaling faster and faster. The city at night is a playground, and we are a pack of kids riding its swings upside down.

As the warehouses give way to residential streets, I cut

through the fleet of cyclists to the front of the pack. Red BMX and Purple Mongoose and I keep pace with one another, our bikes humming beneath us like generators. I've lost track of Skunk again, but it hardly matters. At this speed, there's no way we could talk, no way to do anything but watch the houses and trees and bus stops flash past like frames in a stop-motion movie. The Granville Street Bridge is a roller-coaster. We fly over it in a blur of metal and blinking lights and veer left as a single body.

Guys in tight jeans wave and whoop for us as we thunder down the hill toward English Bay. Music pounds inside the nightclubs on Davie Street, and the smell of beer and salt water makes even the air seem drunk. On the water, I can see Sukey's ships, dark cities of their own. They are objects I will never touch, places I will never stand, sleeping giants that would not be disturbed even if all the shimmering lights and pretty buildings on land crumbled and fell down. Maybe we all need ships to hold our dreams, to be bigger and steadier than we ever could be, and to guard the mystery when we cannot, to keep it safe even when we have lost everything.

I keep my eyes on them as long as I can, falling behind the others as we cruise along the sea wall to the dark, forested path that borders Stanley Park. I startle when Skunk rides up beside me. I'd fallen so deep in thought I'd practically forgotten he was here.

"How's the bike feel?"

"Oh. You know. Like a total death trap."

I smile at him so he knows I'm kidding.

"I ant to ear oo ay um time," shouts Skunk, scraps of his words torn away by the wind. I angle my bike closer to him.

"WHAT?"

"I want to hear you play sometime."

I nod to show I've understood him.

"Make you a deal," I shout.

"Another one?"

"Uh-huh."

"I want to hear you too."

He opens his mouth to protest, but I curl over my handlebars and scream, "Race you!"

Before he can answer, I've shot ten feet ahead of him, the bike path melting into mercury beneath my tires. Up ahead where the seawall curves, a bronze sculpture shines brightly in the moonlight. I blast toward it.

When I'm halfway there, a huge black shape streaks past me.

It's Skunk. Cutting through the night like a sailboat. Flying down the path as if he weighed nothing at all.

I tip my face into the wind and charge after him, leaving the ships far behind. I know they will be there, waiting. But as my bicycle carries me deeper into the forest, it feels like I'm carrying them with me too.

chapter twenty-three

It starts raining after we cross the Lions Gate Bridge back into Stanley Park. Soon, it's a full-on downpour. The pack dwindles as people peel off in various directions to ride home. Red BMX and Purple Mongoose evaporate into the night somewhere around Denman Street, and by the time we hit Granville, it's just me and Skunk. The nightclubs have emptied out and the heat lamps have been pulled inside. Granville Street is empty except for cop cars and the leftover drunks and homeless people shouting at each other on the sidewalk. My clothes are soaking wet and suctioned to my skin, and my tires are slick. We bike slowly, floating over the shining pavement.

"You headed home?" says Skunk.

"I guess I should."

The rain's soft music has lulled me into a trance, and I hadn't even realized we'd drifted past Burrard Street, where I should have turned off for the bridge.

"You left your shopping bags in the shed this afternoon," he says.

"Perfect. I'll come get them."

As we coast through the deepening puddles, listening to the muffled sound our tires make slashing through the water, I take another shot at digging for clams.

"So why don't you smoke pot?" I ask.

Skunk wipes the raindrops off his forehead.

"I used to. I was a big-time stoner when I was twelve."

"When you were *twelve*? Where does a twelve-year-old get pot?"

Skunk laughs. "In Montreal, you can do anything when you're twelve."

He pronounces it *Mo-ray-all*, with this whiff of a Quebecois accent that makes my insides go limp. As we bike to his neighborhood, Skunk tells me about growing up in Montreal: smoking cigarettes at recess, skipping school to play in bands, moving out of his mom and stepdad's apartment when he was sixteen to live in a shared house with the Band That Shall Not Be Mentioned.

"So you'd what, blaze and do multiplication tables?" I say.

"Yeah. Or just sit in my room and play bass."

"What happens if you smoke weed now?"

"My paranoia gets worse."

I give him a funny look.

"It gets worse? You mean you're just generally paranoid all the time? Are you paranoid right now? Are you paranoid about me?"

I swoop my bike closer to Skunk's and give him my best evil stare.

"I am plotting to kill you, Skunk. Kiri Byrd in the toolshed with a bike wrench."

He gives my handlebars a light push. I veer away, laughing.

"How do you know I'm not plotting to kill *you*?" says Skunk. "I could have sabotaged your bike and you wouldn't even know it. Your tires might blow up the next time you go over a bump."

I swoop closer again, rain falling lush and heavy on my skin.

"You're not that evil."

"Try me."

"You just think you are because you have tattoos. Speaking of which, should I get one? I was thinking about getting Beethoven's face right here."

I point to a spot on my arm. Skunk grimaces.

"Please don't."

"Why? What's wrong with Beethoven? It would make me more legit as a pianist. I'm going to be in this big piano festival soon, and I want the other contestants to know I mean business. When I flex my bicep, Beethoven could scowl at them menacingly."

"Or you could scowl at them menacingly."

"Trust me. I've got that part down."

"You're a little crazy, you know."

"Look who's talking, Bicycle Boy."

When we get to Skunk's house, the rain is still pouring down. We wheel our bikes through the iron gate and down the side of the house, flower stems slapping wetly against our legs. Skunk unlocks the shed and lifts his bike onto its pegs. He finds my plastic shopping bags stowed under the workbench and hands them to me. I feel the ridiculous shape of the acorn squash and the straw hat. The piano lesson I had this afternoon feels like something that happened years ago, to a different Kiri altogether. My legs are slick with bicycle grease and rainwater, muscles aching from the ride. I want to freeze myself in this feeling like a fern in amber.

I saw the ships, I want to tell Sukey. I know she'd know what I mean.

Skunk closes the shed door and hooks the combination

lock through the metal latch. We stand in the courtyard, rain splashing off our shoulders. I think of my empty house and nudge my kickstand down, playing for time.

"Mind if I use your bathroom?"

I do need to pee, but mostly I just don't want to go home. When I think of everywhere I've been tonight, the warehouses and the sea wall, my house seems lifeless, a plastic Monopoly piece in a world full of brick and glass and water and wood and stone.

Skunk plays with his keys.

"Sure. We have to be quiet, though. My aunt and uncle are sleeping upstairs."

"No problem. I'll be in and out."

I leave my bike in the courtyard and follow Skunk to the house, waiting as he unlocks the sliding glass door and pulls it open. I can't help but feel a little excited. I'm finally being admitted to the inner sanctum. The Sanctum Skunkorium. The cave of mysteries.

He goes in first, and I follow. As I step inside, I forget all about my need to pee. My senses reel.

Skunk's room is one of the most bizarre and beautiful places I've ever seen.

The entire room is filled with old radios. It reminds me of nothing so much as an aviary, each radio a different bird, some with gleaming wooden coats like sparrows and some with green plastic shoulders like parrots. They perch on ledges and shelves, peeking down from windowsills and peering out from in between stacks of old books, their antennas perked at quirky angles, their dials glowing faintly in the dim golden light of an antique lamp. Some of them look ancient, with curved wooden cases and glass-plated dials, and some are squat and cheerful. I even think I can hear birds in here, a faint hooting and scratching, until I realize one of the radios is turned on with its volume low.

There's an unmade bed loosely covered by a black-and-green quilt. A row of red Chinese lanterns hangs above the bed, their bellies glowing. The ashtray on the bedside table is littered with the stubs of incense sticks. I glimpse the soft curves of an ornate velvet armchair piled with clothes. Behind the armchair hangs a painting of the Hindu goddess Kali, her four arms held at right angles, tongue stuck out. The room smells like something I've only smelled one time before. It takes me a moment to place it: myrrh.

Skunk plants his hand on the wall and slides off his wet shoes.

"Bathroom's through there." He indicates a little hallway with his chin. "The light switch is sort of hard to find. It's on the wall under the mirror."

His face is turned toward the floor, concentrating on his shoes. Rainwater slips off his hair and the back of his neck and drops to the floor, making little wet polka dots on the hard-wood.

I'm not listening to his instructions about the light switch. Something in the corner of the room has caught my eye. "My grandma had that radio."

Skunk looks up, smiling. He's peeled off his wet socks and balled them up inside his shoes. His bare feet are surprisingly pale and hairless.

"Oh yeah?"

"The blue one with the clock on the front. She kept it tuned to this crazy Christian station where they were always telling you to put your hands on the radio and pray for healing."

"The blue one's my second favorite," he says.

"Which one's your first favorite?"

"See that little red one on the top ledge?"

I scan the wall until I see it.

"The plastic one?"

"Yeah."

"It's cute. Where'd you get it?"

"I found it sitting next to a fire hydrant. I was walking past and thought I heard something, and it was this radio sitting on the sidewalk, running on batteries. It was like it had wandered out into the world and gotten lost and it was calling out, hoping someone would find it."

"Aww. That's sweet. What was it playing?"

Skunk grins.

"Marilyn Manson."

I go to the bathroom, and when I come back the rain is slapping horizontally against the glass door. Skunk is sitting on the floor, putting on dry socks. I put my hand on the door. I know this is supposed to be the part where I go home.

But what would happen if I didn't?

"Well, it was nice riding with you," I say, reaching up to brush the wet hair out of my eyes. "Next time we race, I get a head start."

I realize, to my simultaneous horror and exhilaration, that I'm flirting with him.

Skunk pulls on a wool sock, his face carefully composed, as if he's trying to figure out how far into his private universe he should let me intrude, and for how long.

Stop it, Kiri! says the part of me that's shocked by my boldness.

The other part says, *Why?*

I smile at him and cast a mischievous glance at my wet tank top, knowing Skunk's eyes will follow.

"I wish it wasn't raining. But I guess it doesn't matter, since I'm already soaked. Anyway. See you later."

I turn around to slide the door open before he sees the half-mortified, half-triumphant expression on my face. My heart is beating like a castanet. *All right, flirt-monster. That's enough for one night. He obviously doesn't like you.* My fingers find the plastic handle.

"Wait," says Skunk.

chapter twenty-four

The rain doesn't seem to be stopping anytime soon.

So I stay.

Skunk tiptoes upstairs, and when he comes back down he's carrying a small clay teapot and two tiny cups without handles. We sit cross-legged on the rug in the middle of the floor, drink our tea, and talk in whispers so his aunt and uncle won't hear. I can't stop looking around the room, stealing glances at the radios, the lanterns, the junk-store painting of Kali, the quilt on Skunk's bed. I still can't quite believe I'm in here. Part of me's on my wet bicycle, making her disciplined, hard-working, and responsible way home. It takes all my self-control not to chicken out and follow her.

Between thimblefuls of smoky, earthy tea, I make Skunk tell me the story of every radio in the room.

The boxy green one he found on top of someone's trash.

The antique one in the walnut cabinet someone left at the bottom of their driveway with a FREE sign the morning after a garage sale.

The digital clock radio he stole from a hospital room.

The vintage 1960s transistor radio his dad gave him a week before he committed suicide in his apartment.

I tell myself I'll only stay until we're finished our tea, but the teapot never seems to run out. Every time Skunk lifts it to fill our cups, more tea trickles out. He asks me about the Imperial, and I tell him everything I've found out since the night we met.

"Are you sure you want to hear this?" I ask, remembering Lukas's reaction, but in the cozy lamplight, it feels like there's no secret too terrible to say. Skunk gives me a sweater to wear, a big brown woolen one that drapes over my whole body like a warm, fuzzy tent. I feel self-conscious wearing it, like I'm taking a nap in his bed. But it also makes my chest tingle. *Get real, Kiri,* I tell myself. *This isn't going anywhere.*

Every few minutes my eyes flit to the clock on the little red radio. *It's four thirty a.m., I should go home. It's five a.m., I should go home. It's five fifteen, I should go home.* At six a.m. there's noise upstairs, and we can hear Skunk's aunt and uncle taking showers and making breakfast.

"I should probably leave too," I whisper. "I really need to practice."

"At six in the morning?"

"Why not?"

"It's still raining."

"I'll get wet."

"At least finish your tea."

"That teapot is enchanted. It never runs out."

"I know."

"So you're saying you're trying to enchant me?"

Skunk presses his lips together. "Wait and see."

I sip my tea, trying to play it cool. But I can't help it. I spring to my feet. "I really need to go."

Skunk waves his arms. "Oh no! She's fiending!"

"I am not *fiending*."

"How many hours has it been since your last hit?"

I count. "Nine and a half."

"Fiending," says Skunk.

"I swear I'm not a junkie," I say. "It's just that my piano will explode if I don't practice for long enough each day. It's sort of like a bomb in that respect."

Skunk goes to the wall and turns on a radio. He tunes it to a classical station, and the slow first movement of Beethoven's *Moonlight Sonata* comes pouring out.

"I'm playing that piece in the Showcase," I blurt.

Skunk kneels on the floor and pours me more tea.

"Tell me all about it," he says.

In the afternoon we go upstairs to make breakfast before Skunk's aunt and uncle come home from work. Their house is a mysterious planet of vitamin bottles and piled-up mail, as different as could be from the warm, cluttered radio temple below. There's a stack of cookbooks on the counter with titles like *Lo-Carb Italian Cooking* and, disturbingly, *The Zero-Calorie Solution*. I page through them while Skunk puts on a kettle of water for coffee and gets out the ingredients for an omelet. Between reading recipes for celery salad and low-carb meatballs, I pace around the kitchen, taking in the stacks of clean dishes and bowls, matching white mugs with square handles, sets of espresso cups and saucers. There's some sort of work schedule taped to a cupboard door.

"What does your aunt do?"

Skunk puts a carton of eggs on the counter and turns back to the fridge to rummage around in the vegetable drawer.

"She's a nurse," he says over his shoulder.

"What about your uncle?"

"Auto parts manager."

"When do they get home from work?"

"Six."

"I should probably go before then. I really do need to practice."

Skunk snorts. I plant my hands on my hips. "What are you laughing at?"

"You sound just like my aunt."

"Why? Does she play piano?"

"No, she's on a diet. *I'm going to lose sixteen pounds. No, twenty pounds.*"

"You're such a jerk! I only have to do eight hours if I leave right now. I can do them before bed."

"Is piano your job or something? Are you going to get fired if you miss a day?"

"It's called discipline, fool. I'll have you know I've been playing piano since I was a kid, and I take it very seriously."

"What about your band?" says Skunk. "I bet you don't play synth for eight hours a day."

"That's different."

"Why?"

"Nobody *needs* me to be in a band."

"And they need you to play piano?"

I scowl at Skunk, piqued. "This had better be the best freaking omelet I've ever had."

He drops his hands on my shoulders and steers me to a chair at the kitchen table. "Consider this an intervention."

He pours me a big mug of coffee to drink, then goes back to

the fridge and takes out arugula, goat cheese, wild mushrooms, and fresh herbs. While he's cooking, a fat orange cat comes out of the living room and slinks around my legs, meowing plaintively.

"That's Gingerly," says Skunk. "Don't feed her, she's a mooch."

Skunk reaches into a cupboard, takes out sea salt, and shakes some into the omelet. I'm so hungry I squirm in my chair. "Is that food almost ready?"

"Good things take time."

"The smell's driving me crazy."

"You're already crazy."

"Oh no, I'm not. Not yet. Okay, now I am."

And for the last three minutes before the omelet's ready I'm fluttering around the kitchen in my socks, light as a moth and practically translucent with hunger, saying, "When-when-when-when-when?" and spinning around with the affronted cat in my arms. Skunk lifts the cast-iron pan off the stove with an oven mitt, and when he puts it down on a hot pad on the kitchen table, I rush up with the cat in my arms and almost kiss him I'm so hungry, but stop just short and stand there, panting slightly, my head dizzy from spinning, our faces just inches apart.

I'm conscious of Skunk's height, of his bigness. He's like a brontosaurus or a bison or a bulldozer, some strong, solid word.

He still smells like something that's been out grazing in the sun, even though it's been raining since last night. There's a fleck of rosemary stuck to his forehead. A smudge of bicycle grease on his wrist. I feel a flutter of fear, then a wingbeat of certainty.

"I want to kiss you," I say, "but I seem to be holding this cat."

Skunk lifts his hand and touches it to the side of my face. His fingers are warm from carrying the hot skillet to the table. He regards me very seriously, and for a moment I wonder if he's about to tell me we should Focus on Bicycle Repair. Instead he just looks at me for a very long time.

"You're beautiful," says Skunk, "and completely batshit."

Then, cat be damned, I do kiss him. I'm either swooning or having a hypoglycemic meltdown, take your pick, because I'm starving and in love with Skunk and because nobody's ever said anything like that to me before. Halfway through the kiss, the cat twists out of my arms, drops to its feet on the floor, and streaks away. I step in and close the space between our bodies and we kiss, Skunk and I, like all the bicycles in the world are gliding down a long, steep, swooping, tree-mad hill.

Somehow we eat our afternoon breakfast and get the dishes done and put away. We wipe down the counters, push in our chairs, and turn off the lights. Every time a car passes, we shoot each other panicked looks and bolt toward the stairs. Suddenly, it's a game: How long can I stay until we get caught? How much of this can we get away with?

We scamper downstairs and kiss until our lips are swollen and our cheeks are pink and Skunk's shape, his vast lovely architecture, has become as familiar to me as the rooms of my own house. We drag the black-and-green quilt off Skunk's bed, lay it on the floor, and roll in it like snow, hands tangled up in one another's hair. *Bicycle Boy, my brontosaurus of love, my love-bison.* I cling to his sweater like a cat, pawing at his heart with my little hooked claws, mewling, memorizing his scent. Every so often my mind flits back to my house, the piano, the thirsty azaleas and the mailbox stuffed with flyers. I finally open my fist and let go of these worries, and like a bunch of helium balloons they float up and up and up until they're tiny specks in the corner of the big blue sky.

At six o'clock, we hear Skunk's aunt coming home from work. We freeze on the rug, listening to her footsteps on the kitchen floor. A few minutes later, Skunk's uncle gets home too. They talk—a low rumbly voice and a sharp medium-high one—and there's the beep of a microwave and the sudden bright loudness of a TV commercial. I snuggle into Skunk.

"I should go home now, right? Right?"

Before I can say anything else, the door at the top of the stairs squeaks open, letting in a bar of yellow light.

"Philippe?" calls Skunk's aunt. *"T'es en bas?"*

Our bodies go rigid like lizards playing dead. I'm sure she sees us, but Skunk motions for me to stay where I am. He jumps up and rummages noisily through his dresser.

"Ouai, tante Martine. J'viens. Un moment, j'suis en train de me changer."

"D'accord."

She shuts the door. My body goes limp, but Skunk is quaking with silent laughter.

"I told her I was changing. I have to go upstairs for a while," he whispers. "Don't worry."

He climbs the stairs. Before he opens the door, he looks over his shoulder to cast me a mischievous grin.

"Hey, Aunt Martine. What's for dinner?" he says more loudly than he needs to. I have to bury my head under the quilt before I laugh so hard I give our secret away.

When Skunk comes back down, he lights big beeswax candles and tunes one of the radios to this station that plays detective shows from the 1940s. We lie on the floor and listen, the quilt wrapped around us. I lift his hand and very gently bite the tender perfect acorn of his finger. He murmurs and pulls me in close, and we spoon while the radio detective comforts a hysterical woman whose husband has just been found poisoned in bed.

"It was the butler," I whisper.

"No way," murmurs Skunk. "It was definitely the wife."

"No way."

"She's having an affair with the butler."

"You're smoking crack."

"Just wait."

I sigh and nest my body more snugly into Skunk's. The show goes on. It turns out it was the hysterical wife. Skunk was right.

We listen to another one starring the same detective, and this time Skunk predicts the killer again. "You've listened to way too many of these," I say.

"You always think it's the obvious suspect. It's never the obvious suspect."

"Thanks, Inspector Gadget."

"It's always the last person you'd ever guess."

"I still don't get why the groundskeeper killed Dr. Knight."

"He'd falsified his brother's will so Harry wouldn't inherit Birch Pond anymore. The only way to get it back was to kill Dr. Knight."

"You *have* listened to way too many of these."

"Let's listen to one more."

I prop my head up on my elbows and look down at him. "Aren't you getting tired? Don't you ever sleep?"

"We'll sleep," whispers Skunk. "But let's listen to another one first."

I start to protest. Skunk reaches up and touches my hair, and before I know it I'm kissing him again. Soon neither of us is paying enough attention to the show to figure out who killed who.

All night we drift in and out of sleep, waking up just long enough to kiss and tangle and fall asleep again with our limbs in a knot. It feels like we're living in a dream, like there's no way what we're doing is possible. But it is. And we are. And I don't ever want it to end. I think back to Lukas and the disaster with the wine, and it seems hilarious now, like I've traded in a jar full of pennies for a bar of gold. It's amazing how quickly the things you thought would make you happy seem small once you stumble on something true.

Beautiful, I think to myself as I float back into sleep, my whole body thrumming with a tender, exhausted state of exhilaration. Beside me, Skunk's body is warm under his T-shirt. The last thing I see before falling asleep is the Kali painting on Skunk's wall. Her blue-gold body is draped in equal parts flowers and severed heads—as if beauty and horror were interchangeable and what matters most is trusting in the dance. I gaze at her until I can almost hear the clink of bells, the thud of drums. My eyes droop shut, and then I'm gone.

Sometime around noon on Saturday we both take showers in the tiny downstairs bathroom. Skunk gives me a soft old T-shirt to wear and a pair of his aunt's sweatpants he finds in the dryer. They're big in the butt and they make me look like an orangutan, but at least they're clean. Oh, Skunk! Oh, Bicycle Boy! This afternoon's omelet features Asiago and leeks. When did Lukas ever feed me? When did Lukas peel off my borrowed socks and do a weird and vaguely pleasant shiatsu thing to my feet?

That evening when Skunk comes downstairs from checking in with his aunt and uncle, he does a silent victory dance in the middle of the floor.

What's going on? I say with my eyes.

He just smiles and keeps dancing.

No, tell me!

I pound the bed with my fist in mock frustration. High heels click on the floor above our heads. Do Skunk's aunt and uncle have company over? Are we about to get busted? Is Skunk getting some kind of sick pleasure out of almost getting caught?

I'm about to bolt for the alley when Skunk slides onto the bed beside me and whispers in my ear, "They're going to an engagement party in Surrey. They won't be home until eleven."

When Skunk's aunt and uncle leave for the party, we go upstairs and play house. We snuggle up on the couch and watch movies on the big-screen TV. We play with the cat. I climb onto Skunk's aunt's elliptical machine and swing my legs so hard I almost break it. When I discover the waterbed in Skunk's aunt and uncle's room when I'm walking through after using their bathroom, I shriek so loud, Skunk comes running in to save me.

We stare at it, then at each other, both of us waiting for the other person to say what they're thinking first.

"We shouldn't," says Skunk.

So we do.

When the rain stops, just past ten, we're lying on the floor of Skunk's bedroom flushed and breathless, our teacups abandoned nearby. We both hear it at the same time: the sudden silence, where the patter of rain had sounded in the courtyard ever since we come in from our ride. I burrow my hand in the soft black tangle of his hair. "Time to go home."

I feel a pinprick of uncertainty when I say it. Maybe it *was* crazy to stay here. Maybe Skunk thinks I'm a big easy sloot, and all those sweet things we did were just games to him. *If you'd only been responsible like I* told *you to be, you wouldn't have to worry about those questions,* says the version of myself that went home and practiced piano on Thursday night. For one perilous moment, my heart hangs in the air like a flipped coin. I know by the time I get home, that coin's going to have landed either on drunken elation or crippling regret, and I don't want to wait that long to find out which one it's going to be. I decide to do a test.

"There's something I want to do before I go," I say. "I need to whisper it, though."

Skunk tilts his head, and I murmur it in his ear. When I pull away, he grins.

"Do you . . . want to?" I say.

He nods and starts to unbutton his jeans. We undress quickly, dropping shirts and underwear, and I glimpse Skunk's body, pale and lustrous as a pearl, his tattoos dark on his arms. When we're both naked, I reach for Skunk's hand.

The glass door slides open easily. The wet concrete in the courtyard is cold and rough under our feet. I glance at the sky and let out a happy whoop.

We gambol, star-clad, while the last few raindrops splash around us and the pear tree shakes its wet, white blossoms on our heads.

chapter twenty-five

When I get home, I plug my dead cell phone into its charger and discover a million messages from Lukas, asking where I am and when we're leaving for Battle of the Bands, which is on Saturday night at nine, which is—oh God—an hour and a half ago.

Shitshitshitshitshit.

I mash Lukas's name in the call log and practically pee my pants while I'm waiting for him to pick up, because the full awful truth of how badly I've just screwed up is dawning on me in all its horror. If we miss Battle of the Bands because of me being a huge irresponsible sloot with Bicycle Boy, I'll never be able to look Lukas in the face again.

Pick up, pick up, pick up, I plead to the cell phone gods, and when Lukas finally picks up, he shrieks, "WHERE ARE YOU?" and I shriek, "AT HOME COME PICK ME UP!" and a minute later Petra's car screeches into the driveway. I scurry out with my synth under my arm and cords dangling everywhere and cram myself into the backseat without even bothering to put my gear in the back of the station wagon.

"I'm so sorry. *So* sorry," I babble while Petra bombs through a yellow light and heads for the bridge. Lukas's dad cringes in the passenger seat. He's a safety freak, and Petra's driving is cause for alarm on the best of days.

Lukas looks at me with his eyes bugged out and says, "I called you fifty-one times! My call log says fifty-one times!"

"We were worried about you, Kiri," says Petra, cutting off a bus that was going too slowly for her taste and merging into the left lane. "I was about to have Lukas break into your house in case you had slipped in the shower and hit your head."

"My phone was dead," I blurt. "I went out of town and forgot my charger. I went to visit Denny in Victoria. I just got back, like, five minutes ago. The bus from the ferry took longer than I thought."

"You went to visit *Denny*?" Lukas says.

"Um. Yeah."

I don't mean to lie, but the truth is suddenly too complicated to explain, especially to Lukas, especially in front of

Lukas's mom. How am I supposed to tell them I just spent the better part of forty-eight hours snarfling with Bicycle Boy? Lukas doesn't even know about Skunk except as that sketchy guy who fixed my tire the night I biked to the Downtown Eastside. There hasn't exactly been time to give him an update. And Petra would flip if she knew the truth. Plus, I haven't eaten anything except omelets and toast for two days; that alone would be enough to make her call in the riot police.

Lukas looks different tonight, and it takes me a moment to figure out why. Then I realize he's wearing all black, like he wanted us to do so we'd look like a serious band. Then I realize I'm still wearing Skunk's aunt's big-butt sweatpants and Skunk's old T-shirt with no bra. *Real smooth, Kiri. Way to make a hot first impression for your band.*

"Next time you remember to tell somebody where you go," says Petra, casting me a stern look in the rearview mirror. She's wearing glasses with dark green frames, which make her look even more stern than usual. "I called your mother, and she said you were probably sleeping over at the house of a girlfriend. But if you were gone for any longer, I would have called the police."

Petra pulls up in front of the venue and lets us out. She drives away to find parking while Lukas, his dad, and I hustle the gear up the stairs. I bang my synth on the wall by accident, and the seam holding the two pieces of silver plastic together pops apart.

"Crap."

"What's going on?" barks Lukas. We stop in the middle of the stairs, staggering under our armloads of gear.

"I think I just broke my synth."

"Are you kidding me?"

"It's not my fault. If I wasn't carrying your cymbal, I could have—"

"Can you fix it?" he squeals.

"I don't know, it looks like—"

"Pop it back together. It doesn't look like the electronics are damaged."

"I don't think I can—"

"Just try."

"God, Lukas. Chill out."

I feel around the edge of the synth. The top and bottom halves have completely split apart. I think a screw must have popped out when it hit the wall.

"Let's just go upstairs, and I'll figure this out when I'm not carrying half a drum kit," I say.

Lukas stomps up the stairs. I pause to adjust the instruments I'm carrying so the edge of Lukas's cymbal stops slicing into my arm. A few steps later, I stop again because I'm close to dropping a drumstick. By the time I get to the top of the stairs, Lukas and his dad are nowhere to be seen. I spot some of our gear in a pile by the wall where they dumped it. The

Train Room is packed and loud, and it's too dim to see anything except a crowded mass of horny underage bodies. I stand in the doorway, craning my neck.

Up onstage, there's a punk band playing—one of our rivals, assuming we even get to play. All the kids in the band go to our school: straight-edge Alex with the Mohawk, Derick Mason, Ayo Ngebi, and that girl Nikky Sharp, who won't even talk to you if you're not punk. They sound like a shitty version of the Dropkick Murphys, all raspy-voiced shouting and bashing drums.

I drop my gear and go to hunt down Lukas and his dad. I find them at the back of the room, talking to a short, tightly built guy in his twenties with a black beard like a massive halo engulfing his whole face. I join them, panting.

"Hey. What's the word?"

Lukas doesn't even look at me.

"I can squeeze you guys in at the end," says Blackbeard, squinting down at the clipboard he's holding, "but you only get one song, not three. That's four minutes, tops."

"Can't we get a little more time if we set up fast?"

Lukas loses his attractiveness when he pleads. His voice gets whiny like a little kid's. *Shush, Lukas,* I beam to him telepathically. *Just be thankful he's letting us play.*

Blackbeard crosses his hairy arms over his chest and shakes his head.

"Sorry, guys. Venue closes at midnight. We need everybody out of here."

Lukas's shoulders sag, and I can see him gearing up for another round of begging. I butt in, casting Blackbeard a knowing smile. "One song's fine. Thank you."

Blackbeard looks grateful to be talking to someone who isn't hysterical. He nods at me, uncrosses his arms and walks away. Lukas moves to chase after him. I grab his arm. "Don't worry about it, Lukas. We still get to play."

"One song?"

"We can kick ass with one song. Plus, this gives us time to fix my synth. D'you think your mom has any duct tape in the car?"

Lukas looks at me like I've just asked him if his mom keeps a bazooka in the glove compartment. "I don't know! How am I supposed to know?"

I don't think I ever realized this before, but Lukas really doesn't handle stress very well. "Come on. Let's find your mom."

Lukas's dad, who has been standing there silently this whole time, starts pushing his way back toward the entrance. We follow him, avoiding each other's eyes. I can't tell if Lukas is pissed at me for being late, or if he's just embarrassed to be seen with me in this outfit.

The Dropkick Sucktards play for another ten minutes, during which Lukas sulks and I do my best to cobble my synth together with a box of Band-Aids the manager gives me from the first aid kit, which he says is the only tapelike substance he could find. As long as I don't bang on the keys too hard, it should hold together for one song. I can fix it when I get home.

Lukas's parents sip coffee from the refreshment booth and browse the internet on their phones, seemingly unaware of how out of place they look among all the teenage scenesters. That's one thing I love about Lukas's parents: they always seem comfortable wherever they are. My parents would last about two minutes in here before saying it was too loud and going home.

After the punks vacate the stage, there's a twenty-minute set change. A drippy indie band from another high school goes on. Their lead singer is a girl with bleached-blond hair and purple highlights who seems more interested in looking cute than in getting the notes right. She *oohs* and *aahs* her way through the chorus until I'm ready to throw up. As if that wasn't bad enough, they play three minutes overtime and Blackbeard doesn't even stop them.

When Blackbeard finally gives us the nod to set up, I feel a stab of guilt. It's already eleven forty-five. Lukas made a big point of signing up weeks ago so we'd get to play first. Now, even the judges look tired.

"We got this, Lukas," I hiss while we're slapping together the drum kit.

Lukas tightens the screw on the high hat.

"Careful with that. You'll scratch it," he says.

I leave him to it and go back to my busted synth. While I'm crouching to plug it in, I sneak a peek at the crowd. A bunch of kids who were here to see the blond girl's band went home after the last set, but there are still enough people left that the room's not totally empty. Lukas's parents are waiting patiently, still nursing the dregs of their coffee. I wonder where my parents are. I imagine them sleeping in a big white bed in a Luxury Berth with waves lapping the porthole; moving slowly down the breakfast buffet; petting manta rays; reading trashy romances on the deck; pawing through a rack of pink coral necklaces at a gift shop, trying to decide which one to buy for Auntie Moana.

"Kiri."

Lukas is calling me.

"You ready?"

"Oh. Yup." I spring up and get into place behind my synth. Blackbeard ambles onto the stage and announces that Sonic Drift will be playing a quick set to wrap up the night.

I shoot Lukas a we'll-discuss-this-later look. Sonic Drift *my ass.*

There's sparse applause. Skeptical glances. People are staring at my sweatpants, which I already forgot I was wearing. I wonder if it's really obvious under these stage lights that I'm not wearing a bra. A riptide of regret starts to pull me under. *Sorry, Lukas.* But there's no time to apologize now. I hear Lukas count to four and then it's on.

The moment we start playing, the last two hours of panic and lateness and getting yelled at by Lukas fade away, and I'm left in a golden dimension of sound. The synth possesses me. The purple stage lights are hot on my skin. Knowing we're screwed just makes us play better. There's no way we can win, therefore we have nothing to lose. I blitz up and down the keys, launching chords like bombs and deploying sixteenth notes like heavy artillery. At the end of the song, the last chord I play sends the synth flying. It sails through the air and explodes when it lands, people dodging the synth-shrapnel left and right. You can tell it's the greatest thing that ever happened to them, this synth-bomb. The crowd goes wild. I fall to my knees and yell, "Good night, beautiful people!"

I could listen to them cheering forever.

chapter twenty-six

While we're packing up our gear, Blackbeard comes up and tells us the judges want us to play in the finals next week.

Lukas practically faints with happiness, and I dance around him, singing, "We did it! We did it!" until I'm hoarse. The car ride home is victorious. Petra pulls into an all-night diner, and we order garlic fries and watch the video Lukas's dad took on his phone again and again. "It is incredible how you kids play," Petra says, and she sounds so genuinely *incredulous* I sort of fall in love with her.

After Lukas and his parents drop me off at my house, I'm too wired to go to sleep. I can't stop marveling over the coincidences, the way every little thing slid into place. If I hadn't gone for that bike ride on Thursday night, I wouldn't have run into Skunk at midnight mass. If I hadn't run into Skunk, I wouldn't have made us late for Battle of the Bands. If we hadn't been late, we wouldn't have played like we did, raw and driven and wild. If I hadn't banged my synth against the wall, it wouldn't have exploded so spectacularily. If my synth hadn't exploded, the crowd wouldn't have gone wild, and we wouldn't have been chosen to move on to the next round. Every disaster, every whim, every seemingly random decision came together to make this night happen. There are no mistakes, I realize—just detours whose significance only become clear when you see the whole picture at once.

Even though it has started to rain again, I decide to celebrate my official launch into musical stardom by taking my bike on a personal midnight mass. I want to go back to Stanley Park and visit the totem poles and cross the Lions Gate Bridge again and turn around and look at the city lights from the North Shore, but this time I want it to be just me, like a pilgrimage, a victory lap, a way of saying, *Hello, Universe! Thank you for all the mystical wonders that have been sprouting up in my life, like Skunk and finding Sukey and Battle of the Bands and Om Shanti Om and also Hare Krishna, O Universe, Amen.*

First thing I do is change out of the sweatpants and put on clothes that are more befitting of the occasion—gold tights and green boots and a stretchy black dress that makes me feel like Catwoman. I don't bother with a raincoat. I want to be wet. I want to be kissed by all two million raindrops in the sky. My hair is a mess. I brush it and sweep it into a towering updo. Now my neck is bare. I shiver.

Good.

I hunt around my room for my iPod so I can have the right music, then stand in the kitchen mixing orange juice and brandy and vodka and Perrier because the Universe demands a ritual dram. I pour it into a pink frosty mug I find in the freezer door. I declare a toast to the Universe and drink the ice-cold witches' brew standing right there in the kitchen in my boots. I mix another one. But once I've drunk the second drink, I still don't feel ready to go, and the words *drunk* and *drink* start a little war in my head, *drink-drunk-drank*, then morph into raindrops that plink and plunk like a toy piano.

It comes to me in a flash. The shoes! Sukey's silver shoes. I wrestle off the boots, scamper upstairs, grab the shoes, and sit on the stairs, strapping them onto my feet. The high heels make it hard to wobble down the stairs, but I do it with the grace and poise of a young Marilyn Monroe. I grab my iPod, bust through the garage door, and crash around in the garage, trying to find my bicycle in the dark because the motion-detecting light refuses to come on and I'm too busy to find the button that turns it on manually.

There's a strange music surging out of my bones, the rhythm pulsing, the volume getting louder and louder. Maybe it will drown me out if it keeps going.

Maybe I don't care.

When I put my hands on the metal post of my bicycle, it's like getting an electric shock. The cold flashes through me, touching a match to the weightless golden kindling that's been building up inside me all night, and I feel such a burst of delight I let out a high animal yip that reverberates circuslike on the cement walls. I wheel my bike out through the side door, not bothering to lock it. When I swing my leg over the frame, it's like that moment in *Frankenstein* when the monster comes alive: I feel my bicycle tense slightly, ready, alert, its honed aluminum heartbeat syncing up with my own.

It's windy tonight, damp gusts filled with raindrops. As I charge down the street, the leaves shimmy in the treetops and the stop signs flex and bang on their poles. Sukey's silver shoes are slippery against the pedals. Wind reaches down to tug my hair out of its updo. As I ride along the beach, I greet the lampposts and street signs and telephone booths as if they're everyone I know lined up to see me off.

Why, good evening, Nelson Chow, fancy seeing you out here! Fancy seeing you as a lamppost, a straight and tall and devious disguise.

Lukas, hello, you street sign! Kelsey Bartlett, hello, you sewer grate! Skunk, you lovely caterpillar, hello!

I go through everybody, one by one. I chatter to the streetlight of Petra, the phone booth of Dr. Scaliteri, and the construction pylons of my mom and dad.

Soon I'm at the bridge. Soon I'm at the top of the bridge. Soon I'm over it and down the other side.

I save Sukey for English Bay, and for Sukey, I don't address a streetlight or a concrete bench. I save her up until I spot the magnolia tree.

Sukey—

I pedal hard, keeping my eyes fixed on the magnolia tree. It breezes, sighs, as if it's thinking about what it wants to say.

Come on, Sukey. Come on.

I push, I pant, I pedal, I strain. The magnolia's scent pulls me closer, reels me in.

All at once it happens: The magnolia tree erupts into light. I lift off from the ground and cartwheel in slow motion through the rain. My bicycle tries to split away, but I clamp my legs around it and we fly through the air like conjoined twins. The streetlights and street signs all lean in like a crowd of people pointing at a strange object streaking across the sky. My bicycle and I flip once. The Sukey-tree leaks into an ice cream swirl of pink and white. For one sparkling moment we hang halfway between heaven and earth.

Then gravity wins. My bike and I fly apart, briefly careen through the night sky alone and land with a crunch on opposite sides of the road.

My head whips back from the impact and my ribs twang like a dropped guitar. The sky spins above me like a penny. My bike has dematerialized, and my iPod is strewn across the intersection in a million glittering pieces. When I try to move, ten different parts of my body light up at once, like someone's pressing all the buttons at an anatomy exhibit. The magnolia tree blows me a kiss of perfumed air, and I can't decide if what I'm feeling is incredible bliss or excruciating pain. This might just be the greatest moment of my life. It's possible. If it is, I don't want to waste it lying around in the middle of the road. For a single, golden second I breathe galaxies.

A car door slams and someone wearing noisy heels gets out.

"Are you okay? I couldn't even *see* you in that black dress. You're bleeding. Okay. Oh my God."

The stopped car's headlights are shining in my eyes, blinding me with their yellow glare. I can't see the woman standing over me dialing 911 on her cell phone.

"Can you talk? What's your name? Oh God. Is your neck broken? Can you hear me?"

I realize this woman is alarmed because she does not understand the situation. The situation is that I have been transformed into an invincible angel who feels no pain. I realize I must elucidate the situation before she calls an ambulance. I leap up from the ground. The woman's alarmed look is nothing compared to the way the branches of the magnolia tree begin to riot in the wind. I scuttle across the street and snatch up my bike. Straddling it, I flash her the devil horns.

"Hail Satan."

I ride away, wobbling, as fast as I can.

chapter twenty-seven

I'm fine and my bike's fine and the situation is 100 percent under control.

I would be exaggerating if I said that my skin is in shreds or my bike looks like it's been beaten by thugs or if I claimed there was any kind of problem at all.

In fact, I have made it home safely and stowed my bike safely in the garage and all the doors are locked and the lights are on.

There is only one bloody handprint on the garage door to suggest—incorrectly—that matters have exceeded my ability to deal with them. There is only one wrecked pair of gold tights in the kitchen garbage can to indicate that anything has veered even slightly off course.

My thoughts dart from one bright thing to another. I sit on the kitchen counter smoking a joint and drinking electric lemonade while drops of purple-black blood run down my shins and make fascinating splatter patterns on the kitchen floor. I make seven bowls of oatmeal, one for each day of the upcoming week, stud each one with razors, no, raisins, swaddle them in Saran Wrap, and line them up in the fridge. This is what I will eat this week. These are my monk's rations. I draw up a new and improved practice schedule and tape it to the wall; it's as big as a map of the world and contains all my plans.

What I need to do is get Serious. It's time. I've had my fun. It's okay to be free but not so free you lose track of what's Serious. If you ever get that free, you need to reel yourself in, because the edges of the world are as sharp as glass, and if you ride over them you're going to get torn up. I wanted to hear that secret music, so I let it play and now that I've played it, it's time to turn it off and be Serious again.

I rearrange the living room furniture, pushing the couch and coffee table against the wall and dragging all the lamps into a circle around the piano. It is time, I decide, to learn some new music. Something daring. Something bold. Something the judges at the Showcase have never heard before. I rifle through my collection of sheet music until I find the tattered folder marked *Sesquipaedia*. It's a piece I've wanted to play for years but never had time for: thirty-five pages long, devilish timing, written by a little-known composer called Stanley Otter Fish, who was run over by a bread truck at the age of twenty-three.

Sensational, sniffed Dr. Scaliteri when I showed it to her last year.

But if I'm going to make an impression on Tzlatina Tzoriskaya, that's exactly what I want my performance to be.

I take out the sheet music and lay it out neatly on the floor, pages and pages of notes like tiny black beetle eggs. I walk through the rows of music like a maze. Someone once told me that it's possible to play any piece of music after hearing it a single time, without ever looking at the notes. Everything we see and hear gets stored in our memory, whether we realize it or not, and it's only a matter of coaxing it back to the surface. I circle the room in my bare feet, listening to the music in my head and trying not to peek at the pages on the floor. As I circle, I can feel the Prokofiev concerto being ripped up like weeds and tossed into a gnarled heap. If I can learn music, I can unlearn it too. I can unteach my fingers to play the notes I spent so long mastering. I could make the whole keyboard foreign again if I wanted to. I could rewind and rewind and rewind until the whole thing became unintelligible. Or I could circle and circle and circle until I knew everything, everything, and I could hear all the music I had ever heard looping through my head.

I circle and circle, my knees weeping blood, until the pages are stained and torn and I can't see the notes at all.

When the sun comes up, I stop circling and march up the stairs. Birds are chirping in the backyard trees, industrious feathered machines, reminding me of all the work I have to do. I had better get some sleep so I can wake up, eat the first of the oatmeals, and go back to the piano refreshed. Sleep is important for memorization—that's another thing I've heard. I ought to have been taking naps all this time.

I go into my parents' bathroom and click open the medicine cabinet. I twist open the Costco-sized bottle of ibuprofen, gravely dispense myself six orange tablets, and swallow them with water from the tap.

I go to my room and lie on my bed with the lights off, but nothing happens.

Something needs to happen.

I need to go to sleep so I can wake up so I can practice piano so I can get Serious.

I lie in bed five more minutes and don't fall asleep at all. Reality whangs horribly in my ears. I feel like a glow stick that's still glowing the morning after Halloween.

I need to sleep so I can wake up so I can practice piano so I can snarfle with Skunk so I can wake up so I can get the situation completely under control.

I can't sleep.

Why can't I sleep?

A minute later I still can't sleep. I get up and go downstairs and smoke two medicinal-sized joints, then go upstairs and take ten more ibuprofen and a handful of sleeping pills I find in my parents' bedroom, then go back downstairs, throw on some smooth jazz, and lie down on the floor under the piano.

In a few minutes or half an hour or maybe the next day a blue haze comes over me and I don't know if I'm dreaming or tripping or what but whatever it is it's heavy and strong and it hurts a little less than whatever the fuck was happening before.

chapter twenty-eight

Denny is here, and I'm so confused when I wake up and he's dragging me out from under the piano that I promptly roll onto my stomach and puke.

"Nice, Kiri," he says, arching one eyebrow appraisingly. "Real classy."

When I lift my head to look at him, another squirt of puke shoots up my throat: flecks of pink and orange. Electric lemonade.

I want to be back under the piano. It's cozy down there. Like curling up under the car you've just been hit by and going to sleep. I grab a piano leg with one hand and start pulling myself back under. The piano is a big, kindly whale looming over me in a comforting way. As long as I'm under there, nothing can crush me.

Denny crouches and grabs my ankle to thwart my return to the mother ship. I make a grunt of protest and thrash my aching leg.

"Damn, Kiri, how'd you cut up your legs like that?"

I groan louder, succeed at twisting my ankle out of his grasp, and clamp my knees to my chest. There. Much better. I am a turtle sleeping with the whale, and Denny is a bothersome crab that keeps trying to drag me away with his pincers. *Go away, crab. Go away, Sir Crabulous.* I have a vague memory that I went to the sea last night. There were ships and clouds and a magnolia tree that picked up and flew like a bird. Also a woman, some sort of witch, who followed me in her car until I dodged her at Granville Island. I remember being wet. Soaked, in fact. I think I was dipped in sacred water like Achilles. I might have taken a swim.

Oh, I remember. I did take a swim. And the witch-woman stood on the pier and screamed, not realizing I was a turtle.

"You smell like dead fish," says Denny.

Naturally. I am a turtle.

"Why are your piano books wet?"

It doesn't matter. All that music is memorized. I summoned it in my sleep.

"Would you sit up and answer me?"

Someone spins around my turtle shell, and the rusty blade of Denny's face appears over mine.

"Kiri? Hey. Kiri?"

Turtle out.

The next time I wake up, there's loud music playing and male voices talking in the kitchen. I hear Denny.

"Yeah, I think she's just hungover. But, like, hella hungover, dude."

I pull my head back into my shell. Whatever.

The time after that, the lights are off and the house is quiet. Whoever was here has gone away. I gurgle and spoon the piano leg. Love.

I close my eyes. Turtle in, turtle out.

The next time I wake up, I hear a basketball game playing on TV.

The next time I wake up, I smell microwave burritos.

The next time I wake up, Denny pulls me out from under the piano again and slams a plastic bottle full of water on the floor next to my face.

"Sit up and drink this."

I make a strangled murmur of revolt and close my eyes. Bad move. Denny grabs my shoulders, hauls me up off the floor, and tosses me onto the couch. He puts the bottle in my hand.

"Drink it."

Denny's wearing his summer uniform, scruffy board shorts and a dark blue T-shirt, and sporting a new angular haircut that makes him look like a backup dancer for a B-list pop star. He plants himself in front of me and watches while I unscrew the plastic cap and take a slow dribbling sip of water. As the water wets my throat, the turtle part of me swims away. I am Kiri, sitting on a couch drinking water. This is my brother, Denny. My tongue feels around for language.

"What are you doing here?" I say.

"Dr. Patel went on vacation. I got two weeks off."

Two weeks off. The words set off distant alarm bells, and I'm not sure why. *Just when things were going so nicely,* I think, then wince as the first pangs of a headache lance through my skull.

Denny picks up the Ziploc bag on the coffee table and helps himself to a chunk of my weed. He takes a Tic Tac container out of his pocket and tucks the weed in for safekeeping.

"Hey," I slur woozily. "That's my stash."

Denny comes back to the couch and brings his face close to mine. He has a new piercing, I notice—a small silver hoop in the cartilage of his left ear. It looks infected. I'm about to tell him so when he grabs my arm.

"Drink *all* that water, Kiri. You listening? You're probably really dehydrated."

I nod and try to retract my arm. He doesn't let go.

"When you finish drinking that water, clean up all this crap. I don't know what you got up to last night, but if Mom and Dad saw this place, they'd freak."

I glance at the sheet music strewn across the living room floor, the half-smoked joint on the coffee table, Sukey's silver shoes like fallen stars near the piano bench. It looks like an artist lives here—a passionate and tormented soul. Maybe even a genius. Sukey would be proud.

"I'm a real musician now, Denny," I croak.

"I can see that," he says, rolling his eyes.

He lets go of my arm, stalks to the kitchen, and picks up his keys and cell phone off the counter. I strain my neck to watch him, holding the water bottle between my knees.

"Where are you going?"

He yanks open the front door without answering.

"Where are you going, Denny?"

"Enjoy your hangover," he calls, slamming it shut behind him.

I sit on the couch in stunned silence, the water bottle dribbling onto my lap.

Denny is here.

Denny is *here*.

I feel exposed, like an inventor whose secret workshop has just been raided by the CIA. I'm a trapdoor spider whose trapdoor has been pried open. I'm a fetal pig pulled from its bucket of brine, my inner workings sliced open for all to see. Nobody was supposed to be here. Nobody was supposed to walk in and become a witness to the fact that things weren't proceeding in an utterly Serious manner. Especially not Denny.

Maybe it's not too late.

This was just a blip, an accidental quiver on the otherwise even Richter scale of my Seriousness. Yes. Okay. All is good. I need to hide Sukey's things and clean the house and practice for at least eight hours. There is utterly and regrettably no time whatsoever to sleep anymore, not until at least Monday. I put the water bottle on the floor, stand up, limp to the bathroom, and bow over the sink, splashing water on my face for what seems like a very long time.

I scrape my hair into a ponytail and throw a sweatshirt on over my dress. My knees are bloody mosaics of scabs. No time to deal with them now. I shake out a handful of ibuprofen and knock them back with coffee. Time to clean up my act. I scoop up all the sheet music from the living room floor and pile it in a high, unsteady tower next to the piano. The pages are mottled and water-stained, and some of them are ripped from being walked on. "Sorry," I whisper to Stanley Otter Fish, doing my best to smooth the paper out.

I clean up the puke with a towel and throw the towel in the washing machine. I clean the kitchen floor with another towel and throw that towel in the washing machine. I grab another towel and use it to lovingly polish every inch of the grand piano. Soon every towel in the house is thumping around in the washer like a family of poor bedraggled beavers trapped in a whirlpool. I dump in more detergent, and the beavers disappear under a mushroom cloud of bubbles.

I clean up the kitchen and wash all the dishes and put them away. I unwrap one of the bowls of oatmeal from the fridge and eat it cold. It's gray and congealed. The raisins are plump and gross from absorbing water. I pick them out and put them in a bowl, in case Denny wants them. Waste is bad.

As I move around the house, my head feels like a public swimming pool during open swim: shouts and splashes, echoes, impossible to swim in a straight line without bashing into someone's hairy leg. My emotions keep flipping between pride and rage and guilt and self-defense, like the shiny red pointer on a game-show wheel.

What do I owe Denny, anyway? What do I owe Mom and Dad? Clean carpets and a pleasant phone voice. That's all they've ever wanted, and all I've ever given them. That's all I've ever given them, and that's all they deserve, because if it wasn't for their precious carpets, Sukey wouldn't have escaped to the Imperial and she wouldn't be dead.

I think this as I haul out the vacuum.

I think this as I plow it murderously around the living room.

That's all they deserve, those liars, those fakes, but when I'm finished ranting, the carpet is clean.

At ten p.m. the phone starts ringing, but I absolutely must practice so I don't answer it, even when it rings again at ten fifteen and again at 10:18 and again at 10:22. I sit at the piano with my back to the squalling phone, practicing scales and arpeggios. I won't answer it. I won't.

I tell myself I won't answer it because I'm finished with telephone voices, but really the sound of the telephone fills me with a cold and queasy dread.

I'm afraid it's my parents calling to tell me they know, they know, and they're coming home directly. I don't know what my parents know or what they're coming home to do to me, but I'm sure it's shameful and sinister and absolutely devastating, so I don't answer the phone.

The phone rings again at ten thirty and three more times between 10:35 and 10:40. It's not Skunk, because Skunk has my cell number, not the home phone, and even if it was Skunk, I couldn't answer because although I haven't gone to the garage to look, I know that something shameful and sinister and absolutely devastating has happened to my bicycle, and when he sees it he'll know all about the trap-door spider and the fetal pig.

At eleven thirty I hear Denny's car in the driveway. The house is spotless. I even cut flowers from outside, daffodils and azaleas and bright pink cosmos, and put them in vases all around the room and on top of the piano. When Denny walks in, I'm polishing the wineglasses and placing them back on their shelf in perfect rows. He glares.

"Don't you pick up the phone? I called, like, twenty times."

He roves around the kitchen, yanking the fridge open and shutting it, banging all the cupboard doors. "There's no freaking food in this house. I wanted you to pick up yam rolls before Kits Sushi closed."

He swipes a pizza coupon off the fridge door and starts dialing the number. I inspect the last wineglass for smudges and carefully lift it into its spot.

"Did you know Sukey used to go watch the ships?" I blurt.

"What the hell are you talking about?"

I adjust the wineglass by a quarter degree. "She used to sneak out to Kits Beach and watch the ships."

"So what?"

I glance back at him. "I just thought you should know that."

Denny's expression is unreadable. He pauses and slowly lowers the phone into its cradle.

"I found out," I warble, a little too loud.

"What do you want, a medal?"

The wineglasses look perfect now, three sparkling rows of three. I gently close the cupboard door and start in on the knives.

"I went to the place where she was living," I say. "I got that frog that used to sit on her windowsill. And her quilt."

"Put that knife down," says Denny. "You're freaking me out."

"I'm cleaning them."

"They're already clean."

"Jars of paint, too," I say. "They're not even dry."

I polish the knife and slide it back into the wooden block, its blade as flawlessly reflective as the mirror on a ballet studio wall. Denny leans across the counter and snatches the dishcloth before I can clean any more.

"Quit it," he says. "Are we talking real life here, or are you still tripping on whatever is it you took last night?" He stares at my eyes, which are admittedly a little red. "Oh my God. You're on meth."

"I'm not on drugs, Denny."

"You were passed out under the piano."

"I was hungover. It was Battle of the Bands."

Denny shakes his head. "No. No way. It's not alcohol. Look at you—you're all tweaky. You're hopped up on something. Drinking doesn't do that. What is it? Coke? E? Your eyes are all bloodshot. You look fucking insane."

"I smoked some pot. A lot of pot."

"Oh, really. Speaking of which, where'd you get all that pot?"

I lift my chin. "None of your business."

He narrows his eyes. I can see the thought forming in

his head before he does. I make a grab for the phone, but he snatches it first.

"Maybe I should call Mom and Dad," he says.

I lunge across the counter, clawing at Denny's hands as he starts to dial. "The only reason you would ever do that is to be an asshole."

"They would be so worried if they knew their perfect little pianist was on drugs. They might have to cut their trip short and fly home to take care of you. What a shame. Let me just dial this number, and—"

I pant, the counter edge cutting into my stomach as Denny and I do a slow-motion arm-wrestle for the phone. "You don't really think I'm on drugs," I say through clenched teeth. "You're just trying to avoid the conversation."

"What conversation?" he says.

"*Exactly.*"

Denny relaxes his grip on the phone. I swipe it and hold it behind my back, its plastic case hot in my hand. "Why didn't anyone tell me?"

Denny watches me warily. "You were *twelve*, Kiri. You hung on Sukey's every word like she was your guru. You couldn't have handled it then, and by the looks of it you can't even handle it now."

I glare at him, outraged. I know how I must look right now, with my scraped-up knees and bloodshot eyes and the

trembly-tense posture of a first-time gangster holding up a convenience store. But it's not fair. It's a misrepresentation. I'm the
strong person here, the one who stayed nice when everyone else
was slamming doors, the one who filled the house with music
when grief had drained it to a creeping silence, the one who
rode to the Imperial on a freaking bicycle to bring a piece of
Sukey home. If there's something I can't handle, it's being told
all of that means nothing. My face heats up.

"Well, I know more than any of you now. You want to
know who killed her? A kid with a sideways nose. You want
to know how I got her stuff? Her alcoholic neighbor kept it in
his closet for five years because nobody from our stupid family
cared enough to go down there and clear out her studio after it
happened."

Denny sighs and runs a hand through his idiotic haircut
like a long-suffering adult trapped in negotiations with a three-
year-old. "It's not that simple. You don't even know all the
details."

The condescension in his voice hits me like baking soda on
vinegar. I erupt.

"'You don't know the details. You don't know the details.'
I'm the one who went down there, so don't give me that crap
about details."

Denny smirks. "Oh yeah? You know about her tiny little
pill problem?"

"Lots of great artists use mind-altering substances."

"You know she owed people money?"

I don't answer.

Denny keeps going, his voice oh-so-casual, drumming on the counter with his fingernails.

"You know what great artists with tiny little pill problems do to *get* money?" he says.

The sentence hangs in the air like a tossed grenade. Denny's eyes pin me to the spot. I writhe like one of the sea urchins he tortures in his lab, dark possibilities crowding into my mind.

"Mom and Dad should have helped her," I bleat.

"They *did*. Do you know how many times Dad tried to—"

"She was working on a painting. A big one. Which you and Mom and Dad would know if you'd actually believed in her."

Whatever scrap of sympathy was in Denny's eyes before burns away instantly. "I don't know what kind of warm, fuzzy story this alcoholic neighbor told you, but she wasn't there on a freaking art residency."

"It's true. She was working on it when she *died*."

Denny gives me a look of such utter incredulity that it appears he is considering, for real this time, the possibility that I may actually be insane.

"Oh, right," he says, his hands dropping to his sides in disbelief. "Our dear, sweet, innocent Sukey was hard at work on a lovely painting in her lovely art studio when this random drug dealer just happened to walk in and stab her to death. If that's true, where's the painting? Don't tell me her alcoholic neighbor saved that stupid frog but let this supposed masterpiece get thrown out."

"Maybe it got blood on it," I say, but my mind is already racing to the stains on the quilt. Doug *would* have saved the painting. Maybe he still has it. Maybe it's the one thing he couldn't bear to give away. Or maybe he brought it to an art gallery, just like Sukey was planning.

I must look distraught, because Denny reaches across the counter and pats my hand.

"Hey. She was my sister too."

I yank my hand away, and Denny shakes his head, his pity giving way to exasperation.

"Come on, Kiri. If you're going to make a stink about how nobody told you the truth, you should at least stop lying to yourself."

He stalks out of the kitchen. I stay there smoldering, hating Denny, hating our parents, trying to think up the perfect comeback to prove them all wrong.

But five minutes later, I haven't come up with one, and I'm still standing in the kitchen alone.

chapter twenty-nine

The next morning, I can't stand to be in the house. Denny's words from the night before are like a stone in my shoe, their truth a grinding presence I can't ignore. *He's wrong*, I tell myself again and again. But there's a ten-pound weight in the pit of my stomach that says otherwise. The fridge buzzes and tiny spiders crawl out of the flowers I cut from the backyard until there's nothing I can do but grab my keys and wallet and catch a bus downtown. I tell myself I'm only going to drop in on Doug for a friendly visit, but Sukey's painting is all I can think about as I hurry to the stop.

The minute I get on the bus, I start to regret it. It lurches along, hardly traveling six feet before an iguana-faced senior citizen pulls the cord and makes it stop again. A tall, pimply boy sits down next to me, takes out a spiral-bound notebook, a pen, and graphing calculator, and starts working on a long and seemingly impossible math equation, breathing loudly through his mouth. I think of Goth Girl from *The Adolescent Depression Workbook*. Maybe they should date.

"Need some help?" I ask in a friendly way, but he just glances at me with a terrified expression and scribbles more numbers down.

The bus crawls along West Broadway, getting more and more crowded at every stop. It would have been faster to ride my bike, but the front wheel is bent and there are splinters of pain in my kneecaps when I walk, so I can't imagine trying to pedal. I grit my teeth while people pull the cord and get off at the most mundane and pointless places: the Laundromat, the bank. It seems so petty of them to keep doing that, I can hardly contain my frustration. *Let's go, let's go, let's go.* Math Boy's shoulder jostles mine, and the old lady sitting behind me unwraps a breath mint that smells like industrial detergent. The only thing that keeps me from flipping out completely is when Skunk texts me WHERE'S MY CRAZY GIRL? and I text back ON A MISSION and he texts me COME OVER LATER? and I text YES YES and he texts OK BEAUTIFUL.

When I finally get to the Imperial, Doug is sitting on his mattress, his blue fleece blanket gathered around his scrawny legs, beer can plugged into the hollow of his hand. Snoogie's munching greedily at the cat food I brought for her the other day. I can hear the star-shaped pink pellets cracking between her teeth. I sit down beside her on the dirty floor and break open the pomegranate I bought at MONEY FOOD before coming in. Some days call for strange fruit.

"My brother wants to know what happened to the painting," I say, doing my best to sound casual and nonthreatening in case Doug really did keep it for himself or sold it for beer money one day when he got desperate.

"Whassat?" Doug burps.

"Sukey's masterpiece. The one you said she was working on when"—my throat constricts—"when it happened."

My voice sounds high and cartoonish, like I just took a hit off a helium balloon. I wonder if there's something wrong with me. I've felt strange inside myself since the night under the piano, rushed and dizzy. My thoughts feel like a TV with the volume all messed up: one moment, everything sounds normal, then suddenly it's BLARING LOUD, then normal again before I can be totally sure the loud part even happened. I pinch myself on the leg, annoyed. *Just quit it.*

Doug gazes down at his speckled yellow hands and says nothing. I pick up a chunk of pomegranate and sink my teeth into it, tasting the bitterness and the rush of sweet. When I've finished sucking the juice out I look around for a place to spit the seeds. I settle on my hand.

"Don't worry," I say between spits. "I won't be mad if you wanted to keep it for yourself. But you can't not show it to me at all. I have to see it."

I pick up another chunk of pomegranate and go to work on it. The pile of seeds in my hand is growing into a warm, chewed-up heap. I tip it out onto the floor.

Doug looks up, sees the pomegranate, and scowls.

"Put that thing down, you're getting crap everywhere. What the hell kind of fruit is that, anyway?"

"Pomegranate."

Doug sighs. "I don't have no painting," he says.

"What do you mean, you don't have the painting?" I say, my voice false-cheerful. Even as I hate myself for asking, hate the sound of my own pathetic hopefulness like the tinny jingling of cheap bells, I can't help but push on. "Did someone steal it? Did you give it to a gallery?"

Doug scowls down at his blanket, avoiding my eyes. I keep at him, pleading. "You said she painted all the time. You said she used to lock herself in there for days. Artistic privacy. Come on, Doug. You at least saw her last painting, didn't you? Can't you at least tell me what it looked like?"

In the room below us, someone throws something heavy onto the floor and starts shouting, a long caterwauling invective that makes the floor vibrate. Doug says nothing. The silence hanging between us is thick and awful and spreading in size like a stain.

"Forget it," I say quietly.

"Oh, honey."

I get up, brushing pomegranate seeds off my jeans, and pick my way toward the door. The strange feeling in my head is getting stranger. The utter bizarreness of my presence here, in this dingy hotel talking to this dingy old man, presses on me with an urgency akin to panic.

What the hell am I even doing here?

I fumble for my phone so I can text Skunk on my way down the stairs.

"Aw, hell," says Doug. "Honey, wait."

I trip over something and almost bail, but catch myself and keep heading for the door. Denny was right. I guess I know what Sukey was really doing when she locked herself in her room for days at a time, and it didn't involve a paintbrush.

"*Wait*," says Doug, and there's something so raw and urgent in his voice I turn around.

"What?" I demand. He motions for me to sit down, but I remain standing, hands on my hips. Whatever he has to say had better be quick.

"Your sister—," he begins. He stops and looks at the floor. I make an exasperated noise and turn to leave, but Doug starts talking again and I freeze, the promise of a story a drug I can't resist.

"The first time I saw Sukey-girl," he says, "I'll never forget it. She was wearing a blue polka-dot dress, and she was sitting on the sidewalk with a stack of paintings she was trying to sell. It looked like she'd been on the streets for three-four days tops. I was guessing she was one of those runaway kids from the suburbs, Surrey or Burnaby. She didn't look a day over sixteen. 'Go on home, honey,' I said. 'You look like you come from a real nice family.'"

The image catches me off guard, and in my surprise and bewilderment I burst into tears. On Columbia Street, a car drives past pumping rap music. The beat carries through Doug's window, *boom, boom, boom*, a disorienting reminder that in the world outside this hotel room, the words Doug is passing to me like tarnished silver mean nothing at all. The car recedes, its noise like a fly that alighted on Doug's shoulder and is buzzing off again. I strain my ears, but I can't hear its thumping anymore.

"We got to chatting," Doug says. "Some tourist had just bought a painting off her for fifty bucks. It was the first time she'd ever sold anything, and she was so happy she had this glow. She asked me if I knew about a cheap place to stay. I said, 'Go home, girl. You're having fun now, wait until you end up like me.' You want to know what she said?"

I'm really crying now, tears silently licking my cheeks. I'm not sure why Doug has elected to tell me this story now. Maybe because he's saved the saddest part of all until the end. Maybe because I'm the only person in the world who can lift it from his shoulders now that he's carried it for so long.

"What did she say?"

"She said, 'The soul has a home of its own, and I want to live in that one.' Some line from a movie. I had her write it down for me, eh, but I lost the paper. It knocked me out—this beautiful girl in a polka-dot dress sitting there on the sidewalk, selling her paintings and pulling out lines like that. Every single day, I told her to go home. Every goddamn day."

"Why didn't she?" I say, even though I know the answer.

Another car passes by with its stereo blasting, this time a nattering top forty host whose words I can't make out. I'd never realized how loud the world was, how filled with cold and impersonal noise. It's a wonder we ever find each other at all in its clamoring thickets. It's a wonder we still try.

The mattress groans as Doug leans over to get his crutches "Come on, honey," he says. "I got something to show ya. It's maybe not what you wanted, but I bet Sukey-girl would have liked you to see it."

He maneuvers himself up from the mattress. I watch him warily, my tears drying up but my cheeks still hot. I don't think

I'm ready for more surprises, no matter what they are. I want to be home with my head under a pillow, muffling as much of the world as I can. Doug works his way across the room, lurches past me, and goes into the hall. "Down this way," he grunts. I follow him at a distance. "I've already seen her old room," I say, remembering the porn magazines and the stench of old cigarettes.

Doug shakes his head in disgust. "Sukey-girl never spent hardly any time in that shithole anyway."

He crutches down the hall quickly, as if he's afraid I'll find some excuse to leave if we don't get there fast. The floor creaks beneath us like something that's already breaking, even though the demolition notice taped to the door of the hotel when I came in this morning pins the date a few weeks away. Doug stops when he gets to the fire door at the end of the hall and leans on it with his shoulder.

"Isn't the alarm going to sound?" I say.

Doug ignores me. "Give that door a push, honey."

He shuffles out of the way, and I reluctantly take his place. The door scrapes open when I shove it, revealing a rickety fire escape. Doug blinks at the blueness of the sky like he's seeing an alien landscape. I gaze out apprehensively, my eyes wandering down through the metal slats to the alley four stories below.

"I don't know what you're going to find up there," he says with a rueful glance at his crutches. "Maybe nothing. But

Sukey-girl was always sneaking up to that rooftop, so you may as well have a look around."

I glance at the spindly staircase climbing up the brick wall, and my stomach twists up like a wet shirt. I hate heights, hate-hate-hate them, and the fire escape looks like it would collapse if you blew on it too hard.

"Go on," says Doug.

"I don't know."

"You want to see what your sister saw, this is as close as you're gonna get." He pats me on the arm, gazing up the fire escape with an expression of such naked yearning I feel ashamed.

"You stop by when you come down," he says, "and tell me what it's like up there."

The fire escape clangs each time I take a step. I grip the rusty handrails, silently uttering threats to the Imperial Hotel: *If I die climbing this stupid fire escape, I will come back and burn you to the ground before they even get a chance to demolish you.* Cars rumble past on the street below, and the smell of their exhaust pricks my nose. I can hear the bass thump of someone's sound system and see the white splatters of pigeon droppings on the tops of faded awnings. *Look at you, sneaking up fire escapes,* laughs the Sukey in my head, but I'm so mad at her I don't even answer. Each rattling step sends my heart racing. Every time I glance down, my guts contort. I can smell the cloying stink of the Dumpster in the alley below. That's where I'll land if the fire escape gives out.

The higher I climb, the more I start to worry about the most random and trivial things, as if my brain has given up on trying to distinguish the important stuff and is just firing at everything that moves. I wonder if Math Boy found the solution to his equation. I wonder if Stanley Otter Fish would have been a famous composer if he hadn't gotten run over by a truck. I wonder what would happen if I died, and the last fruit I had ever eaten was a pomegranate.

I tell myself there are worse things than having a pomegranate be your last fruit.

After a dozen more rattling steps, the fire escape ends and this weird iron swimming-pool ladder goes up the rest of the way. I clench my teeth and scramble up it, scraping my knees against the top rung in my hurry. Once I'm safely on the roof, I'm so dizzy with pent-up dread and relief I don't even look around, I just crouch down and squeeze my eyes shut and breathe. While I'm crouching there, so close to the roof's heat and dusty smell, the height and the climb and the whole situation overwhelm me all at once and I almost start to cry again. My knees hurt and I haven't slept, and when I tried to fix my synth this morning, the power light flared and flickered and then winked out and I couldn't make it come on again.

I'm not supposed to be here, I think. *I'm not supposed to be here and my brain is not supposed to be doing whatever it's doing and I'm not supposed to know about Sukey and everything is wrong.*

Maybe if I wave my hands, someone will see me and call 911 and the fire department will come and get me down, not just from the roof but from everything, from Sukey being murdered and my thoughts going loud and then normal again and from this whole entire wreckage of a summer.

I pinch myself again, viciously this time. *Do you* ever *shut up? There's nothing wrong with you. You're just looking for excuses not to be brave.*

I huddle there by the ladder, the strong side of me bullying the weak one, until the feeling evaporates and just like that I'm fine again. I lift my head and look around.

In the middle of the roof, there's a sagging plastic lawn chair. Beside it there's a pile of cigarette butts, an old Discman, and a faded Coke bottle filled with rainwater. A chipped clay flowerpot has rolled under the lawn chair, spilling out a heap of black soil spotted with white pearls of fertilizer.

I'm psyching myself up to investigate more closely when something catches my eye: a splatter of dirty yellow paint beside my right foot. I reach out to touch it and immediately spot another one a few inches away. I freeze, my pulse quickening, as my eyes pick out more and more of them, scattered all around me in a cloud. The colors have gone dull and filthy from years of dust and rain, but they're still there, still visible, layers and layers of drips and splatters and spots.

Sukey.

I shift onto my hands and knees to get a closer look, ignoring the roughness of the rooftop on my grazed skin. Rubbing away the grime, I make out raspberry, purple, sea-foam green, like droppings from a psychedelic pigeon. Sukey must have stood over this place with her easel while she painted. These drips of paint must have flown off her brush as she lifted it to the canvas, splashing onto the hot roof. *Sukey made art here,* my brain keeps thinking, sounding it over and over like a bell—my Sukey, the one I remember, not the strung-out stranger that was starting to replace her in my mind. Even if she was screwing up and getting lost and making all the wrong decisions, at least she was still searching. At least she was still trying to get to that place her soul was from. And maybe, in spite of everything, she found it.

As I climb back down the fire escape, I tell myself there's no reason to be sad anymore—no reason to crash bicycles or fight with Danny or have stupid, fretful worries about the people on the bus. The world is good and I am good and love is good and if I'd only stop freaking out long enough to realize that, I wouldn't have any problems at all.

chapter thirty

All day long, I carry Sukey's rooftop around with me like a pocketful of gumballs, an ecstatic secret I can hardly keep contained. I want to be good for the world—pure and true and wise and somehow saintly, somehow illuminated. I want to have experienced something that has changed me, and so I act changed.

I take my synth to Skunk's house, and we fix it in the shed using bike tools. The pieces of the exploded synth fit back together perfectly. You can't even tell it exploded in the first place, and when I plug it into the extension cord, the power light glows bright blue. I play for Skunk for a little while, saying things like, "This is where Lukas goes ba-ka-ka-ta-ba-ka-ta on the drums," until Skunk picks me up, moves the synth out of the way, sets me down on the workbench, and kisses me with his hands in my hair. "Love-bison," I say, but he can't hear because my mouth is smothered in kisses.

When I leave, Skunk gives me a little black book with yellowing pages. I read it on the bus ride home. It starts, "The Way that can be experienced is not true; the world that can be constructed is not real." I flip it over. The cover says *Tao te Ching*. By the time I get home, I've read the whole thing twice. I send Skunk a text I THINK MY BRAIN IS ON FIRE, and he texts back IT PROBABLY IS, and I text back THE WAY IS A LIMITLESS VESSEL, and he texts back USED BY THE SELF, IT IS NOT FILLED BY THE WORLD, and I text back IT CANNOT BE CUT, KNOTTED, DIMMED OR STILLED, and he texts back ITS DEPTHS ARE HIDDEN, UBIQUITOUS AND ETERNAL. We keep texting lines back and forth until we've texted practically the whole *Tao te Ching*, then Skunk calls and says, "I miss you already, Crazy Girl," and I get off the bus, cross the street, catch a bus in the opposite direction, go right back to his house, and kidnap him for an expedition to the Chinese bakery before his aunt and uncle get home from work.

That night, Lukas finally texts back after I've already sent him a million texts asking when we're going to practice now that I've fixed my synth. I go over there for dinner, and Petra's made potato-and-cheese pierogi. She comments on my outfit, which is somewhat more daring than what I usually wear, and I tell her now that our band is famous, I need to look the part. Lukas still looks the same, but that's because he's the drummer and drummers are never fully in the spotlight, it's kind of a rule of drumming. He doesn't say much during dinner, just picks at his pierogi. Lukas's parents and I do most of the talking.

"Where are your parents now?" says Petra.

"Paraguay," I tell her, "taking care of sea tortoises."

"I thought Paraguay was landlocked," says Lukas.

I lean forward confidentially.

"Not anymore."

We go downstairs to jam, and Lukas goes straight to his drum kit and sits. I look at him expectantly. "Don't you want to smoke first?"

"No."

"Why?"

"Seems like you already did."

"No, I didn't."

"Why are you acting so weird?"

"I'm not."

"You haven't been the same ever since you found out about your sister."

"I'm not the same. How could I be the same?"

He picks up his drumsticks and starts playing, and even though I try again and again to catch his eye, he won't look up. Something about that scares me. I stand there with my fingers hovering over the keys of my synth.

"Lukas?" I say.

He stops drumming. "What?"

A dozen possible things-to-say swim nervously around the edges of my brain. A few weeks ago, Lukas knew everything about me, and now there are so many things he doesn't know, and so many things I don't know about him. It's scary how a friendship can change like that, so fast, so completely. It's like walking past your old elementary school the week after graduation: The swings and slides and buildings are the same, but suddenly, incomprehensibly, the place doesn't belong to you anymore, and you don't belong to it.

I want to tell him about Sukey's rooftop, and the fact that I now have a boyfriend, and that I've found the perfect person for Goth Girl to date.

I want to tell Lukas all this, but the way he's glaring at me over his drum kit—annoyed, impatient, sick of my bullshit—I feel small and queasy and not very illuminated at all.

"I'm sorry," I say, and he gives me a quick, embarrassed shrug, and for the rest of the jam session we don't make eye contact again.

The next day, Skunk and I are exchanging lustful embraces on the floor in the radio temple, and when I shimmy out of my jeans he notices the scabs on my knees. He springs up with a look of alarm and pulls my legs onto his lap to inspect them.

"What happened?"

I yawn and try to pull him back down to kiss me. "Oh, nothing."

"No, seriously."

He runs his fingers over the scabbed parts, touching the bits of gravel I never managed to pick out. Some people have such warm hands. Skunk's feel like old pillowcases fresh out of the dryer. "I fell off my bike."

"When?"

"Like a week ago."

"What were you doing?"

I give him a mischievous grin. "Ridin' dirty."

Skunk traces his thumb over my kneecap. "What did you do, cut off a bus?"

"No-o-o. I got hit by a car."

Skunk freezes. "You got hit by a car and you didn't tell me."

I swing my legs off his lap and sit up. "Whatever, homey. The Way is an invincible fortress."

He looks at me all pop-eyed and distressed. "What color was the car?"

I reach out and smooth Skunk's hair. He looks like he's about to faint.

"I don't know. It was just some car."

"Are you sure you don't remember what color it was?"

I lean forward and lick his ear. "Relax, Bicycle Boy. As you can see, I am alive and well."

Skunk's body has gone all tense, like he hears a strange noise: a mouse in the wall, or a burglar. "Was it following you?"

I sit there blinking at him. "No. Well, actually she did follow me for a while after it happened, but I think she just wanted to make sure I was okay."

"Oh God," says Skunk.

"What? What?"

But Skunk holds his head in his hands and won't even start to relax until I get up, tiptoe across the room, and quietly turn on a radio.

Later that day, when Dr. Scaliteri calls me in for an extra lesson, I tell her all about my new practice regimen. I've been practicing constantly, I tell her. Now that I've realized I can do it in my head, I have basically been practicing piano twenty-four hours a day.

"How many hours does Nelson Chow practice per day? Probably just four or five, right? I can teach him my technique, if you want. It could really help him out when he's at Juilliard.

He'll want to practice on the subway."

I hear the front door open and Nelson Chow walk in for his lesson. I hear him stop in the hall to take off his shoes.

"Hey, Nelson," I shout. "How many hours a day do you practice?"

No response. Nelson is the kind of person who always pretends he hasn't heard you. "Hey, Nelson! I said how many hours?"

Dr. Scaliteri calls out to Nelson that he should wait in the hall. She leans forward so her speckled old cleavage is practically falling out of her silver blouse and hisses, "I will not have this behavior in my studio."

"What behavior?" I say. "I'm trying to help him."

"Kiri," she says, "I have never before had this kind of behavior in my studio. You will go home now and practice."

"I just told you, Dr. Scaliteri. I already *am* practicing. I've been practicing the whole time we've been talking." I point at my temple. "In my *head*."

On my way out of the room, I realize the stained-glass fruit bowl is glowing a little too hard, like someone installed neon tubes behind the glass.

Denny and I get sushi most nights because I threw out all the food. Denny always gets an avocado roll and a yam roll. I always get a yam roll and a California roll. I rip open the foil packet of soy sauce and pour it over my sushi like pancake syrup. Denny can hardly contain his disgust.

"That's not how you're supposed to do it," he says, pouring soy sauce onto his tray and mixing in a dainty green dab of wasabi with the tip of his wooden chopstick. "You're supposed to dip it in the soy sauce. Like this."

I pay close attention, marveling at Denny's mastery of the simple things in this world, thinking if I could only learn to mix my soy sauce correctly, maybe my life would make perfect sense.

I read the *Tao te Ching* over and over until I have it memorized.

I text Lukas over and over about band practice, and when he doesn't text back I show up at his house with my synth and my own stash of weed. I'm pretty sure he's dating Kelsey Bartlett; his phone beeps ten minutes after I show up, and he gets all awkward and says he has to go.

I bring my bike to Skunk's house, and we snarfle in the shed with pear blossoms knocking on the door.

I sit in the hall after my lesson, listening to Nelson Chow's lesson and taking notes.

I follow Nelson Chow to the bus stop when he comes out and read him my notes.

I sit next to Nelson Chow on the bus, questioning him about his practice habits until he pulls the yellow cord and gets off.

I text Lukas about buying a new amp, and when he doesn't text back, I go on eBay and order one to be delivered to his house.

I smoke weed and practice piano until Denny says, "When did you turn into a fucking pothead? Don't you sleep?" and then I practice inside my head, pacing and pacing around the living room very slowly like a Zen monk doing walking meditation in a garden of very tiny bonsai trees.

Skunk makes me promise to call him at once if I am hit by any more cars, or if I have even the slightest suspicion that I am being followed by secret agents. We fix my brakes and he sniffs my hair like a flower. We listen to radio mysteries and I climb onto him like a branch. We read the *Tao te Ching* out loud to one another and suck on guavas. We ride bikes to English Bay and build a nest in the sand. We make love ten thousand times and then make omelets. I call him Bicycle Boy. He calls me Crazy Girl.

Denny says, "Where are you always going on your bike?"

chapter thirty-one

Since Lukas doesn't seem to think we need to practice anymore, I spend the last few days before Battle of the Bands finals keeping a close eye on Skunk. He doesn't like to talk about his paranoia-thing, but ever since my bicycle crash I've been noticing the ways it slips out when he's not paying attention, like a foreign accent or a stutter he's worked hard to tame.

Sometimes when Skunk wakes up he's really groggy and disoriented, and he squints at me suspiciously like I'm a Russian spy whose motives are not to be trusted.

Sometimes when I show up at his house without calling first, I catch him standing outside smoking with a pile of cigarette butts at his feet, his face blank like an open document with all the text deleted.

Sometimes when we snarfle he gets embarrassed, and when I ask him why he's embarrassed, he gets apologetic and says he didn't always used to be this fat.

I tell him he's my love-bison and to stop apologizing.

I silently take note of all the things that trigger his paranoia and steer clear of them when we're together. I do this so masterfully that Skunk thinks he's the one looking out for *me*.

"You should really wear a helmet," he says, and I pat his big warm hand. "Oh, Bicycle Boy," I say. "Most things in life feel better when you don't have a chunk of Styrofoam strapped to your head."

We ride our bikes to the university and go to the Nitobe Memorial Garden and walk around looking at the little stone pagodas and drinking tea Skunk brought in a silver thermos. I make up stories about everything we see: This is the temple where the Frog King lost his teeth, this is the pond where the Riot Snake wrestled with a lightning bolt, causing daffodils to be invented.

"Oh, Crazy Girl," says Skunk. "I love to listen to you talk."

On the ride back to Skunk's house I count all the billboards for new condo developments.

LUXURY LIVING IN THE HEART OF GRANVILLE ISLAND

LIVE. WORK. SHOP. PLAY.

AN EXCLUSIVE WATERFRONT LIVING COMMUNITY

From the looks of the billboards, it appears that people who live in condos spend most of their time shopping, drinking cappuccinos, and doing yoga. As a matter of fact, the new condo developments are basically ashrams: billboard after billboard of slender white women in yoga pants doing the lotus position in front of windows showing blue-white views of the North Shore. Prices starting in the high four hundreds. Om Shanti Om.

Later, at home, I Google the Imperial Hotel, and just as I feared, the top hit is for a yoga condo that will soon be taking its place on Columbia Street. A month ago this wouldn't have bothered me, because the Imperial is a horrible murder-hole unfit for human habitation, but now that I've met Doug and found Sukey's rooftop it feels like a profound injustice, and I immediately fire off an email to the developers, informing them of my objections.

That night I sneak back to Skunk's house very late, after Denny has gone to bed. I rap softly on Skunk's sliding glass door, and he answers it a moment later.

"Oh, Crazy Girl," he says, and lets me in.

We're sitting in the radio temple, drinking pine-needle

tea and taking turns reading the *Tao* out loud, when we hear footsteps creaking upstairs, and then Skunk's aunt appears at the top of the stairs wearing those big-butt sweatpants I borrowed the first time I stayed over. I've never met Skunk's aunt or uncle before, because so far we've managed to evade them. But here she is. She stops when she gets halfway down the stairs and stares at me like I'm an escaped baboon Skunk has been harboring in her basement.

I'm about to offer her some tea, since she seems to still be awake at four a.m. anyway. But then I realize maybe she's awake at four a.m. because the sound of us reading woke her up. Skunk has been more worried than usual about thought control, and we have been reading the *Tao* to throw the agents off. I smile and say hi, assuming she will realize in one look that her nephew and I are hopelessly in love and give us one of those wistful glances like the old couple we walked past at the Zen garden.

She looks right past me to Skunk.

"What's going on?"

Her voice is sharp. Maybe she wasn't already awake. I don't see how we could have woken her, though—we were being very quiet. I lean my face down to the teacup Skunk's holding and lap it with my tongue like a cat.

"Kiri, this is my aunt Martine."

I swallow my tea. "Hi."

She frowns. She has a pale, puffy face that says I Have to

Work in Three Hours. A face like a day-old hamburger bun. She looks at Skunk.

"What are you doing up this late?"

Skunk indicates the teacup.

Martine sighs and rubs her forehead like he's giving her a headache. The way her glasses sit on her face looks unnatural, like she's a person who normally wears contacts and on the rare occasion she actually wears her glasses people look confused and say, *Whoa, I didn't know you wore glasses.* She takes off her I-didn't-know-you-wore-glasses glasses and presses her thumb and forefinger into her eye sockets. Her hair is cut short in that I-don't-have-time-for-hair style that my mean kindergarten teacher had. Her face is square and droopy. With her glasses off, she looks like a haggard dingo.

"It's four in the morning. You should be asleep. Don't you take your meds at eleven?"

Skunk stiffens. "Not always."

"You're supposed to take them at eleven. *Every* night at eleven."

"Only if I need them." Skunk's voice is strangely petulant. I get the feeling they've had this exact same conversation before. Martine's hand flies off her eyes.

"*Mon dieu.* Does this mean you haven't been—"

"Can we talk about this later." He doesn't say it like a question. I glance back at him and see a coldness I haven't seen before. His face has closed up like a cardboard box. He won't meet my eyes. On the stairs, Skunk's aunt is shaking her head and muttering swear words in French.

Maybe a little mediation's in order. I sit up.

"Sorry we woke you up, Martine. We were trying to be quiet."

She glances at me, then raises her eyebrows at Skunk. Her jaw tightens.

"Who is this?"

I can feel the muscles in Skunk's arms clench like he's trying to bench-press a minivan.

"Kiri's my girlfriend."

Even though my presence here is obviously getting Skunk in trouble, I feel a pleasant tingle when he says that. Martine's glance swoops over me.

"What's she doing here at this time of night? Why isn't she at home?"

I'm not sure why she keeps talking about me as if I'm not in the room. I clear my throat. "Actually, I don't have a curfew."

She ignores me.

"Did you tell her, Philippe? Does she know about your condition? Does she know you need to be careful?" I'm assuming she's talking about Skunk's paranoia thing, but I don't know why she has to say it like that, like an accusation. Look, lady, people are gonna worry about *your* condition if you talk to my boyfriend like that.

Martine the Dangerous Dingo takes another step down the stairs and looks around with a brief, disapproving glare. I try to fend her off telepathically: *Away, dingo! Out of our temple!*

"Explain to me why I am seeing this, Philippe. Why did we have that long talk full of promises and today already you are not taking the medicine like you're supposed to, like you promised Dr. Winterson you would?"

Martine has a bit of a Quebecois accent. You can hear it when she says "Philippe." Which is Skunk's other name. I reach down and squeeze his ankle. *Hi, Philippe.* He puts down the teacup.

"I *am* taking the medicine. I take it when I need it."

"You need it every day, Philippe. It's only been six months. You're not better yet. Do you understand what could happen if you stop taking your meds now? *C'est un problème, Philippe. Un grand problème.*"

"I'll decide when there's a problem—"

Martine holds up her hand.

"No. Don't interrupt. We've talked about this before, Philippe. We agreed that as a condition of you living here you would do everything Dr. Winterson said. You're supposed to be taking your meds, seeing the counselor, going to the support group, and getting your life on track. If the doctor says meds at eleven, it's meds at eleven. Every night. No four a.m. tea parties.

And no overnight visitors in my house."

Skunk's aunt looks at me again, then lays into him in French.

"Vraiment, Philippe. T'es imbécile. C'est pas à toi de choisir si tu vas les prendre ou pas les prendre. C'est à Dr. Winterson à dire."

"On peut parler plus tard, Martine? Ecoute. Ecoute-moi, là. S'il te plaît. On peut parler plus tard?"

They go back and forth like that in sharp bursts, as if they've both forgotten I'm here. I do the best I can to mentally translate: Martine's general vibe right now is *It's not up to you to pick! It's not up to you to pick it!* Skunk keeps saying, *We can talk later? Please. We can talk about this later?*

I thought he was tensing up out of anger, but no. My poor dearest love-bison is quivering with humiliation. This has to stop. I have to stop it. She can't be allowed to hurt him like that.

I wave my hand in the air.

"Martine?"

She looks at me like she can't believe I'm still here.

"How did you get here, Kelly?"

"On my bike."

"Bon. It's time for you to ride home. Take all your things. Philippe and I have a few things to discuss in private."

chapter thirty-two

When I get home from Skunk's house, it's almost five in the morning. I tiptoe in through the garage and slip upstairs to my bedroom. There's no point going to sleep now, so instead I lie on my bed practicing *Sesquipaedia* in my head until I finally hear Denny get up, and then I go downstairs to start some coffee brewing and do my house-sitting chores, the garbage and the recycling and the azaleas.

When I take the mail in, there's a big white envelope with the words INTERNATIONAL YOUNG PIANISTS' SHOWCASE printed on it in a fancy font. I rip it open. Inside, there's a copy of the official program, a printout of directions to the concert hall, and a checklist of things to bring to your recital. I scour the program until I find my name:

KIRI BYRD, 2:07 P.M. SUNDAY

J. S. Bach, Italian Concerto

W. Beethoven, Sonata in C-Sharp Minor, op. 6, V. 2

F. Chopin, Nocturne in D

C. Debussy, *La cathédrale engloutie*

A. Khachaturian, *Toccata*

I'm listed again under the master class heading, along with *Prokofiev: Concerto No. 2*.

I call Dr. Scaliteri.

"The program came!"

"Kiri, I am teaching a lesson right now."

"I have a question."

"Kiri—"

I hear someone plunking keys in the background. "Make the left hand float," says Dr. Scaliteri to someone, probably Nelson Chow.

"Dr. Scaliteri. Dr. Scaliteri? I've decided to change which piece I'm playing for the master class."

"You cannot change this piece."

"No, it's fine, I'm learning a new one with that technique I told you about. It's a little-known composer, very obscure. It's going to be a world premiere."

"Kiri, I have no time for this nonsense. You will play the Prokofiev."

Whoever's on the piano bench plunks away. "Good, Nelson," says Dr. Scaliteri. I knew it.

"You just haven't heard me play it yet. How about I come over this afternoon?"

"Excellent, Nelson. Your sound is flowering."

"Dr. Scaliteri?"

"Have I already talked to you about the recital in October?"

"What recital?"

"Oh, that's right, you'll be at Juilliard. It would be worth flying back from New York City."

She's talking to Nelson. Why is she talking to Nelson? She's supposed to be talking to me.

"Dr. Scaliteri? Should I come over?"

"Well, think about it. I'll give you the information."

"Dr. Scaliteri? I can come over now."

Nelson starts plunking, oh excuse me, floating. There's a click and a rumble like Dr. Scaliteri just put down the phone on her desk. Did she seriously forget she was just talking to me? Or is this a subtle way of letting me sit in on Nelson's lesson without letting Nelson know that I'm listening? Maybe Dr. Scaliteri is trying to show me something, let me listen in so I can give her my input later. I'm starting to think we're in on this whole Nelson Chow business together.

I keep my ear pressed to the phone, listening intently for the next twenty minutes, until Dr. Scaliteri starts dialing a number, like she's forgotten we never hung up. I pick up the program for the Showcase, find the number on the back, and make a call of my own.

I bike to Skunk's house so I can see him before Aunt Martine gets home from work, but when I knock on the glass door he doesn't answer, and when I try to open it, it's locked. There's a big pile of cigarette butts on the concrete. I go to the Chinese grocery store and buy him a dozen dragon fruit and leave them in front of his door in a circle of pear blossoms with a note that says *The Way that takes its meds at eleven is not the true Way. Love, Kiri.* There are brown birds chirping in the tree, and Skunk's van is not in the alleyway. I wonder where he's gone. I call his phone, but he doesn't pick up—I can hear it ringing inside.

Text from Lukas: WHY DID FEDEX DELIVER AMP 2 MY HOUSE?
Text back: B O B SAT NITE NEED MAX SOUNDAGE OBVS

"Stop pacing around the house like that," says Denny. "You're making me edgy."

"I don't know where Skunk is."

"Who the hell is Skunk?"

I prop up the cream-colored International Young Pianists' Showcase program on top of the piano and play my entire recital all the way through six times.

"Stop playing like that," says Denny.

"Like what?"

"Like there's someone holding a machine gun to your head."

I remind him that the Showcase is in sixteen days, Mom and Dad are due back in fifteen days, and it's my personal responsibility to ensure that they come home to the kind of impeccable performance they have come to expect.

Petra calls to invite Denny and me to dinner. She assumes my parents finally saw reason and sent him home to babysit me, and I don't correct her on that point. When I decline the invitation, she asks if she can speak to Denny.

"He's not here right now," I say with a rush of paranoia that makes my hair stand on end. *Why does Petra want to talk to Denny? What's she plotting, anyway?*

"You tell him to make sure you are eating real food," says Petra. "I can give him instructions for roast chicken, if he doesn't know how."

My suspicion dissolves into relief, and I remember how much I love Petra.

"He knows how to cook a chicken," I say.

* * *

As the day progresses, I become more and more worried about Skunk. What if Martine took him to some evil mental hospital and had him committed because he goes to bed at four a.m.? She's a nurse. They would believe her word over his, even though Skunk is obviously and thoroughly sane. Too bad he doesn't have his phone, because then he would be able to call me for help.

I try calling him one more time just in case, but all I get is the same constipated robot voice telling me the subscriber has not set up their voice-mail in-box.

I start calling hospitals.

"Is there a Philippe in your psychiatric ward?"

"Philippe who?"

"He's really big. Like a bison. He has tattoos all over his arms."

"What's the last name?"

"Could you just go look if he's there?"

Denny comes home from skimboarding.

"Denny, can you drive me somewhere?"

"No, get a license."

"It's extremely, extremely, extremely urgent. I need to go a psychiatric ward."

"No shit."

276

"I need to find someone."

"If they're in a psych ward, they're probably not allowed to see you anyway."

"Please."

"I told you. Get a license."

I go on the internet and look up the symptoms of psychosis. Somehow I end up taking a self-scoring suicide quiz on a mental health website. According to the quiz, I have an 87 percent risk of committing suicide. This sounds serious. I wonder if maybe I'm on the verge of suicide right now. Maybe that means I can join Skunk in the psych ward. The website says there's a hotline you should call if your score is over 50 percent. I call the hotline. It rings busy. When I hang up the phone, it rings immediately. I think it's the hotline calling back, but it's my parents calling from Lithuania, where they are eating herring and snurkleberry jam.

"I am bringing you and Denny some snurkleberry jam," titters my mother.

"Maybe you could study piano in Lithuania," says my dad. "Then we'd have an excuse to come here all the time."

"I haven't slept in three days," I say.

They chortle as if I've made some funny joke.

"There'll be plenty of time for sleeping after the Showcase," says my dad.

"If you're stressed, you can borrow my gym card," says my mom. "It's in the basket on top of the fridge."

"I don't think—"

"They have something called Hot Yoga. That might be relaxing."

I stare at the ceiling. *I don't need to relax, I need to find Skunk.*

"Is the computer working okay?" says my dad.

"They have Sunrise Pilates on our ship," says my mom.

I am not sure how to decode this. Surely we must be talking about something bigger than computer viruses and ambiguously spiritual exercise regimens. There must be something buried deeper, a subtext I've been too thick to parse.

"I'm dying," I say carefully, trying to load each word with as many layers of meaning as I can.

"All right," says my mom. "Go take a nap."

chapter thirty-three

When I answer my ringing cell phone on Saturday morning at four a.m., Skunk's voice whispers, "The Way that can be experienced is not true."

I hold the phone close to my face and whisper, "The world that can be constructed is not real."

I hear the crackle of a radio in the background. Sometimes Skunk tunes one or more of his radios to static when he's feeling paranoid. I spread my legs out on the kitchen floor, where I am sitting and organizing the cleaning supplies, soaps and detergents and powders and sprays.

"Hi, Kiri."

"Hi, Skunk. Are you listening to the radio?"

Pause. "Yes."

"How many radios?"

Pause. "Three."

"Is this a three-radio alert?"

Pause.

"I was worried you were in a mental hospital. I called all the mental hospitals asking if they had you. I was afraid your aunt Martine had brought you in for not going to bed when she wanted. She seemed like kind of a, excuse me, bitch."

There's a very long pause. Skunk says quietly, "I was in a hospital. Not this time. Six months ago. I had a thing. That's why she's so afraid."

This time, it's my turn to pause. "Afraid of what, Skunk?"

"Afraid it will happen again."

"The Thing?"

"The Thing."

Pause. "Where did you go this time?"

Pause. "Guess."

"Not a mental hospital."

"No."

"Um." Pause. "Um." Think. "Lucky Foo's."

"No."

"Montreal."

"No."

Pause.

Pause. "Give up?"

Skunk's voice is very quiet. I picture him sitting on the floor in the radio temple with his hand cupped around the phone, trying to hide the sound from his aunt Martine. Maybe he's using the radio static as a foil. Wouldn't Aunt Martine hear the radio static and take him to a mental hospital?

"Skunk?"

"Yeah?"

"Are you sure your aunt's sleeping right now?"

Pause. Static. "Yes."

"Okay." Pause. "Are you smoking a cigarette?"

Pause. "Yes."

Pause. "Be careful."

Static.

Pause. "I went to the marshlands."

"What?"

Pause. "I went to the marshlands."

"You are a friend of marshlands."

"Yes."

Static. I pick up one of the brightly colored bottles on the floor in front of me and inspect it.

"Which do you think is more trustworthy, Windex or Toilet Duck?"

Pause. "Windex."

"Why?"

Pause. "You should never trust a duck."

"Oh."

"Especially not a toilet duck."

I peer at the label on the bottle in my hand. "They write too much on these things."

"People like to know how things work."

"Hm. But why all the science? Why the diagrams about breaking down bacteria? Why not something else? Why not say Toilet Duck works by channeling the spirit of ducks? Why all the crap about chemistry?"

Radio static. I hear Skunk exhale his cigarette smoke.

"People like to think everything can be explained by chemistry."

"Yeah, but toilets?"

Skunk laughs. I silently award myself one point for cheering him up.

"Are you burning incense?" I ask him.

Pause. "Yes."

It's amazing how well you can get to know a person if you actually pay attention. People are like cities: We all have alleys and gardens and secret rooftops and places where daisies sprout between the sidewalk cracks, but most of the time all we let each other see is a postcard glimpse of a floodlit statue or a skyline. Love lets you find those hidden places in another person, even the ones they didn't know were there, even the ones they wouldn't have thought to call beautiful themselves. I decide to test my knowledge of all things Skunk.

"Are you wearing your 'Sed Interdum' T-shirt?"

Pause. "Yes."

"Are you wearing white socks?"

Pause. "No."

"Are you wearing no socks?"

Pause. "Yes."

"Are you sitting on the floor?"

Pause. "Yes."

"Are you afraid of your aunt Martine?"

Pause. "Yes."

"Are you afraid she'll kick you out if you don't do what she wants?"

Pause. "Yes."

"Does she think you're having a Thing?"

Pause. "Yes."

"Do you think so?"

Pause. "No."

"Is that why you went to the marshlands?"

Pause. "Yes."

"Will you come watch my band tonight?"

Pause.

"Skunk? Hey, Skunk?"

Pause. Static.

"Can I come over?"

Pause. Static.

"I can be there on my bike in twenty minutes."

Static.

"Okay, I'm getting on my bike."

"No."

Pause. "Why not?"

Pause. "You should sleep."

Pause. "Why?"

Pause. "It's four thirty, Crazy Girl."

"It's four thirty, Crazy Boy."

Pause. "Make you a deal. You go lie on your bed and I'll go lie on my bed."

"Oh, I know! We'll fall asleep at exactly the same time, and we'll both have a dream where we go bike riding together."

"Yes."

"And we'll ride around Stanley Park in our dream, and we'll break into a condo in our dream, and we'll take a long steamy shower together in the finely appointed bathroom with stunning views of Burrard Inlet."

"Yes."

"Okay."

"Yes."

"Then you'll come hear my band tonight."

Pause. "I love you," he says.

My body goes so bright and hot I'm surprised the cell phone doesn't melt in my hand.

"I love you too," I say in a rush, like in the city of myself I've just stumbled on a fountain.

chapter thirty-four

"My mom thinks you're having a hypermanic episode."

I happen to be carrying a very heavy, very expensive, very brand-new amp when Lukas says this. It starts to slip out of my hands, but my left knee shoots up to catch it before it falls.

"Urff."

Lukas keeps walking down the Train Room's steep, narrow stairs.

"I don't know much about it, you should really talk to her, but—"

"Urrrh! Urrhh!"

The amp is teetering preteeterously on my rapidly tiring

thigh. If Lukas doesn't turn around and help me soon, there will be one more piece of high-tech music gear for me to fix in Skunk's shed using only a socket wrench and a set of tire irons.

"Urrrrrrgh!"

Lukas finally turns around, sees me balancing this giant amp on my knee, and scrunches his nose.

"What are you doing with that amp? It's going to fall and break."

Heaven forbid Lukas come back up three steps and assist in said amp's timely rescue. He stands there watching me struggle with it until I manage to slip a hand under the leather strap on top of the amp and lower it to rest on the stair. He scratches a zit on the side of his head.

"I'm just saying it seems like maybe you're having some issues," he says.

I can't believe what I'm hearing. We just won Battle of the Bands, for chrissakes, which means that next Saturday we get to headline our very own show. We just did our Invincible Gods of Time and Space thing where our minds meld together and the force of our collective vibrations could shatter the ceiling in the Sistine Chapel. An indie photographer with chunky glasses took our photo for an obscure music zine. Straight-edge Alex and Nikky Sharp even gave us high fives. A nerd from CiTR-FM asked if we had a demo. That's how hot we were. Hotter than the freaking sun.

"What?" I shriek. "But I'm fine. I'm acting totally normal."

I know that flipping out will only prove Lukas right, but the thing is, I tried really hard to keep it together tonight. I've been alert and lucid, polite and serious and humble and helpful and friendly and kind. It felt like things were finally good again. Why is he wrecking it now?

Lukas raises a hand as if to fend me off. "My mom's a social worker, Kiri. If she thinks you're hypermanic, you probably are."

I stare at Lukas. Sandy yellow hair. Tight T-shirt. Black jeans. Standing three steps below me on the stairs going down to the street after Battle of the Bands, Final Showdown Edition. This is the Lukas whose earlobe I touched on his birthday. The Lukas in whose basement I played music every afternoon after school. The Lukas at whose kitchen table I sat drawing album cover after potential album cover for the ~~Bucket of Skulls~~ ~~Snake Eats Kitten~~ ~~Sonic Drift~~ debut EP. The Lukas in whom I used to take such irrational delight, just because he was a Lukas and I was a me.

Who the hell is Lukas, anyway?

I am carrying a four-foot-long synth, a tangle of cords, and an amp that weighs more than I do. Lukas is carrying a pair of drumsticks and a green sweater. His parents have gone down ahead of us carrying his drum kit and stool.

"Would you take something? This is kind of a lot to carry."

Lukas gazes up at me skeptically. "I'm carrying this sweater."

"Never mind."

"I guess I could tie the sweater around my waist."

The thing is, Lukas is serious. He seriously has to consider the fact that he is carrying his sweater, and seriously has to arrive at the conclusion that, okay, maybe he could make a slight adjustment to his sweater-carrying configuration and give me a hand with the amp. It is slowly dawning on me: This is just how Lukas is. He will never know how to turn off a smoke detector. He will never be able to start watching a movie half an hour later than he planned. He will never look at me close enough to see more than a postcard. He won't even try.

Lukas ties his sweater around his waist.

"Hand me those cords," he says.

"Hypermanic meaning what?"

Suddenly, carrying the cords and the amp and the synth myself is of utmost importance. I snatch the cords out of his reach.

"I don't know," says Lukas. "It might have been some other word. She said you're a monomaniac."

"A monomaniac."

Lukas looks away. "Or something."

"Your mom said this?"

Nod.

I silently strike Petra off my list of People I Would Take a Bullet For. A monomaniac. *Moi.*

"She's been worried about you ever since the last time you came over for dinner."

"What happened the last time I came over for dinner?"

"You spent half an hour talking about some secret technique you have for learning piano pieces."

"It's not a *secret*, it's a scientifically proven method for—"

"Kiri—"

"If she's so worried about me, why hasn't she said something? Why is she down there waiting in the car while you tell me you all secretly think I'm a monomaniac?"

"Because—"

Lukas presses his lips together several times as if crushing the false starts of sentences he decides not to say. I glare down at him, wielding our expensive new amp like a wrecking ball. Finally:

"She said you might listen if it came from your best friend."

A hot, hollow bomb of humiliation and outrage explodes in my chest. Our eyes meet briefly and we both look away. He stomps up the stairs and tries to grapple the amp out of my hands. "Let me carry that stuff."

"No."

"Come on, let me carry it."

We struggle for a moment, coming dangerously close to falling down the stairs, amp, synth, and all. Finally, I shove all the equipment into Lukas's arms.

"Fine. Take it. And you know what? You can tell your parents I'll get my own ride home."

"Come on, we'll give you a ride."

"No."

"My mom won't leave without—"

"Denny can pick me up."

Lukas looks dubious, but at least he quits arguing. He casts me a wounded glance and makes his way down the stairs. I stick my hands on my hips and shout after him in my most monomaniacal voice.

"Great bands don't psychoanalyze!"

I stomp back up to the Train Room, pushing through the swinging doors into the dark, still-crowded venue. I go all the way to the back and hide in the sound booth. After a minute, I see Petra and Lukas come in through the doors. They split up and look around. When they can't find me, they meet up again and have a short, stressed-out conference, then turn around and go back out.

Ten seconds later my cell phone starts ringing, but I turn it off and shove it back into my purse. I've had enough of Lukas's hysteria for one night. Before we went on, he was worried the new amp wouldn't work. Then he said his shoulders hurt and he might have strained a muscle. Then he kept checking his dad's phone obsessively to see what time it was. Then I developed an alarming case of monomania.

Also, Skunk never showed up.

I walk up to the refreshment booth and ask for a ginger ale. The guy working the booth recognizes me from our set and lets me have it for free. He has a red beard and alarmingly straight shoulders, like someone squared them off with a ruler. He shovels ice into a plastic cup, squirts in the ginger ale with a flourish, fits a lime wedge over the edge of the cup, and slides it across the counter to me.

"You guys rocked. It's on the house."

"Why, thank you. Did you know I have monomania?"

"Is that like mononucleosis?"

"It's much worse."

"I'm sorry to hear that."

"Don't be. It's the rarest form of monomania in the world. It's the kind of monomania only gotten by famous musicians."

"Wow."

"Jimi Hendrix had it."

Amused sparkle of eyes. "I didn't know that."

"Well, now you do. Thanks for the ginger ale."

"Good luck with the monomania."

"Oh yes." I take my drink and slink my way to a vacant stool. My silver shoes flash like knives. I alight on the stool and bring my glass to my lips. When I take a sip, I let the ginger ale swim around in my mouth for a second, fizzing, before it goes down.

Someone pokes my arm, and when I look it's this kid from school holding a curved aluminum flask.

"Top up?" he says, and I hand him my cup. Something clear and alcoholic glugs out of the flask. He winks, hands it back, and disappears.

I cross one leg over the other and eye the other people in the Train Room. I take another sip of my new and improved ginger ale. I am grooming myself for my new life as a monomaniac. In my new life as a monomaniac, I sip cocktails and brazenly fang the crowd. In my new life as a monomaniac, I wield the silver scissors of my own Way.

I think about Lukas and feel a stab of betrayal so sharp it makes me gasp.

The next sip of doctored ginger ale blossoms hotly in my throat like a flaming flower.

I feel like I should have a top hat and a monocle. A monocle for the monomaniac. A monocle and a motorcycle. I would go monocling around Stanley Park in the dark most monomaniacally. Where's a good top hat when you need one?

I know I should try to stop this—this, this whatever it is— but part of me doesn't want to and part of me doesn't think I can. I feel like a tire rolling down a hill, heavy and fast and completely indestructible, and if there was ever a point when I could have slowed down, that point is teensy-tiny far behind me now.

All these kids I don't know keep coming up to me to say hey and give me props on Sonic Drift: music nerds who want to know what kind of synth I'm rocking, clusters of tank-topped ninth-grade girls who want to know if Lukas is single.

It's like I have become magnetically attractive, sitting here on my stool, fixing the room with a savage glare. I inform each one of my admirers that I am a monomaniac. Most of them look impressed. There are fist pumps and high fives. A girl and a guy in full Native American sun dance regalia slip me another drink. It appears I am very amusing. Amusing or perhaps amazing. A college kid in a World War II flight suit asks for my opinion on microtonality. I squeeze my lime into my cup. "Between you and me, microtonality is about to hit the mainstream in a big way."

Sage nod.

"Fascinating."

A red-lipped girl in an eighteenth-century nurse's uniform asks me where I got my silver shoes. I tell her I am a monomaniac whose shoes belonged to a murder victim.

More people gather around to hear me talk about my murder shoes, and soon I'm telling them the story of how Sukey was strangled to death by a Russian pimp. I don't tell them the truth. Sukey's life is too precious to be handed around like that. As a registered monomaniac, it's my job to control what stays in the rare books collection and what passes into general circulation. I am the Librarian of Life Experiences. I am the Curator of Truth. I walk my disciples around the fantastical gallery of my imagination, and they ooh and aah and nod as if they knew. I could almost do this as a career. I should make business cards: Kiri Byrd, Monomaniac-at-Large. It would be huge.

The photographer kid comes back and snaps a photo of my murder shoes. The boy from my school reappears with his flask. I've attracted quite an audience. No surprise, really. I'm the only monomaniac in the room. Hell, I might even be the only monomaniac in the city. These people might not get a chance to see another one. I'd better let them have it while it's good. I laugh and tip my hat and raise my monocle. *Quite right, quite right, quite right.* The Eighteenth-Century Nurse says I could probably sell those shoes on eBay for five hundred bucks. I tell her eBay doesn't allow the sale of murder shoes. She looks duly corrected.

"Oh, sorry, I didn't know that."

"No murder shoes," I tell her. "No murder shoes and nothing infested with mange."

When I'm finished with my latest drink, I dismiss the coterie with an imperious wave of my arm and saunter over to the women's bathroom. When I come out of the bathroom, a black-haired man in a motorcycle jacket asks me if I want to party. He's older than most of the crowd here. I wonder if he's a talent scout for a major label. I grin. "Monomaniacs were born to party."

We go out onto the fire escape, and he pulls a wrinkled joint out of the pocket of his black leather jacket. The jacket is stiff like armor and blackly shiny. My eyes keep on being drawn to it as if I'm hoping to see my reflection, but you can't quite see your reflection in the leather's muffled light. We smoke the joint. It's strong. Sometimes joints aren't very strong, but this one is. I feel like the space inside my chest is expanding and all my organs are floating apart. Is that supposed to happen? Motorcycle Man is smiling like he's pleased with something. He takes out a small plastic bag with some yellow pills in it.

"You have a very attractive body," says Motorcycle Man.

Monomaniacs are known for their physiques.

"Want to try something?"

Monomaniacs will try anything.

He shakes out two pills. "Enjoy."

I swallow them. A monomaniac always enjoys.

My internal organs that are floating apart start to glow with heat like baked yams. The best yam in the world is the garnet, because it is a jewel. It is a jewel and I have six internal organs, six glowing jewels that shine through my skin like flashlights. Motorcycle Man's hand floats toward my waist and sticks there. Is this what is meant by an attractive body? A body to which other bodies are summoned like migrating butterflies? I start to recite Shakespeare. I am the beast and Juliet is the gun. No, I am the feast and Juliet is the bun. If I click my silver heels together, I will wake up on my bicycle. I will sail through the air with my monocle planted firmly in my eye socket and my hands wrapped around the handlebars like vines.

Skunk, damn you, you should have come.

Motorcycle Man is whispering suggestions in my ear. His latest suggestion: Come for a ride with me.

I don't think we're making out, but maybe we are. The glowing jewel of my brain struggles with the distinction. His hand is attracted to the part of my leg that is just barely covered by the otter-slickness of my black dress. I'm trying to guess how old he is. Numbers float out of my head like bubbles.

"Thirty-three," murmurs Motorcycle Man.

I turn the number over and over like a secret code. Thirty-three. As in 4:33. As in the piano piece by John Cage that is four minutes and thirty-three seconds of nothing but rests.

An untraceable blur of seconds passes. I count to 4:33.

Then I am in a car with black leather seats and a stereo that glows like a slot machine.

chapter thirty-five

"Kiri. Kiri!"

On Hastings Street I am so very busy and walking so very fast that when I hear Skunk calling my name it takes me almost three blocks to turn around. My knees are scraped again, but I don't think it's from crashing a bicycle since I'm not riding one. Then I remember—I was in a car with a man, some kind of label rep, but the stereo played evil music so I screamed, "Pull over!" and clawed my way out onto the sidewalk like a shipwreck survivor washing up on a rocky beach. Sukey died in a car crash—at least she did originally—and I did not like the way his hands strangled the wheel like white tentacles and his eyes were twin heat guns on my skin.

I stop on the sidewalk, and Skunk swoops up next to me. Skate shoes. No helmet. He brakes, jumps off his bike, and catches me in his arms like I'm a blown-away newspaper he's been chasing down the street.

"Kiri. I've been looking all over for you. Whose car was that?"

I give him a once-over. Sunshine is streaming out of his head in a huge pink-and-gold halo despite the fact that the rest of the street is still dark. His black bicycle is glazed in neon light. When he talks, his words reverberate weirdly, like he's speaking into a microphone with a delay line. I think I might be dreaming, or the subject of a very elaborate hoax. I put my hands on my hips and squint. "Are you a trick?"

"No. I promise, no."

"How can I tell?"

He sticks out his arm for me to smell. I put my nose against his sleeve. American Spirits. Lapsang souchong. WD-40.

I nod reluctantly.

"Okay."

Skunk glances up and down the street as if he's afraid there are spies in the doorways or snipers on the roof. Maybe he's worried about the homeless men trundling down the middle of the road with their shopping carts full of empty bottles. Maybe there are secret cameras hidden in their clinking, clanking loads.

"We can't stay here," says Skunk. "We have to get off the street. Can you ride on my handlebars?"

Skunk's bicycle is glowing like Christmas lights. It looks magical, sleek, like a time machine. It's almost too beautiful to touch.

"Can you do it?" pleads Skunk. "Here, put your hand on my shoulder."

He lifts me onto his handlebars and climbs on behind me. The metal is lightning-cool under my thighs. I lean back and Skunk puts his arms around me. He grabs the handlebars and pushes off with his foot. Soon we're zigzagging through the streets in a convoluted route of Skunk's own devising. We cut through alleys, roll across construction sites, and slip through the vast hollow silence of a parking garage. I understand without asking that what Skunk is doing is throwing the secret agents off our trail. Nobody could follow us in a car, not with the shortcuts he's taking. They'd have to be on bicycles, and we haven't seen another bicycle since we started.

As we jag through the city, I have the unsettling sensation of being caught in a dream, an imaginary world Skunk and I have silently agreed to call real. The buildings and lampposts and street signs reel past in a seasick parade, and I'm not sure if we're escaping something anymore or just clinging together while we drown.

"Love-bison," I say, but now it sounds desperate, like a thing you scream before you both burst into flames.

When we roll to a stop outside a twenty-four-hour diner, Skunk's T-shirt is soaked in sweat.

"Wait here," he pants, clutching the brakes while I jump off.

He whips around the corner and reappears a minute later, on foot. His forehead is beaded with sweat, and his hands are shaking from squeezing the handlebars so tight.

"I locked it up in front of an apartment building," he says by way of explanation. "Come on. Let's go inside."

We go into the diner and take the booth at very back, next to the bathrooms, far away from the door. We both squeeze into the same side of the booth. Skunk's body is damp and hot like a rain forest. He scans the diner.

"I think we're okay here," he says, but his eyes keep checking and checking.

The waitress comes and slaps menus down on our table. Skunk's too distracted to order. I sit up and take charge.

"We need six grilled-cheese sandwiches and a gallon of coffee."

She blinks.

"Coffee comes only in mugs this size. But you get a free refill."

I flutter my hand. "Do what you can."

When the waitress goes away, Skunk turns to me.

"Kiri."

"Mm-hmm."

"Now that it's safe to talk, you can tell me. Who was the man in the car?" His brown eyes are huge with concern. It occurs to me, suddenly, what a strange coincidence it is that Skunk was out for a bike ride at the same time I was swimming through the strange leather-and-glass aquarium of Motorcycle Man's car. Our connection must run deeper than I ever imagined; Skunk must have sensed that something was afoot.

This being said, my memory of the preceding hours is becoming more and more slippery. I peer into Skunk's eyes, which are glowing like little planets.

"I don't remember."

Skunk's smoking hand keeps moving to his cigarette pocket and back to the table, as if it keeps sneaking away on him and he has to constantly herd it back. His eyes strain into mine, as if he thinks if he looks hard enough he'll be able to see the memories I can't piece together. "Try, Kiri. Try. What did he say to you? What did he want?"

Before I have the chance to answer, the waitress comes carrying six plates of grilled-cheese sandwiches and two cups of coffee, which she unloads onto the table. Each sandwich comes with a bright green pickle. I pick one up and eat it. Its firm, cool pickle bones snap in my mouth like a frog's. My thoughts are woozy and colorful. It's like being at a carnival. Each time Skunk asks a question, I cast my little plastic fishing rod and reel in a different prize. I sit up suddenly, remembering something.

"Four thirty-three," I say to Skunk. "That's the message he gave me."

"Four thirty-three."

Our eyes both snap to the greasy white clock on the diner wall. It's 4:32. Just when the minute hand slides forward, we hear the scream of police sirens on the street outside the diner. We hold our breath as the sound crescendos to a brain-cracking whine that seems to hover outside the diner interminably before rushing away.

"Oh God."

Skunk squashes his fist against his mouth, blinking rapidly. I pick up my grilled-cheese sandwich and dispatch it in six bites. It's delicious. Golden brown on the outside and traffic-cone orange on the inside. The coffee is hot and watery in its white china cup and comes with a mean little spoon, which I hide in a crack in the booth's leather lining. Beside me, Skunk is knitting and unknitting his fingers on the table and muttering worriedly to himself. I reach under the table and unbuckle my murder-shoes. They clatter onto the dirty diner floor. I pull my bare feet under me and sit cross-legged on the leather seat. Now that I have eaten my sandwich, the world is coming into sharper focus. When I look around the diner, I see people eating pancakes, not blurry rainbows like a moment ago.

"They've been following you," says Skunk. "They used me to get to you."

I pluck another sandwich off a plate and sink my teeth into it. Hungry. I've never been so hungry in my life.

"They tried to kill you once before, and tonight they tried again. Both times it was right after you played at the Train Room. It's a pattern, Kiri."

I slurp up my coffee, and the waitress swoops in to refill it. "No shoes, no service."

"Oh, sorry."

I slip my feet back into Sukey's shoes without buckling them and take a sip of my coffee. The lights and color of the diner have started to quiet down, like someone in the kitchen has adjusted a knob.

Skunk is staring at the patterns in the tabletop as if they reveal a horrifying picture he's never put together before. He looks at me. "Promise you won't go back to the Train Room."

I feel like I'm waking up after a long sleep in a strange bed. For the first time since he appeared on his bicycle, Skunk's face comes into focus, and his words start to make sense. I put down my coffee cup.

"What do you mean, don't go back to the Train Room? Me

and Lukas just won Battle of the Bands. We're going to play our own show next Saturday, which you would know if you'd actually come. Speaking of which—"

"Don't go back to the Train Room," says Skunk. "Don't go back there and don't go to my house. Where's your phone?"

I stupidly hand it to him. He opens my contacts list and scrolls down to his name.

"Hey—what are you doing?"

Skunk presses a button and hands me back my phone. The screen reads CONTACT DELETED.

"What the—why'd you do that?"

He takes out his phone and does the same thing to my phone number while I sputter at him, outraged.

"It's too dangerous, Kiri. They're using me to track you. As long as we're together, they'll keep trying to kill you. You have to stay away from me. They've already come too close."

Our four remaining grilled-cheese sandwiches are growing cold. Skunk hasn't touched his food or coffee. His face has stiffened into a mask of grim resolve.

My brain fumbles for an appropriate response and arrives clumsily at rage. I jerk away from Skunk.

"There's nobody trying to get me, Skunk. You're having a Thing."

Skunk shakes his head in a maddeningly knowing way.

"You don't understand it now, Kiri, but you will someday.

I'm just trying to keep you safe. If you go to the Train Room again, they'll be waiting for you. And if they see you with me—"

"Stop it, Skunk. You're paranoid. You need to go outside and smoke a cigarette. You haven't been taking your meds."

Skunk doesn't stop. He keeps on speaking in a low, insistent drone, as if he's not even listening to what I'm saying. The waitress comes again to take our plates. I thought the yellow pills were finished, but apparently not: Her face is slice-mouthed and awful, like an evil marionette's. All of a sudden, I can feel the world spiraling out of my control just as clearly as you can watch an escaped balloon heading for power lines. I wriggle out of the booth and stand up. My unbuckled shoes make me unsteady. I sway briefly, clutching the table.

"Come on, Skunk. Come with me. We're going to my house."

Skunk pauses just long enough to give me an icy stare. He doesn't move from his spot on the leather bench.

"If you need to communicate with me," he says, "use a radio."

I stare at him, my beautiful mysterious love-bison turned hostile alien. And I honestly don't know who I'm seeing. And I don't know who I am, either, pleading with him in a twenty-four-hour diner while my head thrashes in a sea of chemicals like a cat trying to find its way out from under a heavy blanket.

I am a heartless monomaniac.

I don't know what to do.

I spin on my silver heels and bomb out of there just as fast as I can possibly limp.

chapter thirty-six

Sometimes, a problem looks so small you can crush it between your fingers. Then you wake up one morning and it's eating you alive.

When I leave the diner, it's like the world comes unplugged. I run around pressing buttons, but nothing is working and nothing makes sense.

First, Denny and I get into a huge fight because I start practicing piano as soon as I get home without even bothering to change out of my murder-shoes or my scotch-smelling dress. I start practicing piano because I don't know what else to do. There is nothing left to do. There is nothing left to do except what I was supposed to be doing in the first place, all summer long: practicing. I play Bach, Beethoven, Chopin, Debussy, and Fish, Fish, Debussy, Chopin, Beethoven, and Bach. I drown out the worries that snake through my brain. I block out the touches of spiders and skunks. Ladies and gentlemen, this is a five-piano alarm.

Denny comes down the stairs, white-hot furious with sleep-puffy eyes.

"Where the HELL have you been?"

"Battle of the Bands."

"I drove around looking for you for TWO HOURS. Your friend's mom called at midnight and said I had to pick you up, then you weren't even there."

"Leave me alone. I'm practicing."

"It's six o' clock in the FUCKING MORNING."

"It's not my fault you sleep all the time."

"You're FUCKING INSANE."

He snatches the wooden metronome from on top of the piano and throws it hard at the floor. Like everything else in the world, it explodes into a million splintery pieces. I keep playing.

"You'd better listen to me, you psycho BITCH."

Denny's voice has a high-pitched strain to it like wind screaming in a chimney. I don't care. I need to practice. The International Young Pianists' Showcase requires my presence at 2:07 p.m. on Sunday, July 30. Now that I've scared off Lukas and abandoned Skunk, piano is all I have left. *Triplets, triplets, left hand plays triplets. Right hand floats above.*

Denny grabs my shoulders. Before I realize what's happening, the piano bench topples like a kicked colt. My chin cracks against the floor. I am down. I have been downed. Kiri down. An ache springs up where my jaw hit the hardwood. My head floats dizzily from the surprise fall. I hear Denny stomp back up the stairs and slam the door.

For a moment, I lie there, stunned. I get up, lurch up the stairs, and pound on Denny's door. "Denny—"

"Piss off."

I talk at his door in a loud, fast, choppy gurgle.

"I'm sorry, Denny. I didn't mean to wake you up. Maybe you could wear earplugs or something. The Showcase is in two weeks, and I basically need to practice nonstop until Mom and Dad get home."

He crashes around his room. I hear him dial a number on the cordless phone. It's sixteen digits long, which can only mean one thing.

The cruise ship.

"Mom? Hey. Kiri's lost her mind."

No.

I grab the doorknob, but it's locked. Denny speaks nice and loud so I can hear.

"Yeah, she never sleeps, and she starts practicing piano at six in the morning, and I'm pretty sure she's on drugs."

No. No, no, no.

I jiggle the doorknob frantically and strain against the door with all my weight. "He's lying!" I shout.

"What's that?" says Denny, his voice dripping with responsible-older-brotherness like a switchblade dipped in honey. "Sure, you can talk to her. Hang on."

The door pops open. Denny smirks as he hands me the phone. I snatch it and stalk down the hall to my room. By some miracle, I hear my own Responsible Voice spool out, calm and reassuring.

"Hi, Mom. I don't think Denny understands. The Showcase is in *two weeks*."

I sound so convincing it's scary. I keep going, amazed at my own skill.

"I know, but he didn't even try asking nicely. He can't just come home out of the blue and expect me to work around his slacker schedule when I have so much to do."

This is going well. This is going better than well. I press on. "I don't know what he's talking about. I *told* him I was sleeping over at Angela's last night, but he doesn't listen to a word I say. Ha-ha. Okay. I'll tell him. Thanks, Mom. How's the cruise going?"

Through my bedroom wall, I can hear Denny turn up his music to drown me out. I smile ferociously into the mouthpiece, hearing precisely nothing of my mother's reply. "Ha-ha, sounds awesome. Say hi to Dad for me. Talk to you later. Bye."

When I hang up, relief is coursing through my veins. I take the phone downstairs and drop it into its cradle.

"Mom says to let me practice!" I shout up the stairs.

I go to the piano, right the toppled bench, and start up where I left off without even getting ice for my chin.

Denny doesn't come down again.

At one p.m. I take a quick lunch break, scarfing chips and salsa in front of the computer. There's an email from my mom, saying it was nice talking to me on the phone this morning, but she just got a very worrisome email from Petra Malcywyck, who says that I seem to be having a rough time, and is there something going on that she should know about?

I reply to inform her that I have in fact been having a lovely time. I have been attending Hot Yoga classes at FitCity thrice a week, I have been learning the art of bicycle repair, I have been cooking organic macrobiotic three-course meals using the grocery money she left on top of the fridge, I have been practicing piano like a child of traditional Asian parents, I have been reading all the links to supposedly fascinating physics articles my friend Teagan has been emailing me from physics camp, and, oh yes, I have been watering the living crap out of the azaleas.

I write a similar email to Petra that is slightly more acerbic in tone.

A few minutes later, Lukas calls. I almost don't answer. Then I do. I have a couple things to say to him. But instead of apologizing for being a treacherous narc, he says his great-grandma's sick and they're going up north to be with her next weekend so, um, sorry, but he can't play our victory show at the Train Room on Saturday and is throwing everything we've been working on since September on the stink barge.

I tell Lukas to have fun at IndieFest with Kelsey Bartlett next weekend, whereupon he mumbles something about dropping off my gear and hangs up.

A little after noon, the phone rings again. It's Dr. Scaliteri. I take the phone into the kitchen with me and press a pack of frozen peas to the bruised part of my chin, thinking, *Dr. Scaliteri, if you knew how much I've suffered for my art—does Nelson Chow have to stand up to vicious thugs every time he practices piano? Does Nelson Chow have slivers of shattered metronome stuck to the bottoms of his feet?*

It turns out Dr. Scaliteri did not call to congratulate me on my fortitude.

"Kiri, I am thinking we will cancel your lessons. It has been a very bad summer for you, and I cannot be teaching you if you are not doing serious practice."

I lift the frozen peas off my chin.

"But I *have* been practicing. I've been practicing constantly."

I've been practicing since six in the morning, in spite of brutal beatings and an awful comedown from those yellow pills that's left me queasy and dry-mouthed.

"Yes, yes, I understand this, Kiri, but you know, if you are not serious about piano, it is not right you should be taking lessons from me. The rest of my students, they are very serious, and it's not fair to them. Besides this, I have received a call from the Showcase, and they tell me you are wanting to change which pieces you play."

"Yes—I'm going to play *Sesquipaedia* instead of the Prokofiev. Remember, I showed you the music last year?"

"This is completely unacceptable."

"It's a great piece. Risky, sure. But I think I'm up to the challenge."

There's silence on Dr. Scaliteri's end. I pace to the window and look out. Our neighbor Mr. Hardy is pulling up a shrub from his front yard. He plunges his shovel into the dirt and pries it up. Each time he pries, a little more of the tangled, woody rootstock is wrenched up from the ground until the whole plant is lying on its side, naked and wretched and impossible to screw back in. Dr. Scaliteri sighs.

"I have told this Showcase you will not be able to perform. You do not have the discipline for piano."

My body goes numb.

"You can't do that. You can't withdraw me."

"Okay, Kiri. You remind your parents to mail me the check for your last lesson when they come home."

"Wait—I need to—"

"Ciao."

When I take the phone away from my ear, the air in the kitchen is hot and softly vibrating, as if someone just shot a gun. In the living room, the piano looks like it did on the day the movers delivered it to my house: a beautiful bomb shelter, a flotation device in an ocean whose depths I was afraid to see. Maybe it's not discipline I've been lacking all this time. Maybe it's something simpler—something that's been staring me in the face this whole time.

I march to the front hall and open the door. The high noon sun is blinding, and the azaleas are snickering at me. "Hey, Mr. Hardy!" I shout. "Can I borrow that shovel?"

The first azalea bush takes fifteen whacks.

The second one takes ten.

I wrap my arms around the bushes, wrestle them out of the earth, and heave them, panting, onto the lawn. Mr. Hardy gapes at me from his driveway. "Whoa, whoa, whoa! What are you doing to those pretty flowers?"

"They're diseased," I shout back. "You should probably kill yours, too."

I go back into the house, sweating all over and electric with

315

holy rage, and play through my repertoire one last time. I play passionately, brilliantly, as if Tzlatina Tzoriskaya herself was sitting on the living room couch. I drain my entire being into the keys. As I play, I hear things in the music I never heard before. My grief over Sukey. My fury at my parents. My vulnerability, my savage ugliness, my playfulness, my hope. It's all there, laid out with terrifying clarity, where anyone could hear it—where I can hear it myself.

Holy crap, I think, *Nelson Chow was right.*

All this time, I've been afraid of the music, and I'm not afraid anymore.

When I'm finished playing, I lower the piano's heavy lid and slide the curved wooden cover over the keys. Shuttered like that, it almost looks like an instrument again instead of the massive winged creature with polished white teeth it had started to become in my mind. Leaving the living room, I glance over my shoulder, but it stays like that—placid, benign—and I know the next time I play, it will be from love.

I want to see what the world looks like from the ground. I ride my bike to the Salvation Army thrift shop and buy a lime-green radio, then bike to Skunk's house and leave it on the patio outside his door, tuned to the mystery station.

Next stop is the Imperial. I spy an old microwave someone put on the curb with a STILL WORKS sign and decide to bring it to Doug. On my way up the stairs, I make a list of all the things I need to remember to tell Doug about the microwave. Number one, don't put metal in it. Metal will make it spark. Number two, don't put anything in it for longer than five minutes. Longer than five minutes and even the rock-hardest frozen thing will be reduced to a hissing, bubbling goo. Number three, never put cat food in it. There is no reason to ever put cat food in a microwave, and I know you're going to be drunk some night and try it. Number four, don't let a crackhead sell this microwave for crack. Number five, do not make any part of this microwave into a deadly weapon.

When I get to the fourth floor, Doug's not in his room. I unplug his hot plate and thunk down the microwave in its place. I plug it in and stand there, setting the time. Doug would never in a million years bother to set the time.

I'm about to pay a visit to Sukey's rooftop when I hear a grating yowl. Snoogie has wandered out of the closet and is skulking across the room in my direction. She gets close and starts pressing herself around my legs, doing that round-the-leg figure-eight thing cats do. I bend down and scoop her up, a skinny hot bag of bones with fur like a ragged bath mat. She sticks out her legs, claws extended, and rakes them against my shirt. I flip her around so her back is against my chest and her razor collection is sticking out in front of us as protection against crook-nosed Kids who might be roaming through the hall.

"Let's find Doug," I whisper, and she meows in response. "He needs a microwave tutorial."

The usual suspects are drinking on the front steps of the hotel. I say hi to Jasmine, who is wearing a stretchy purple tank top, leopard-print sweatpants, and sparkly pink eye shadow that goes all the way up to her eyebrows. She's sucking on a cigarette like it's a stick of honey.

"Aw," she says. "Doug wanted you to have that kitty."

"I brought him a microwave," I say. "I left it in his room. Where is he?"

Jasmine stubs out her cigarette. "He's dead, baby. He passed on Tuesday night."

I stare at her, stricken. "What? How?"

"He'd been sick for a long time, baby. HIV. He didn't like people to know."

"Does he have any family?" I say, but Jasmine says no.

I hurry back up the stairs to Doug's room, blinking back tears. *I will pack up his things; I will keep them in my closet until someone who loves him picks them up.* But when I get there, there's a skinny, sunken-cheeked, green-skinned elf in the room with the microwave under one arm and Doug's blanket under the other.

"Hey," I say, and he turns and snarls at me with a face of such pure, ugly, Gollum-like desperation that I take Snoogie and bolt before he kills us both.

Snoogie doesn't stop yowling the whole bike ride home, and I have to hold her in one arm like a tattered, flea-bitten baby to keep her from twisting away and getting run over by a bus. When we get home, I drag us to the top of the stairs and pull my bedroom door open, ready to collapse on the floor.

But there's already something on the floor. A smashed thing.

Blue shards crisscrossed with looping silver. The splintering angles of a broken frame.

I look at the wall. The nail is bare. I look back at the floor.

Sukey's painting.

I die.

chapter thirty-seven

Someone's knocking on the front door of my house.

I'm sitting in bed with my knees drawn up to my chest, licking the salt on my scabs. Snoogie is roaming around my bedroom with her nose to the floor, tail erect, her ragged ear oozing. Sukey's painting is spread out on the blanket in front of me in sixteen splintery pieces. I'll never be able to put it back together, or put anything back to the way it's supposed to be. It's still Sunday, only Sunday, but Doug is dead and my band has dissolved and the azaleas are lying, unscrewed, on the lawn.

Someone's still knocking on the front door. I hug my knees

tighter and squeeze my eyes shut, willing whoever it is to go away.

I think it's a mailman coming after me with a bushel of accusatory letters from the Showcase.

I think it's my mother and father and Petra Malcywyck coming to cart me away and electrocute me until I confess to being a monomaniac.

I think it's Motorcycle Man coming to confuse me with yellow pills.

I think it's Dr. Scaliteri and Nelson Chow coming to stand around the piano and cast damning glares at me while I play, weeping, through all one hundred pages of Concerto No. 2.

I think it's Doug's druggie friends dragging a body bag.

I think it's policemen and firefighters and emergency room doctors coming to declare me legally dead after I cut my wrists with a pair of scissors.

I think it's all my teachers from school coming to click their tongues and shake their heads over how far I've fallen after such a promising year.

I think it's Lukas and Kelsey coming to squint at me like an animal at the zoo.

I think it's a murderer.

I think it's a vampire.

I think it's the bizarro version of myself, and when she sees me sitting on her bed in a cave of blankets, we're going to fight each other to death like wolves.

Someone's knocking on the front door, and I'm too messed up to go downstairs and answer it but too scared to stay here listening, not knowing who's there.

I wrap my quilt around my shoulders like a cape and go downstairs. As I walk toward the front door, I can see them all standing there on the front step: the mailman, my parents, Petra, Dr. Scaliteri and her Serious Students, the burnouts from the Imperial, the police, my teachers, Kelsey Bartlett, Lukas, the murderer, the vampire, and my own indignant double, all shaking their heads.

With every step I take, I'm conscious of my bare feet connecting with the cool stone floor of the front hall. I'm shivery and feverish. My body is grinding and listing like a broken bicycle. *I'm sorry,* I want to say to everybody who is waiting outside. I especially want to say it to my double. I want to hug my other self and apologize for crashing my bicycle and hurting my leg. I want to kiss her scabs better and not let her take Motorcycle Man's yellow pills. I want to call her a cab instead of sending her limping through the night. I want to tuck her into a clean bed with a mug of Sleepytime tea and a good book to read until she falls asleep. I want to make her some good food and make sure she eats it. I want to hold her hand when Doug dies and tell her she was a good friend. I want to tell her

Sukey would be proud of her, that Sukey would have said any kind of pain is worth it if makes you brave.

I want to do all these things, but I can't because I'm chilly and panicked and wearing a blanket for a cape. I hear the click of Snoogie's claws on the floor behind me. I watch from a distance while I touch the cold doorknob and pull open the door.

It isn't my parents or Lukas or a mailman.

It's Skunk.

He's wearing clothes I haven't seen him wear before, old jeans and a dark blue shirt with a tear on the left sleeve. His face is pale like he hasn't been sleeping either; his eyes are red like mine.

He's carrying his electric bass in one hand and the little green radio in the other.

He starts to say something, but instead he puts down the bass and the radio and gathers me very tightly into his arms.

Skunk and I decide that the best place for us to be right now is my basement. We bunker ourselves down there with the boxes and the spiders and the bass and the synth and the amp and the little green radio and yowling, prowling Snoogie the cat, and we close the door and plug everything in and we play, slow and mournful, a dark dreadful dirge for Doug and Sukey.

The neck of Skunk's bass is cracked. I hadn't noticed it

before. There's a jagged seam running across it where the wood split and was glued back together. When he plays, the bass moans like a broken animal. My synth keens along like a love-lorn bird. Between us, the radio crackles.

As we play, I start to cry, and when I look over at him, I see that Skunk is crying too.

"How long has it been since you played?" I ask him.

"Six months," says my beautiful tearstained love-bison. "Not since before the Thing happened."

"Last night at the diner," I start. "You seemed like a different person."

"Please, Kiri," says Skunk.

"No," I burst out. "I need to know what's going on."

His fingers travel over the strings as if their melody could answer for him.

"I freaked out," he says. "I even knew I was freaking out—I was aware—but I was so scared when I found you on Hastings Street, I couldn't control it."

"Are you still freaking now?" I say. "Has it stopped? Are you better? You thought people were trying to *kill* me—"

"Please," Skunk says again, but I'm shaking, remembering the look on his face when he deleted his number from my phone.

"Maybe your aunt's right about the medicine," I say.

I feel terrible saying it, like I'm betraying him, but I'm so scared he'll slip back into that cold place again and I won't know what to do.

Skunk casts me a pleading glance.

"I know I messed up this time, but I can get by without the pills if I try hard enough, I really can."

"If the pills help you, why does it matter?"

Skunk's face boxes up. "You shouldn't have to take pills to be okay."

"Everyone does something to be okay, Skunk. That's how the world is. At least the only things you need to muffle to survive are the voices in your head. Some people muffle their hearts."

"I just wish I could be strong for you," he says.

"I wish I could be strong for *you*."

We play on, weeping, until the little green radio runs out of battery and its power light quietly blinks out.

When we come upstairs from the basement, I hear Denny and his friend Chris in the living room, playing Xbox. I'm still a little drunk with tears, and my head feels big and clunky like it's filled with wet cement. Skunk's behind me, his hand warm and still on the small of my back. We go into the kitchen to make a pot of coffee.

The kitchen is blurry and confusing in my post-music stupor. I pull the big tin of Folgers toward myself, peel off the plastic lid, and scoop coffee into a filter. The scoop is red, like the wheelbarrow in the poem. How red the plastic coffee scoop amid the black coffee. I forget how it goes.

Skunk rinses the glass tureen and pours water into the machine, locates mugs. He asks me where the bathroom is, and I point him down the hall. While Skunk's in the bathroom, Denny wanders into the kitchen holding a beer. I drop the coffee filter into its plastic cradle, shut the little door, and press *on*. The machine burbles to life.

"Hey," he says.

I ignore him. Denny smashed Sukey's painting. I have decided he no longer exists. He's an evil ghost. A mean phantom who lives in my house. A thing that will go away if I ignore it for long enough.

Down the hall, the toilet flushes. Denny leans against the kitchen counter, arms folded over his chest. He has that elaborately interested look about him like he's trying to make peace.

"Was that you and Lukas playing? You sound a little like this band called Birdseye."

When he says that, Skunk comes into the kitchen. Denny does a double take. His eyes flit to Skunk's tattoos and back to his face, as if putting something together.

"Hey, man," he says. "You want a beer?"

I slide past Skunk. "I'm going to the bathroom," I whisper so Denny can't hear.

Skunk freezes. "Actually, Kiri, I gotta get home."

"You're not staying?"

"I can't. I'm supposed to be home for dinner with my aunt and uncle."

"You sure you don't want a beer, man?" says Denny.

"No thanks, I don't drink."

Denny is using his cool voice, all casual, super-chill. He leans against the counter like, *Oh, I'm the cool older brother who always takes an interest in Kiri's friends.* He keeps trying to check out Skunk's tattoos while pretending he's not. I have never, ever seen him act like this before.

I put my hand on Skunk's arm. "What about coffee?"

"I'll make some at home. Sorry, I lost track of how long we were in the basement. I'll call you tomorrow."

He walks to the front door. I follow him.

"Hey, nice meeting you," calls Denny. "You should come over and jam again sometime."

Outside, Skunk kisses me before getting into his van.

"What's going on? Why are you leaving?"

"I got shy."

I arch my eyebrows. "Highly dubious."

"Kiri?"

"Mm."

"Give me your phone." I hand it to him, and he keys his number back in.

"Call me any time of day or night if anything's going bad."

"Why don't you just stay?"

Skunk glances at the house. "I just can't. I'm sorry. I have to go."

When I go back inside, Denny has been joined in the kitchen by his friend Chris. They're both holding their beers and watching out the window while Skunk drives away. I glare at them and pour myself some coffee.

Denny looks at me like I have snakes growing out of my head.

"You never told me you were dating Phil freaking Coswell."

I forget I'm not talking to Denny. "Who?"

Chris is still staring out the window, as if there's a chance Skunk will come back.

"Dude, didn't he go psycho?"

chapter thirty-eight

There were the magazine headlines: BIRDS-
EYE FRONTMAN ATTACKS BANDMATE. PHIL COSWELL
ASSAULTS DRUMMER DURING SHOW; BANDMATES BLAME
DRUGS. BIRDSEYE TOUR CANCELED FOLLOWING FRONT-
MAN'S PSYCHOTIC BREAKDOWN.

And the indie music blog posts: *Phil Coswell Finally Loses
His Mind. Phil "Birdseye" Coswell Knocks Out Bandmate with
a Bass Guitar. Birdseye Tour Turns into Psychotic Nightmare.*

And the YouTube videos, shot on cell phones, of the event:
*Watch Phill Cozwel Goin Psyko at Concert. Phil Coswell Los-
ing His #%$* at the Train Room—Part 1. Phil Coswell Psycho
Attack.*

I click through tab after tab of YouTube videos, Pitchfork write-ups, and articles in the *Ubyssey* and the *Georgia Straight*. They're all about a boy named Philippe with a green bass guitar who lost his mind at the Train Room.

There are quotes from bandmates, onlookers, and friends: "Coswell, 18, allegedly swung his bass guitar at a bandmate's head, knocking her unconscious." "Bandmates say Coswell had been 'progressively losing his mind' over the course of the tour." "They describe Coswell as 'volatile,' 'unstable,' and 'really paranoid.'" "Bandmates say he had been abusing drugs for several months leading up to the breakdown." "Tess Elowak, Coswell's bandmate and former girlfriend, says she will not press charges." "Coswell has since been hospitalized for psychosis."

I watch all the videos. At first, I can't believe it's Skunk. He's skinny. He has the same black hair and brown eyes, but he's about a hundred pounds lighter and his face is sharper, more triangular. The only way I know it's really him is by looking at his tattoos. The videos are really low quality, but I can make out the general shapes of the ink on his arms, the bird silhouette and the bass clef. It's Skunk, but it's also not Skunk—it's this wiry teenage rock star clutching a bass like he's drowning.

I recognize the wooden stage at the Train Room with the rusty railway crossing sign nailed to the wall. His band, the six of them, takes up the entire stage with all their gear. They're all dressed in black. Four guys, two girls with ragged haircuts.

Skunk's center stage with his own mic. Whoever's shooting the video is somewhere near the back of the crowded room, holding a cell phone camera high over the sea of heads to catch a bit of the show.

In the first few seconds of video, it's hard to tell that something's wrong. Everyone in the band is playing their instrument, and the crowd is humming along. But slowly, you realize there's something out of place. Skunk isn't singing. He's talking. No, he's shouting. At first, it seems like part of the music, but the song ends and he keeps going: "STOP IT! GET AWAY FROM ME!"

You can hear the person taking the video talking to their friend. *"Whoa, dude. D'you think he's tripping on something?"*

The harmonium player and the electric guitarist put down their instruments. In the grainy video, you can see them huddle around Skunk, talking to him, trying to walk him backstage, but he shakes off their hands like a scared animal, clutching his bass to his chest. The crowd's buzzing now, that greedy, hungry thrum of excitement people make when something bad is happening and it's not happening to them.

"Whoa-ho-ho, man—are they gonna fight?"

The camera tilts toward the floor, showing a dim swarm of sneakers and pant legs, and when it swings toward the stage again, Skunk is locked in a slow-motion wrestling match with the harmonium player, still shouting "STOP!" and "NO!" and all sorts of things in French.

Everything happens in the next two seconds.

Skunk wrenches free and staggers forward, swinging his bass like a club. Most of his bandmates get out of the way in time, but in the midst of the chaos, you can just make out the blond girl's arms flying up to protect her head.

"Dude, I think he nailed her!" says the person shooting the video.

A second later, the video ends.

I sit at the computer wrapped in a blanket, watching it over and over again, until every millisecond of crappy footage is burned into my eyes.

chapter thirty-nine

"They were broadcasting my thoughts through the speakers," says Skunk. "They'd been doing it the entire tour."

It's Monday afternoon and we're at the Army & Navy store on Cordova Street, shopping for cat supplies. As we talk, I grab things and toss them into my basket: a red-and-white bowl, a catnip mouse, bags of litter and food. Snoogie misses Doug, I can tell from the way she sniffs around Denny whenever he opens a beer, despite the fact that I have informed her in both English and cat-speak that we are *not* acknowledging his pathetic existence.

"You mean, you *thought* they were," I say.

"Yeah. I thought they were," echoes Skunk distractedly, as if to him the distinction hardly matters. "I realized they were using my bass as an antenna. I was going to smash it so they couldn't do it anymore."

"And Tess got in the way?"

"And Tess got in the way."

I throw another cat toy onto the pile, some kind of battery-operated ferret that squirms when you pull a string. Snoogie is going to rip its freaking head off.

"Did you try to explain?" I ask him. "Did you tell them about the broadcasts?"

"They thought I was on mushrooms," Skunk says. "Nobody realized what was really going on."

As we wander the aisles, Skunk tells me everything. He tells me how the police and ambulance showed up at the Train Room, their carnival lights spraying all over Cordova Street. He tells me about the hospital ward, with its long, windowless hall-ways, where he bounced like a pinball in the doctors' attempts to Stabilize Him.

Ten medications. He tells me their names: Risperdal. Lithium. Seroquel. Haldol. Lamotrigine. Trazodone. Depakote. Celexa. Wellbutrin. Ativan.

The doctors turned the volume up and down on Skunk, adjusted his bass and treble. Now he was the Messiah; now he was cold and dumb as a potato. He lost all emotion for weeks at a time. Couldn't speak. Lumbered fatly down the hall looking for a window to look out of. Couldn't find any. All communications suspended. The world went flat and fuzzy. Abort.

I kiss him quickly. An old lady looking at salad spinners glances at Skunk's tattoos and edges away. We've drifted into the kitchen section, all translucent plastic picnicware and lemonade pitchers. I gaze at a stack of cups printed with ladybugs. "What did your band do?" I ask, and his words weave themselves into a movie in my mind.

The rest of Skunk's band drove back to Montreal, back to a warm sunlit spring of shows and acid trips. On the West Coast, it rained. The nurses would come into work with damp hair, carrying umbrellas. They kept saying he was almost ready. Almost cooked, like a fat loaf of bread. Yeasty and soft on the inside, blank.

The days crackled by.

When they finally let him out, he was not Philippe anymore. He did not look like Philippe. Under the spell of the pills, he did not feel like Philippe. When he finally made it back to Montreal, people he knew no longer treated him like Philippe. His bandmates shunned him. His mom and stepdad treated him like a criminal. At least on the West Coast, he could hide in Aunt Martine's basement and be left alone.

I listen to this. I listen to this, and my heart swells with love and indignation until I can't contain it anymore. When we circle back to the cat aisle, I stop Skunk midsentence. "Here's our plan."

"We have a plan?"

"Yes. You're going to play the victory show with me at the Train Room on Saturday night. Instead of Lukas. It'll be your big comeback. We have five days to write all our songs."

Skunk is quiet, and for a moment I think he's going to protest. But he's nodding. Skunk is nodding. He agrees with the plan. "What will our band name be?" he says.

I pull the string on the electric ferret. It leaps out of my hands and convulses diabolically on the floor. We gaze at it, this convulsing ferret, like a sign from the gods. I grip Skunk's arm and whisper in his ear.

"Daffodiliad," I say.

After the Army & Navy, we decide we desperately need coffee, so we head down to the Waves on Main Street, where a woman in a purple jacket standing in front of us in line takes a skinny, practically hairless white dog out of her bag, roots around in the bag for her cell phone, puts the unresisting animal back in, and zips it up. The lights behind the counter undulate in a sort of faded neon slurry. We order the biggest coffees we can get.

I talk to Skunk about our new band, Daffodiliad. I tell him exactly how it will go. The Train Room will see that Phil

Coswell has not slunk off into the dark. He is not a monster. He is still as ferociously talented as ever, and as gentle. Our music will be soft, intellectual, peculiar, and lovely. It will hit the airwaves all over the country, and it will be specially engineered to make the other members of Birdseye go insane. We will go on tour in Skunk's van, or perhaps riding our bicycles, pulling our instruments behind us on little red carts. We will play to packed venues all over North America, then put our bicycles on a plane and tour Europe.

We must do all these things. We must do all these things, and we must make love frantically at every possible opportunity.

"Okay, Skunk?"

"Okay."

We collect our bikes from the place where we locked them and ride back to Skunk's house. While we're putting our bikes in the shed, laughing and snatching the blossoms out of one another's hair, a car door slams in the alleyway, and Skunk's aunt comes crunching across the gravel, carrying a bag of groceries. I wave at her.

"Hi, Martine."

When she sees us, she stops.

"Philippe. Dr. Winterson called. You missed your appointment today."

Skunk slowly leans his bike against the shed wall.

"I'm sorry, *tante Martine*. I can't believe I forgot. I started taking the pills again. I've been taking them every night."

Her face doesn't soften. She jerks her head at the door.

"Come with me, Philippe. Your uncle and I want to talk to you."

She glares at me, glares at Skunk, crosses the courtyard, and goes inside.

chapter forty

That night, Skunk calls to say that Martine is *thisclose* to kicking him out. He has been Reckless and Noncompliant, and no amount of promises to take his meds will do. From now on, Skunk has to check in with her every morning at six thirty and every night at ten. She's going to watch him take his meds just like with the patients at the hospital.

There are to be no visitors.

And no midnight bike rides.

And no afternoon omelets when she's out of the house.

When Skunk comes over the next day, we have a grim conference about how best to deal with these constraints.

We decide that Skunk will come over before noon every day, and we'll play music until 9:24. He'll bike home in time to be medicated.

"What about Saturday?" I ask. "You'll need to stay out later than ten o'clock for the show."

He chews on this. "I'll have to ask."

"What if she says no?"

"They might not be home until late anyway. Sometimes they go to this comedy club with their friends on Saturday nights."

"Aunt Martine likes stand-up comedy?"

He nods. I try to wrap my brain around this latest revelation.

"Okay," I say finally. "Let's just hope."

We spend the rest of the week writing songs, drinking coffee, and playing until we collapse on the basement floor. We gambol, star-clad, every night at nine.

I ask Skunk what I should do if he ever has a fit.

"A fit," he says. "What is this, 1852?"

"I don't know, a session. A sesh. What-do-you-call-it."

"A psychotic episode?"

"One of those thingers."

He flips over onto his stomach and regards me very seriously.

"I'm not going to have another psychotic episode."

"But what about—"

He shakes his head.

"Really. The first time, I had no idea what was happening. Now I know how to catch myself before things go that far. I know I crossed the line the other day, but that was an accident. I've got it under control."

I climb onto his back and start biting his ears.

"But what should I do? What are you supposed to do?"

Finally the playfulness returns to his voice.

"Okay, okay," he says. "First you have to fill a bucket with ice-cold water and dump it on my head. Then go into my backpack, grab the giant syringe from the box marked with a skull and crossbones, and stab it into my—"

Laughing. "Come on, Skunk, I'm serious! What would be the best thing for me to do?"

He tickles me.

"Then you have to take off my pants and take off your pants and climb on top of me and—"

Squealing. "You're joking!"

"It's true. That's what you do when someone you love is psychotic."

"You're so full of shit."

More tickling.

"Okay, okay, okay, you win, you win. I'll throw a bucket of water on your head and then jump you."

Since Skunk's on an Enforced Sleeping regimen, he wants me to go on one too.

"I want to know when I'm dreaming that you're dreaming too."

"I don't sleep anymore," I inform him. "I unsubscribed."

"Sleep's not optional," says Skunk. "You can't unsubscribe."

"Yes, you can. It's like cable. You just get it disconnected."

"That's crazy."

"It's true."

"Okay then, how about you meditate and I'll sleep. But you have to lie down so we're both in our beds."

"All right, Bicycle Boy. Whatever you say."

So we each lie down in our own beds, and Skunk's meds knock him out and I burn on, awake, lit up from inside like a neon sarcophagus. I think it's meditation. I see fractals, think thoughts, recite the *Tao te Ching* backward and forward all the way to the end. I text Skunk: R U REALLY SLEEPING?

He doesn't text back, so I guess that's a yes.

We do this four nights in a row. I soon realize Enforced Sleeping Time is the most productive time of my whole day. While Skunk's sleeping, I make plans and speeches, learn concertos, argue court cases, solve for x. I listen to entire albums start to finish. I realize all sorts of previously unrealized facts about science, and music, and physics, and history, and love.

Skunk buys me a bag of loose-leaf tea from an herbal medicine shop that's supposed to help me sleep. The bag has a gold foil label that says FLYING LOTUS TEA FOR CALMING OF NERVOUS, and the tea leaves are little black flakes like curled-up pine needles. The tea tastes like dried mushrooms and dead grass. I boil up a teapot full of it and drink it before Enforced Sleeping Time, but instead of Calming My Nervous I have to get up and pee sixteen times.

Really, sixteen times.

When Skunk keeps waking up to find a night's worth of texts from me, he gets worried.

"If you go for too long without sleeping," he says, "you might be having a Thing."

"A thing like your Thing?"

"Or something like it."

I admit that the possibility has crossed my mind. "Do I seem Thingy to you?" I ask him.

"A little."

"Are all Things bad? What if I'm having a good Thing?"

Skunk considers this. "Does it feel good?"

Now it's my turn to pause, a million contradictory answers crashing into each other like bumper cars. *I feel great. But I'm exhausted. But I'm perfectly fine. But I'm desperate. But there's nothing wrong. But I can't seem to shut myself off. But I could stop anytime.*

"It feels important," I say.

My in-box piles up with emails from my parents, but I'm too busy to read them. They can tell me all about the sea tortoises when they get home. I stop answering the phone when the caller ID shows the cruise ship number. What would we talk about? Snurkleberries?

"Mom and Dad want to talk to you," says Denny, standing in my bedroom doorway with the phone in his hand.

I let him hand it to me, but when he leaves the room, I hold the phone next to my synth and blast it with sine waves.

There is only one time all week when I really fall asleep, and even then it is only for a few seconds.

I'm lying there, making up lyrics to songs, when all of a sudden I slip. I fall into a great yawning cavern of pent-up dreams that come rushing at me, yapping and desperate, like a pack of starving dogs. The dreams had been waiting for me all this time, their faces pressed against the gates. When I fall asleep, they swarm me and devour me, and the shock is so great I am suddenly awake again, my heart pounding, while the dream-dogs, dissatisfied, howl for more.

"Why'd you stop practicing piano?" says Denny. "Isn't your Showcase thing, like, ten days away?"

Denny and I have hardly been speaking since he destroyed Sukey's painting, or rather, he has been speaking to me quite a bit but I rarely speak back. He trails me around the house when Skunk's not here, like I'm some kind of endangered species he has to monitor so it doesn't go extinct.

"Aren't you supposed to be back in Victoria?" I snap.

He looks confused for a second, then something seems to click.

"I was thinking I'd hang around and catch your show," he says.

"Oh really."

"Yeah."

I eye him suspiciously. He takes a step toward me in the hall and wraps me in an awkward sideways hug.

"Hey," he says. "I'm sorry."

I keep my body stiff. "It's fine."

"It's not fine. It really, really sucks, and I'm sorry."

I don't know if he's talking about the Showcase or Sukey's painting or the bruise on my chin, but as he hugs me against his Old Spice–smelling T-shirt and doesn't let me pull away, I can feel something broken in me setting like a bone.

"I'm sorry too," I say. "And Denny? I'm glad you came home."

After that, Denny doesn't go skimboarding with his friend

Chris as much. Instead, he hangs around the kitchen when Skunk and I are downstairs jamming, trying to catch a glimpse of Skunk or get a word in with him whenever we come upstairs to make coffee or get food. Denny, it turns out, was Birdseye's biggest fan. I hear him tell Skunk that their music really spoke to him when he was going through a dark time last year. After Denny says this, Skunk starts talking to Denny a little bit. At first it doesn't get much beyond "Hey, man," or "Cool, man," but after a while they graduate to complete sentences, and then all of a sudden we're all making pancakes in the kitchen, Denny, Skunk, and me, throwing blueberries at each other and listening to the Yeah Yeah Yeahs.

On Friday morning, I go to the print shop to make posters for our show. I copy the design from the card for Sukey's show at razzle!dazzle!space:

Daffodiliad

this saturday 10:00 p.m. at the train room,

e. cordova @ carrall st.

feat. new works by PHIL COSWELL of BIRDSEYE

and kiri byrd of sonic drift

I highlight Skunk's name and the word *Birdseye* to make it extra clear that this is really his show. When the posters are ready, I go out on my bike and tape them up all around the city until my roll of duct tape has dwindled to a cardboard skeleton, my sheaf of posters has thinned out to a few slippery rectangles, and there's no lamppost or bus stop in the whole city that isn't adorned with Daffodiliad signs.

Skunk calls twenty times to see where I am. I give him an assortment of cheerful, reassuring answers.

Oh, I am at the Rocky Mountain Chocolate Factory eating a marshmallow-peanut candy apple.

Oh, I am at Kim Fong Sushi House playing mah-jongg with old men.

Oh, I am at the harbor investigating cruises to Japan.

Oh, I am at the beach smoking hash with a sea tortoise.

He can't know that what I am really doing is announcing Phil Coswell's glorious comeback to the world. Skunk, my modest Skunk, my humble and secretive Bicycle Boy, would never agree to such a plan. I half wonder if TV crews will show up to film the show tomorrow night. I wouldn't be surprised if we were offered a record deal on the spot.

I scuttle up and down Granville Street, making sure I haven't missed a posterable place. A record store owner yells at me for taping a poster on his window without permission, but when I explain the situation, he asks for three more posters to put up inside the store.

"Phil Coswell," he keeps saying. "From Birdseye?"

I nod.

"God," he says. "I was at that show."

My last stop before going home is the Train Room itself. I sidle up to the coat check. When the manager comes over, I slide the last poster across the counter.

"Whatcha got there?" he says, picking it up and skimming the hand-lettered text.

"It's for tomorrow night."

"Daff-o-dilly-ad. I thought your band was called Sonic Drift."

I cast him a conspiratorial glance, lean close, and whisper, "There's been a slight change in the lineup."

The manager looks back down at the poster and whistles. "Phil Coswell. No kidding. Didn't know he was even around. I'll get Hal to throw up an announcement on the website tonight."

I favor him with my most gracious smile.

"That would be lovely."

chapter forty-one

"Oh no."

Skunk stops on the sidewalk outside the Train Room, his bass in one hand and the amp in his other. His face goes pale.

"Kiri. You didn't."

I beam at him. I am wearing my favorite black-and-pink-striped dress, paired of course with Sukey's silver shoes. On the ride here in Skunk's van, I had to distract him every time we passed a bus stop or lamppost where I'd taped a poster. This, of course, turned out to be futile: There's a bright yellow Daffodiliad poster taped to door of the Train Room with the words PHIL COSWELL RETURNS!!! scrawled across it in permanent marker. I'm so excited I can't help but peek my head in. When I open the door a crack, we can hear a loud, low rumble at the top of the stairs. It must be packed in there. You can practically smell the crush of bodies all the way down on the street.

"I can't go in there," says Skunk.

He turns around sharply and heads back to the van as fast as he can with the amp and the bass. I hop along beside him with my synth under my arm.

"You can, Skunk. Yes, you can. Oh, Bicycle Boy. We're going to be famous. It's going to be great."

He doesn't slow down.

"It's not going to be great," he says. "It's going to be a freak show. Come see Phil Coswell, the psychotic gorilla, live onstage for one night only."

We get to the van. He plunks down the amp and pulls open the door. When he lifts his bass inside, his hands shake. For the first time, I realize he's angry.

I put down my synth and clamber all over him, nuzzling his neck and kissing his ears and squeezing him.

"It's going to be okay, Skunk. It's going to be okay. They love you. There's this record store owner, he says he was at your last show, and he told me everyone who was really there agrees that—"

"I'm not going in there."

Skunk's face has frozen over like a pond. He shrugs off my

arms, walks around the van, unlocks the driver's-side door, and gets in.

"Skunk."

I knock on the passenger-side window.

"Skunk. Let me in. Come on, Skunk. Please."

He doesn't unlock the door. He puts the key in the ignition and turns it one notch, then pushes the volume dial to turn on the radio.

I stand on the sidewalk, my heart jittering like a wind-up toy and breaking like an egg, and watch as my dear beautiful love-bison puts his face against the steering wheel and cries.

I dance and knock and plead. Skunk doesn't move and he doesn't look up. I can hear the radio through the van window, some awful party station playing pop songs and ads for discount furniture stores while my love-bison sits there with his head on the wheel. More and more people are arriving for the show. Soon, there's a long line stretching all the way down the stairs and out the door. I can see our fans standing against the wall in their miniskirts and vintage jackets, smoking cigarettes and chatting and texting and complaining about the line. Every time I look over, the line has gotten longer, until suddenly it's gone. Everyone who's going in has gotten in. All they're waiting for is us.

Denny texts me.

WHERE R U GUYS?!

He's inside selling our CDs, and people are getting impatient.

I leave Skunk in the van, walk to the Train Room door, and rip down the yellow poster. I scrawl a note on the back of it, go back to the van, and stick the note facedown on the windshield, where Skunk will see it if he ever looks up.

I knock on the window one last time, wishing he would lift his shaggy head just once so he would see how much I love him.

No response.

I pick up my synth and the amp and hurry up to the Train Room alone.

If there was ever a situation that called for the services of a professional monomaniac, it's tonight. I blaze into the Train Room, proud and twinkling as a star, an hour late but gorgeous, charming, ever so interesting. I do a quick promenade around the room, shaking hands and giving hugs to my many fans. I air-kiss the snack booth tender and the ninth-grade girls from East Van High. I trade ironies with all the hipsters at the corner table. I breeze past Motorcycle Man, cool and distant as a rare white bird, and he stares after me, sulking, his long hands laced in front of him. I swing by the merch table to explain the situation to Denny, but it's too crowded with people buying CDs.

The room is packed and restless. Everyone's ready for the show. I do my best to entertain the crowd while they wait, keeping up a constant stream of banter as I hurry around setting up the amp and microphones and running a long and elaborate sound check. I make jokes and puns and dark insinuations, and when the stage is set up and Skunk still hasn't come, I play through my classical repertoire on my synth, Bach and Beethoven rendered in warbling square waves with a heavy, stonerrific delay.

People clap, but I know what they're thinking: *Where's Phil? Where's Phil? Where's Phil?*

I finish playing my last classical piece and bend down to adjust the buckle on my shoe. While I'm down there, rubbing my ankle and desperately plotting my next move, I hear a low roar. It starts at the back of the room and sweeps forward like a wave. When I look up, every head in the crowd has turned to look at the door, where Skunk, Philippe, Bicycle Boy, my brontosaurus of love has just appeared with his apple-green bass in his hand.

It takes him a long time to make it all the way to the stage because so many people want to touch him, talk to him, fold his big wounded body into their arms like a best friend come back from the dead. At first I think they're asking for his autograph. I expect the cameras to start flashing at any moment.

But no. These people touching Skunk's shoulders, his arms, are welcoming him back. *It was just a thing,* their faces seem to say. *Just an awful thing and we're so, so glad you're okay.*

Finally he makes it to the stage. When he plugs in his bass, the crowd cheers. Before we start to play, he leans over and whispers, "Thanks, Crazy Girl."

I whisper back, "The Way cannot be cut, knotted, dimmed or stilled."

It's from the note I left on the windshield.

Our favorite line from the *Tao*.

We play one song, two songs, three songs, five. The crowd goes silent and hushed. People put down their drinks and sit cross-legged on the floor, staring up at us like kindergarteners at story time. My hands float over the keys and my voice melds and tangles with Skunk's, singing the ancient riddles we wrote down in my basement, the ones that came to me in my waking and Skunk in his sleep. There's a golden force field thrumming between us, a space the universe has rushed in to fill. Up on that stage, I feel more exposed than I ever have before, like I'm climbing a rock face with only a strand of dental floss for a harness. I gaze at the assembled faces.

And I realize that Skunk is the bravest person I know.

As soon as the concert is over, Skunk has to go straight home. Aunt Martine has promised terrible things if he isn't back by midnight. She will torture his bicycle. She will put an alarm on his sliding glass door. She will murder his radios one by one.

We lean against his van and kiss like avalanche survivors

until his phone starts beeping and beeping, and it's his fifteen-minute warning alarm going off like a bird with its nest on fire.

"I'd better go," says Skunk, but his big brown Skunk-eyes are shining like birthday candles.

"Oh, Bicycle Boy," I say. "Oh, Phil. Oh, Skunk. Did you see their faces? Did you hear them clap? There must have been a hundred people in there, and I think some of them were in bands. Did you see that guy at the back, from the radio station?"

His smile is a jar full of fireflies.

"Crazy Girl," he says. "All I saw was you."

I stand on the sidewalk waving, blowing kisses, and turning a lopsided cartwheel as Skunk drives away. The Train Room is spilling out people, who roll away into the night in twos and threes. I feel like how Sukey must have felt on the night of her art show, a feather in her hair. The moon is up. The sky is clear. The world feels big and bright and possible.

"Yo, Kiri."

I spin around on Sukey's silver heels and smile at Denny, who has just come out of the Train Room with an envelope full of money from selling our CDs.

"Denny!" I skip over and pluck the envelope out of his hands. "Are you hungry? Do you think there's a place we could get Mongolian food this time of night?"

"I just got off the phone with Mom and Dad," he says.

I shimmy around him distractedly, dancing to the music in my head. "I'm sure it was fascinating. Hey, you have ID, right? Can we buy champagne?"

Denny stares at me. "You do realize they're coming back tomorrow morning."

I stop dancing and stare back at him, stunned. As the news sinks in, I start to babble. "What? Why? They're not coming home for a week. I still have a week!"

"Don't you check your email? They changed their tickets, like, four days ago."

"Why didn't you tell me?"

"I handed you the phone when they called about it, didn't I? It's not my fault you wouldn't talk to them."

I remember the day I filled the phone with sine waves, and my nerves thrum with foreboding. "What's going on? Why'd they cancel?"

Denny plays with his cell phone, flipping it open and snapping it shut. "Mom has this weird flu," he says.

I cross my arms. "So? How is flying home any better than being sick on the cruise ship?"

Flip, snap. Denny gazes after a bus driving past. "And Dad has some business crisis he needs to deal with."

"You're kidding me. They're on freaking vacation."

"And—"

There's something about that last *And* that makes me think

the first two reasons are fake, and the real reason is something I don't want to hear. I narrow my eyes.

"And what, Denny?"

Flip, snap, flip, snap. I swear I'm going to break that thing in two.

"And what, Denny?"

He still won't look at me. He's watching that bus like he's never seen one before. "And, so, remember last Saturday when you stayed out all night, then came home all cracked out and started practicing piano?"

I blaze with indignation. "But I explained—"

"Yeah, well, Lukas's mom called them and said you were having a nervous breakdown." *Flip, snap.* "And, um, I sort of sent them this email the other day, back when you were still really—"

"Still really what?"

"I don't know."

"Still what? What did you tell them?"

"Nothing."

"Uh-huh. And they decided to cut their whole trip short and—"

The bus turns a corner. Denny finally looks me in the eye. "I swear I didn't tell them to come home. They were thinking about changing their tickets anyway because of Dad's work thing."

The moon, whose radiance was so lovely a moment ago, glares down at me now like a searchlight. The city is nothing but right angles and dead ends; I can feel it contracting around me, shutting off my escapes.

"Yeah, right. You've been trying to ruin my life ever since you came home from Victoria. You've always hated my music, and now that I'm finally starting to get somewhere, you'll do anything to stop me."

Denny throws up his hands in disbelief. "Listen to yourself. Would you listen to yourself? You sound just like Sukey. 'You're not really trying to help me, you're just standing in the way of my art.'"

"Sukey was *right*!" I scream.

"Sukey had a *problem*!" shouts Denny. "It's not about your music. Your music's great. It's amazing. Nobody's trying to take that away from you. But Christ, Kiri, you've been so high-strung—you say you're not on anything, but I know you are; I just *know* it. I was afraid to go back to Victoria in case—"

"Is that what you told Mom and Dad?" I shriek. "You told them I was on some kind of drugged-out rampage? Thanks, Denny. Way to be a liar."

He ignores me. "—in case there really *is* something wrong, because even though you're shrill and unreasonable and completely insane, you're the only sister I have left."

We stare at each other, spent. At the intersection, the walk sign chirps *bleep-bloop, bleep-bloop, bleep-bloop*. Denny puts an arm around my shoulder as if he half expects me to bolt down the street, which I half intend to do.

"What time are they getting here?" I demand as he guides me to the car, my mind already blazing with to-do lists, stratagems, battle plans.

"Who cares?" he says. "Let's get Mongolian."

"There's no time for Mongolian," I say. "Give me your phone."

"Why?"

"I'm going to call them."

"You can't. They're probably on the plane."

"I'll leave a message."

"And say what?"

"Just give me the phone."

Denny hands it to me, and I dial Dad's cell number. It goes straight to voice mail.

"Hi, Mom and Dad," I say. "It's Kiri. I hope you're having a good time on your trip."

Denny rolls his eyes. I make a face at him. "Anyway, I'm just calling to say that—"

Denny is watching me with a curious expression, and for some reason my voice catches. "*What?*" I hiss, but he just shakes his head and waves at me to finish the message so we can go. I swivel away from Denny and plant myself on the sidewalk.

"Anyway—" I start again, but then I glance down at the silver shoes I'm wearing, so shiny against the dull pavement. There's a warm breeze playing with the hem of my dress, and I can smell the salt in the air from the harbor a few blocks away. The sky, stained orange from streetlamps, is still dark enough to show a speckle of stars.

I feel a sudden wave of homesickness, and I don't even know what for—beauty, or freedom, or love, all the wild and dangerous parts of myself that die a little with every carefully sanitized syllable I speak into the phone. What am I so afraid of, anyway? Let them come home. Let them see me as I am for once, and not as they need me to be. I'm braver than they think I am.

Hell, maybe they're braver than I think they are, too.

I flip the phone shut and toss it to Denny.

"Let's get that Mongolian," I say.

chapter forty-two

We don't mention Mom and Dad the whole time we're wolfing down dinner. But on the drive home, my resolution starts to waver, and I ask Denny what he thinks I should do.

"Get some sleep," he says automatically.

I tug at my seat belt. "That's not what I mean. Do you think I can replant the old azalea bushes, or is there a nursery open where we could stop and buy new ones?"

For some reason, the azaleas feel extremely significant— like Mom and Dad will take one look at the ruined bushes and know my every thought, every twitch, every transgression. Who but a monomaniac would pull up the azaleas? What

kind of sinister deviant would broadcast her own broken-
ness in such a public way?

Even though I know there are a million other things I
should be worrying about—like the Showcase, and how to
explain the fact that our magazine-perfect house is now home
to an irascible three-legged cat that I am starting to suspect is
an alcoholic—the azaleas seem to overshadow it all.

"We can't buy new azaleas bushes at three a.m.," says Denny.
"Get some sleep. Anyone would go nuts if they slept as little
as you."

A wave of dread rolls through me. "But what about—"

Denny's hands are calm and even on the steering wheel.
"Tell you what," he says. "You go to bed and let me worry about
the azaleas."

"Promise?"

"Yeah."

My body untenses when Denny says this, like the matter of
the azaleas was a big hairy spider on my shoulder and Denny
just flicked it off. *I'm safe,* I think, drawing a deep, rattled
breath. *The azaleas. Thank God.*

It turns out that when you unsubscribe from sleep, it's actually
rather hard to get started again. The sleep gods don't just let
you back into the club after you've snubbed them. You need
to make some kind of sacrifice or penitence or offering to get

back in. I light a stick of the incense Skunk gave me and wave it around my bed, singing a wheedling sleep chant as my room fills up with fragrant smoke. I say a little prayer, *Oh sleep gods, please let me in,* and climb under the covers. The first few minutes seem promising. I snuggle into my pillow and try to let my brain go still. For a moment, it seems like I might really fall asleep, and if I can really fall asleep, then maybe there's no problem after all.

But a few seconds later, my brain's at it again. I start thinking about all the complicated things I need to explain to Mom and Dad—Sukey's things, the Showcase, Skunk—and spend the rest of the night wide awake, planning for their arrival.

First I think it might be best if I'm sitting at the piano practicing when they show up, and I can twist around with a pleasantly surprised expression on my face as if I hadn't heard the cab in the driveway.

Then I think I should lay out Sukey's things in the living room and stage a family catharsis, talk show–style, and we'll all weep and hug and confess our wrongdoings and emerge from the house hours later, bleached by forgiveness and scoured by tears.

Then I start worrying that Mom and Dad are going to be angry at me for embarrassing them in front of Petra and Dr. Scaliteri. In that case, perhaps a vulnerable approach would work best. They'll walk in and I'll be curled up on the couch, frail and frightened, with Snoogie the cat in my arms, their poor hardworking daughter who nearly practiced herself to death just to make them proud.

The clock on my nightstand glows red, and even though I try all sorts of different sleeping positions and pillow configurations and chants and spells and prayers, the sun comes up in the morning and I haven't slept at all.

My parents materialize like sunscreen-smelling aliens, all rolling luggage and breathable clothes. There's a brightness about them that doesn't seem real, a sanitized freshness like cut flowers gazing out at the world through cellophane.

I come out of the bathroom after brushing my teeth and Mom and Dad are just *there*, as crisp and neat and color-coordinated as people clipped out of a catalogue. The various scripts I'd run through in my head scramble themselves into a dizzying triple helix and instead I just stare at them, raw-eyed from lack of sleep, as they bump around the kitchen, talking at me so fast I can only process a quarter of what they say.

"Kiri," they keep saying like a pair of chirping birds.

They want to know what happened to the azalea bushes.

And where I put the mail.

They have spent their last three days on the cruise ship doing Research on various teen mental health websites. They tell me it's a good thing Petra and Denny observed the Warning

Signs, or I might be in real trouble.

My dad pushes a pile of books into my hands that they apparently bought on the way home from the airport. I scan the titles. *The Adolescent Depression Workbook.*

You're fucking kidding me, I think.

My parents chatter on and on. Petra has recommended a Hip Young Counselor with whom I will be having an appointment tomorrow morning to discuss a possible future in monomania. Petra has also recommended an acoustic guitar–wielding music therapist, who is supposed to be very, very skilled with troubled teens. Since I am so musical, we are sure to be great friends.

They dig out a few little presents for me: the shampoo and soaps from the cruise ship, a necklace made of some sea creature's crushed-up bones. I twist the little pink shells between my fingers, wondering when they're going to ask me what happened, how I'm feeling, what *I* think's going on. Petra's right, Lukas is right, Denny's right, Skunk's right, they're all right—I'm Thingy, I'm having a Thing. I'm exhausted and cracked out and not entirely okay. But I don't even care about that anymore. That seems like something that will get better. It's right now I'm worried about: It's standing here together with so much to say, and not saying anything at all.

I hover there a moment longer, waiting for them to ask me about something, anything, that actually matters.

Dad busies himself with the plugging-in of cell phone chargers.

Mom checks the fridge for milk.

There's an exaggerated kind of industriousness to their movements, bright and false, like kids pretending to be absorbed in taking notes so the teacher doesn't call on them. Mom is unscrewing a giant bottle of vitamin pills that gives off a scent like rubber flowers, Dad's pouring himself a glass of water at the sink, and for the first time since Sukey died I can see us clearly, hovering at the intersection of love and avoidance like lost tourists who can't decide which road will bring them home.

My shoulders start to tremble and my chest swells up like a hot-water bottle filled too fast.

"Mom?" I warble. "Dad?"

They both spin around at once.

"Can we talk?"

It comes out strange and strangled, like words in a foreign language I'm only beginning to learn.

Then they're hugging me in their sunscreeny arms and breathing in my hair with their mouthwashy breath, and I feel like a firewalker who's just crossed hot coals to collapse, on the other side, into cool grass.

"There was a phone call," I mumble into the sleeve of my dad's shirt.

We start from there.

chapter forty-three

That night, I do my incense ritual standing over my bed, and I'm just about to swallow the melatonin Mom left on my dresser when I realize I haven't checked my phone all day. I fish it out of my purse and see three missed calls from Skunk, and two texts from this afternoon: JUST BIKED PAST IMPERIAL. ALL BOARDED UP. ??? And: TALKED 2 CONSTRUCTION GUY. DEMOLITION 2MORROW!!!

I spit the melatonin into my hand and press call back. Skunk answers on the twenty-millionth ring, his voice thick and groggy from his medication.

"Huhllo . . ."

"They're tearing it down *tomorrow*?" I whisper.

"Mmmmmmm."

I don't think he's really awake, or even physiologically capable of being awake. The pills he takes are basically elephant tranquilizers.

It occurs to me in a flash that starting tomorrow, the Hip Young Counselor might try to put me on elephant tranquilizers too.

Skunk makes a sleepy, confused moan. I whisper lovingly, "It's okay, Bicycle Boy, go back to sleep."

I press the end button and sit on my bed, my body straining between rival impulses like a chew toy being pulled in six different directions at once. I know I should go to sleep. I should take the melatonin and get into bed. But when I think about everything that's happened this summer, I can't let it end like this, with a pill and eight hours of chemical oblivion. It would be like skipping Sukey's funeral all over again. It would be like I never went out to find her at all.

The house is quiet. The only sound I hear is the barking of a distant dog through the open window, blocks and blocks away.

Just one more night, I say to myself.

I get up and pad down the hall, pausing outside my parents' door to make sure they're asleep. They kept yawning during dinner and making comments about being on "Canary Island time," and I'm pretty sure they're conked out on melatonin themselves. When I don't hear anything, I tiptoe into Sukey's old room, avoiding the squeaky floorboard by the door. I find what I'm looking for and hurry back to my room. I throw on a sweatshirt and sling a canvas messenger bag over my shoulder, tucking the contraband inside.

Two minutes later I'm silently wheeling my bicycle through the side door of the garage.

For the first few blocks of the bike ride, my senses are on high alert. Every car that passes is my parents coming to bring me home. Every pedestrian is a neighbor or acquaintance who will call them to report my escape.

She's out of control!

She's gone berzerk!

She's biking in her pajamas!

But I feel more solid than I have in a long time, and more certain. My grip on the handlebars is steady. My wheels roll straight and true. The contents of the messenger bag clink softly against my body, their weight reassuring. By the time I get to the bridge, I've stopped worrying about being caught. Ahead of me, the city is still and quiet, the only motion the private dances of the sidewalk trees.

I reach into my bag and pull out the first paint jar from Sukey's set. Anchoring it against the handlebars with one hand, I unscrew the lid with the other, my bike swerving slightly beneath me. When I get the lid off, I hold my arm out and tip the jar over the sidewalk, and a thin stream of paint pours out in one long thread. I look behind me. A trail of marigold yellow follows me down the bridge.

Hey, Kiri. An echo.

I hear you're in a band.

"It's just me and my boyfriend," I say out loud, then laugh at the weirdness of my voice, after midnight, on the bridge.

I screw the lid back onto the yellow paint jar and drop it back into the messenger bag, steering my bike one-handed as I rummage for another jar. I paint a pink dot on Sukey's magnolia tree, and twin streams of cobalt and crimson along the bike trail where Skunk and I raced at Stanley Park. I leave an emerald splatter on the pavement in front of the Train Room and a tiny white blossom on the patio outside Skunk's door, hurrying away on tiptoes before I get caught.

Each time I dip my hand into the messenger bag, my fingers close around exactly the right color. The paints shine up at me like little wet faces from the bottom of the jars.

That's rad, Kiri. You got a demo for me?

As a matter of fact, I do.

The fire hydrants stand stout and friendly on the street corners, and the sly little breezes push me forward through the city, and closer, closer, closer to my goal.

When I get to the Imperial, the doors and first-floor windows are boarded up. There's a new chain-link fence blocking the building off from the sidewalk, with a flimsy plastic sign that says PARAMOUNT PROPERTIES. I roll to a stop, clenching the brakes so hard, my knuckles whiten. There's something scary about seeing a building boarded up, especially if you know who used to live there—it makes you think about your house and all your friends' houses, and imagine the people erased. I gaze up at the dark windows, and the nothingness I see there terrifies me more than the hotel ever did when it was full.

Where did Jasmine go, and Larry and Fink, and Jojo, the dog who trembles all over? Where would Doug have gone? They've been swept out like spiders, scattered to the streets. But even as my heart aches of think of it, another truth drops into my mind as clearly as a stone into a pool of water: If Sukey was alive, she would be right here beside me. She'd point to a fourth-story window and say, "I used to live in that one. Four-oh-nine." I'd follow her gaze, hardly believing that my sister the painter had lived through such a time, when her only friends were an old man named Doug and a three-legged cat, and her studio was the rooftop of a derelict hotel.

We'd stare at that window for a long time, me on my red bike and Sukey on her green one.

"Let's do this," Sukey would say.

And we'd do what I'm doing now:

We'd hop the fence.

We'd scurry up the fire escape without looking down.

And we'd paint one last picture, together this time, in the place where Sukey had always stood alone.

I lock my bike to a lamppost and clamber over the chain-link fence with a clumsiness that would make a ninja cry. It snags at my pajamas and rattles more noisily than a half dozen garbage cans knocked over by raccoons. I land with a *thump* on the other side and hurry down the alley without pausing to investigate the scratches on my arms and the tear on my sleeve. This time, I don't hesitate on the fire escape. It's like the critical moment in capture the flag when you spy a spot of color on a tree branch and there is nothing to do but run, no matter who is chasing you or how the rocks tear at your feet, to grab it and claim it for your own. The fire escape clangs, my bag bounces against my hip, and I swallow the night air in gasping lungfuls.

Just when I've launched myself over the last few rungs of ladder and onto the roof, a car pulls up and a door slams. I drop to a crouch, my pulse a roar I am certain you could hear six stories down. A walkie-talkie crackles.

Security guard.

My body reacts instantly. Before I know it, I've flattened myself against the roof, my arms and legs splayed out. Whoever's down there walks up and down the block, leaving the car idling by the curb. My ears strain to catch every footfall, every scratch of static from the walkie-talkie. *Should have locked my bike farther away.* I think of all the places I've marked with paint—the bridge and the bike trail and the tree. Does that count as vandalism? Am I about to get arrested? I press my face into the roof, as if that could hide me any more than I'm already hidden, thinking, *please please please please please.*

The footsteps move back toward the idling car. The door opens and slams again, and after a thirty-second pause during which I am sure the person inside is dialing for reinforcement, the car drives off and the street is quiet.

The breath I was holding scrapes my throat coming out, as if it had been sharpened into a knife blade in my lungs. My first instinct is to grab my bag and climb down before I have any more close calls. But when five minutes pass and the car hasn't come back, my tensed muscles relax. If Sukey painted here in broad daylight without getting caught, what are the chances of anyone checking the rooftop tonight?

I ease myself up and brush myself off, my ears buzzing faintly from adrenaline. Grabbing the bag, I fumble my way to the place where the drips from Sukey's paintbrush have collected like the petals of an enchanted flower. When I crouch to touch them, the paint splatters are smooth under my fingers, distinct from the roughness of the roof. I unscrew the last of the paint jars, the arsenic and ochre and gold, colors I would have hardly believed existed if she hadn't brought them into my world. They splash onto the rooftop and scatter into a hundred different shapes, joining the cacophony of colors. I don't know what she would have painted with them and I guess I never will, but for now, like this, they are beautiful.

I sit on the rooftop all night long, cradled in the broken lawn chair like a ramshackle bird in a plastic nest. Below me, the neighborhood tosses and turns like a person in a fever. The lamps burn too bright. The street sweats. A bottle breaks on a sidewalk. A police car howls through an intersection.

I wrap my arms around my knees and cry and laugh for a very long time, but mostly I just hold myself very, very tightly, like a piece of dandelion fluff you've finally caught in your fingers after chasing it, leaping for it, again and again on a windy day. The universe, I realize, is full of little torches. Sometimes, for some reason, it's your turn to carry one out of the fire— because the world needed it, or your family needed it, or you needed it to keep your soul from twisting into a shape that's entirely wrong.

So you go, and you come back with paint all over your hands and scabs on your knees and the lingering traces of a song few people have ever heard, echoing in your ears.

I stay until the sky turns pale pink and a flock of small brown birds alights on the edge of the roof, chirping and whistling and flapping their wings. There's a rumbling from the street as someone rolls up a metal screen. The sweetness of steaming buns fills the air: the Chinese bakery. I push myself up from the lawn chair and go to the place where the paint forms a brilliant carpet beneath my feet. *The soul has a home of its own*, Sukey said, *and I want to live in that one*. I feel, as I gaze down at the shining colors, that I am standing in a place I have been forever. A place I will leave without leaving. A place I will find, and yet search for, for the rest of my life.

As I climb onto the fire escape, a blueness catches my eye, so slight and far away, I almost don't turn my head.

But I do stop.

And I do look.

And this is what I see: There, on the horizon, two ships.

Acknowledgments

Thank you to my editor, Molly O'Neill, who was a lighthouse in the stormy seas of revision and a great mentor; and to my agent, Laura Rennert, without whose wisdom and encouragement this ship might have capsized many times over. I'm grateful every day to have fallen into such good hands and am deeply indebted to you both.

Thank you to Lara Perkins and everyone at the Andrea Brown Literary Agency; my foreign rights agent, Taryn Fagerness; Barb Fitzsimmons, Lauren Flower, Tom Forget, Brenna Franzitta, Esilda Kerr, Casey McIntyre, Amy Ryan, Valerie Shea, Megan Sugrue, Katherine Tegen, Joel Tippie, and all the other wizards at HarperCollins who do the magical stuff that makes a book a book; Lynn Lindquist for encouragement in the early drafts; all the INTERN readers whose friendship has been an inspiration and an unexpected delight; and to friends and loved ones in too many cities to name.

May your own adventures be rich and true.